GOD'S SIN

A TIME FORCE INVESTIGATIONS NOVEL

J. R. SIMMONS

This is a work of fiction. Names, characters, places, and incidents portrayed in this novel are either products of the author's imagination or are used fictitiously.

GOD'S SIN

ISBN: 978-0-578-00868-4

Printed in the United States of America
www.lulu.com

For Mom and Dad

ACKNOWLEDGEMENTS

Thanks first to my wife, Debe, and my sons, J. and John, for all they did to make this book a reality. Thanks also to:

Alan Pickrell for his literary advice and more importantly for his friendship.

Barbara "J. B." Duff who reached out from so many miles away to encourage my writing.

My brothers, David and Steven, and sisters, Sue and Sandra, for going out of their way to help any time I asked.

My step-father, Bob, for sharing his life with our family.

Original book cover design and artwork by Rebekah McGrady, www.randomlyvague.com

Edited by S. J. Raduenz

Publishing Coordinator, V. Jade Proffitt

Marketing Director, Andrew McGrady

BACKGROUND

StreamVision Text Message Service (text messages available for all wireless venues. Cerebral Implant connectivity available in most areas.) <u>*August 18, 2263, Boulder, Colorado.*</u> *Dr. Thomas O. Bing held a news conference today, and announced humankind's first documented time travel. Bing and three of his students traveled back to April 18, 2263, and safely returned to August 17, 2263. Bing said that he had confirmed centuries-old hypotheses that time is not linear. Instead, each moment in time occurs simultaneously along the Infinity Loop.*

Time travel takes place in the Time Warp Continuum. According to Bing, the Continuum can be used as an entry point to the Infinity Loop and ultimately any time vector in the past. Once time travelers enter another time vector they are restricted to observing only. People in the target time vector are completely unaware of being observed. Travel to the future has proven impossible to this point.

Bing used the Hyper-Speed Cyclotron in Boulder, Colorado, to propel his student time travelers to the speed of light, which allowed entry to the Time Warp Continuum. Doctor Bing stressed success would not have been possible without the spiritual guidance of the revered Himalayan Lama, Do (pronounced Doe) Chi. It was Do Chi who acted as the bridge for Bing and his students between the scientific and spiritual worlds and aided them in developing the meditation techniques needed for successful time travel.

At a private ceremony prior to the news conference Do Chi presented each of Bing's students with a bright blue feather. He explained that in his country the feather was a symbol of reverence to the past and faith in the future. Do Chi was not at the news conference and was not available for comment.

Bing stated he hoped to see time travel become an effective tool used throughout the scientific community. Noted observers at the news conference included representatives from business, the military, and several international police organizations. END...

BOOK ONE

~ FLASHBACK ~

Chapter One

THE SUSPECT
1994

Jack Mueller could feel the same, insatiable urge coming again. "Tonight," he thought to himself. "I'll kill the bitch tonight." Jack had spotted his old high school girlfriend working as a cashier in a big discount store in their hometown several months ago. Ever since then he had been planning his attack.

Mueller's obsession had driven him to the point of insanity. He kept seeing himself using his knife to slice his ex-lover beyond recognition and finally plunging it into her heart. Mueller simply couldn't stop the scene from playing over and over again in his head.

Jack finally snapped out of his other world and grabbed the knife from his pants pocket. He had found his Turk Blade, as he called it, in Ankara and had carried it ever since. "Tonight's our night," he said almost tenderly to his killing tool, caressing it the way he would a lover. "Tonight!"

Commander Mueller had retired from the Navy as a decorated aviator and a true hero who had flown F-14 Tomcats in the first desert war. After retiring, Commander Mueller tried his hand at commercial airlines, small airport operations, and finally bush pilot training in Canada. He failed at all three.

Mueller looked at his watch. It was almost 2300 Hours or 11:00 P.M. He saw Dianne Welt walk out of the store toward the employee parking area. She had bleached blonde hair, cut short, and was still attractive despite a few extra pounds. A man ran up behind Dianne and said, "Hey there, got time for a quick beer before you go home?"

Jack was beside himself. The man obviously knew Dianne. "You can't go with him. You can't!" Jack almost screamed, but he caught himself and gritted his teeth.

"Sorry, Ted, but I'm in no shape to spend anytime anywhere but my couch, and that's exactly where I'm headed," Dianne responded.

"Sounds good to me," the man said as he fell in beside her.

"Nice try, big guy, but this girl needs her beauty sleep. I'm working a double shift tomorrow. Good night, Ted," Dianne said forcefully.

"Okay, but how about a rain check?," the man asked.

"We'll see," Dianne said softly, and the man peeled off to find his car.

Mueller had parked two rows away from Dianne hoping to keep hidden. They had dated exclusively in high school until their senior year. Then came the messy break-up. Dianne immediately started hanging out with three jocks who made Jack's life a living hell. Mueller was man enough to stand up for himself but not big enough or fast enough to beat three to one odds. The result was a broken nose and a body that ached from head to toe. He swore that somehow, someday, he would pay back all of them--especially Dianne.

The woman from Jack's past got into her car and pulled out of the parking lot. When she was about two miles from home, a red Mazda Miata pulled up next to her at a stoplight. The guy had the top down, and she couldn't help thinking he was familiar. Then the driver turned towards her, smiled, and cried out, "Dianne, Dianne Welt, is that you?"

Dianne couldn't believe her eyes. It had been 20 years, maybe more, but she was almost sure it was Jack Mueller.

"Jack?"

"Yeah, long time no see. What are you doing?"

Dianne chuckled and said, "Just going home from work." Then Dianne made a quick decision--a decision that would cost her life. The light was about to turn when Dianne blurted out, "Jack, why don't you follow me home. It's only a couple of miles, and I'm sure I can get my babysitter to stay a while longer. It would be great to talk, okay?"   "Well, sure. I'll follow you. I have no idea where you live," Mueller lied. Thirty minutes later the two were in Mueller's sports car heading for a bar. As usual Mueller drank too much and so did Dianne. However, tonight Jack kept himself from slipping into total oblivion. He wanted to enjoy what he had planned for later.

Jack spent all night telling Dianne not to worry about the silly things they had both said in high school. "The important thing is we've found each other, and we can move on from here," he said to her. He talked about his life, and she told him about hers. They had both been through bad marriages and were both trying to heal. Dianne could feel herself actually beginning to believe Jack might be her ticket to a new life.

Both of them had another drink, and then Mueller said, "Let's get out of here."

"Where do you want to go?" Dianne managed to answer with a slur.

"How about the lakes?" he quipped.

"Okay, but don't get any ideas. Let's just talk tonight and see how things go."

Jack smiled and said, "Anything you say, Dianne. We can go to the bluffs just like when we were kids."

They both laughed and ran out to Mueller's car. Twenty minutes later they were on a country road 15 miles out of town heading for an abandoned quarry. Mueller had counted on Dianne being too drunk to notice they weren't headed toward the lakes, and she had obliged.

Jack had given her a miniature bottle of vodka as they left the bar's parking lot, and she was asking for another. "Sure, there's more in the side pocket. Help yourself," Jack replied smoothly.

Soon they were pulling into the quarry, and Mueller helped Dianne out of the car. She was very drunk now, and Mueller had to steady her. He pulled out a sheet of plastic from behind the seat and walked Dianne toward the quarry.

Dianne couldn't make out exactly where they were, but she was pretty sure they were getting close to the bluffs.

Jack led Dianne up a steep embankment and found the spot he had picked out weeks ago. It couldn't be seen from the road and was well hidden by a large boulder left over from the days when the quarry was still active. He grabbed Dianne and kissed her hard. There was no resistance. She melted in his arms and then responded to his kiss with a passion all her own, forgetting completely her wish to go slowly. Jack undressed her quickly and then suddenly jumped away from her.

"What's wrong Jack?"

"Nothing."

"Stop it, Jacky. Come here before I get cold."

Mueller instantly became enraged and yelled, "Don't call me Jacky! Only my mom called me Jacky."

"Jacky, she's been dead for years. Why don't we let her rest in peace?" Dianne answered paying no attention to Mueller's warning. She tried to focus on Jack's eyes, but the alcohol wouldn't let her comprehend the danger Mueller posed. He pulled out his knife and opened the blade.

"*Peace*, what do you mean *peace*?" Jack screamed. "That last year of high school you wouldn't let Mom rest in peace. You and your football stars screaming out obscenities as you drove by our house. Telling me she was a slut. Sure she drank too much. You drink too much. Does that make you a slut?" Mueller yelled.

Mueller stepped closer to Dianne and took a quick swipe at her with his Turk Blade. She screamed instantly. The booze was no good stopping her pain and there was so much more pain to come. It lasted for over two hours with Dianne begging for mercy the whole time. Finally in a whisper she implored him, "Stop, please stop! Kill me and get it over. Please, Jack, please."

"Why? Why should I?" Jack answered breathlessly. "I want you to suffer just like Mom, more than Mom!" Then Mueller looked at Dianne, or what was left of her, and he smelled her blood. It was too much for him. With one final blow he stabbed her in the heart just as he had done so many times in his dreams.

Dianne slumped over and was finally beyond Mueller's reach. It was done. Jack looked at his watch; it was 0200 Hours. He cleaned up the area and realized he felt strangely calm. "They'll learn. They'll all learn," he promised himself. Then suddenly he felt a chill and thought someone was watching him. He peered through the dark but saw nothing. He listened intently but heard nothing. "Must be my nerves," Jack whispered.

But Jack was not alone. From the darkness that was hell, a force was watching everything Mueller had done that night and was eager to see more. Centuries in the Future, a man named Jason Law would feel the same chill, and it would put the two men on a collision course to destruction.

Chapter Two

Jason Law and his team peered into the D.C. lock-up and spotted their suspect almost immediately.

The jump through the Time Warp Continuum had been almost flawless. As usual Jason and his team had been momentarily blinded as they entered the Continuum, and the breath was almost sucked out of them. They proceeded quickly to make the jump to their target time vector.

"T-Control, this is Law. We've completed our jump and are monitoring the suspect." Law was a senior agent for Time Force Investigations (TFI). On July 1, 2273, the World Court formally authorized establishing the TFI under the Court Prosecutor's Criminal Investigations Unit. The TFI's mission was to investigate and solve aggravated capital cases from the past. As part of that mission the TFI was responsible for apprehending, arresting, and returning the perpetrators of these crimes to the World Court for prosecution. Jason and his three-member field team had just made the jump from the Time Warp Continuum to 0700 hours, September 12, 1994. Their assignment was to confirm the suspect's identity before an arrest warrant was issued. Sitting in a holding cell in Washington D.C.'s 19th Precinct was Commander Jack Mueller.

Jason looked at Mueller and flashed back to his first prisoner. Confederate Senator Thaddeus Nichols had strangled thirteen lonely war brides who hadn't seen their husbands for months, sometimes years. Like most of his suspects since then, Nichols had threatened to kill Jason. The TFI agent paid no attention to Nichols or any of the others.

6

Jason concentrated on Commander Jack Mueller. The suspect appeared drunk and was muttering, "The guy had it he coming. He had it coming!"

However, Mueller wasn't so drunk he didn't know he was in big trouble. He had been in D.C. for a job interview set up by two old Navy buddies. The three of them told too many war stories and jumped from one seedy bar to another. They ended their spree in a dark, smelly dive called the Tick-Tock at about 0300 hours. Jack was very tired and more than a little wasted. He saw a redhead waiting tables and couldn't resist pinching her backside. Then he staggered to the table his buddies had found.

"One more time and I tell the bartender--got it?" the young redhead warned. "Sure, Baby," Jack replied, and he threw a $10 bill on her tray as she took the order.

"Easy, Jack, no trouble tonight," one of his friends said, and Jack just shrugged his shoulders. He wished he were in his hotel room getting some sleep before his interview. He was also growing very tired of his two friends who had told the same stories over and over. If it weren't for that interview...

The next few moments were a blur to Jack. He remembered seeing the redhead walk by the table and the idiot bartender yelling, "Keep your hands off!" The bartender jumped over the bar, and Jack went for his Turk Blade. He stuck the bartender in the gut and pulled up hard. The bartender was dead before he hit the floor. It was only three hours later that Jack was picked up, identified by his buddies, and arrested for murder.

Mueller almost laughed when he thought what a mess he had made of his last night of freedom. "Wonder how interested the cops would be to find out about the others," he asked himself. Dianne, Larry Johnson, and the others had all paid the ultimate price for hurting Jack and his mother so badly.

Larry Johnson had been the only one who hadn't immediately begged for his life, but after hours of torture even the one-time high school quarterback was on his knees crying out for mercy.

Jason and two of the TFI team members triangulated their positions with TFI T-Control. All of them were within the required 30 centimeters of the suspect to ensure Mueller could be scanned by the TFI Bio-Thermal Forensic Depository Computer or Big T.

"Ready for scanning," Jason reported. Scanning was actually a two-part process. First, Big T confirmed the exact vector of the suspect. Next, the computer performed an aura photo-cellular analysis to confirm the suspect's DNA, physical, intellectual and emotional markers, and a myriad of other forensic data.

Aura analysis had been studied for centuries but it had only been within the last 100 years that science had accepted it as a legitimate scientific discipline. Known as Sub-Atomic Harmonic Physics, it was a fountain of information to the TFI--especially in terms of determining identification and motive. Individual aura analysis was accomplished though readings of aura wavelength, color, light intensity, and temperature. Big T compared the results to cohort aura data stacks, which provided specific target parameters for a suspect.

The team's forensic specialist, Dawn Phillips, was several steps away from the rest of the team, performing her own scan to confirm the suspect's identity. Dawn, or "Phil" as Jason called her, was five feet, three inches tall, had auburn hair, and a knockout figure. She felt she was attractive, but she thought her looks were more of a negative than a positive. All through high school and college guys had been hitting on her. Dawn had almost filed a formal sex discrimination charge against her advanced molecular physics professor, but her roommate had talked her out of it. Then and there she had promised herself she would pass or fail in the real world based on her brain not her bra size.

T-Control wanted an immediate data file dump on the suspect's identity. "Transmitting," Dawn said. The scan would provide information on any specific identifying marks or characteristics that could be used during the investigation. For the most part this was redundant and unnecessary. However, Dawn knew more than once a team had been forced to use body scan information to identify a suspect on the run.

Big T retrieved the data in less than 0.3 nanoseconds including transmission time. Then something unusual happened. Dawn was getting a strong reading that Jason Law and Jack Mueller had a connection sometime in the past. Dawn was unable to get a specific readout on where or when the two had crossed paths, but there appeared to be some kind of connection.

8

"Detective Inspector Law, I'm getting a positive readout on a direct DNA connect between the suspect and you. How do you want me to proceed?"

Jason had joined the TFI to find his mother's killer. She was murdered in front of him when he was only seven, and he had promised himself he would never rest until he found the perpetrator. Twenty-five years in the Sidney Police Department had yielded nothing. It had been the same story in the TFI until now. Despite some very unofficial, clandestine help from a few, select friends in the TFI, Jason had never been able to get a good lead on who had killed his mother.

"Let me take a look at the readout," Jason said to Dawn. "You show a high DNA association probability but nothing on space/time vector. It's probably no more than a DNA association factor," he lied. Jason had never advertised his real reason for becoming a TFI agent and he wasn't about to start now. He might have to go outside the law to make sure the killer received the only justice Jason would accept--a slow, slow death.

The DNA association factor was technical jargon to explain a natural phenomenon. Whenever a TFI agent entered a target time vector and was in close proximity to a suspect, there was a natural mixing of aura-DNA data. In about one percent of the cases the readout became garbled and actually showed an association between the suspect and a TFI member. Scientists weren't sure how this happened, but their best guess was it might have something to do with the Infinity Loop and its impact on time.

"Contact T-Control and get authorization to proceed," Jason said trying to remain calm. Dawn fed the data to the T-Control Master Computer where the anomaly was studied and classified as most likely benign. Jason had managed to make the problem go away, but inside he couldn't wait to get his hands on Commander Mueller.

Once the mission was completed, Jason and his team were transported to their own time where they prepared their status report on Commander Mueller. The DNA results proved that Commander Mueller was indeed the man they wanted.

Mueller felt nothing during the scanning process other than a moment of anxiety that he forgot almost immediately. Later, he would remember that feeling and wish that it had been his last on earth.

Chapter Three

Jason Law was running out of time. He had made 21 jumps back into time. When he reached 30, he would be promoted out of his job. Then he would be offered two choices--take a desk job or retire. Neither choice was acceptable.

Jason had come to the Time Force Investigations Unit after spending a number of years in the Sydney, Australia, Police Department. He had spent most of his time there as a homicide detective. He was a good-looking man with one possible exception, a one-inch scar just below his chin from a childhood incident he couldn't remember. Over six feet tall with dark wavy hair, and blue eyes, Jason cared much more about how well he could shoot than his appearance.

Jason's father had died of natural causes several years before his mother's murder. It was her death that haunted him. Jason kept replaying her cries for mercy in his head. He couldn't forget the killer's long slim fingers wrapped around her neck squeezing the life out of her. Her last words to Jason were, "Run, Jason, run! Don't look back. Run!"

The next thing Jason remembered was being comforted by a female police officer in the back of an ambulance. "Everything will be all right, honey. It's okay. Go ahead and cry. You'll feel better if you let it out." Jason wasn't listening. He was burning those murderous hands into his mind, and trying to understand why God had taken his father and now his mother.

The TFI was Jason's best chance of making sure his mother was avenged. More than once he had steered his caseload back in time to Sydney, hoping to find some clue to his mother's death. Each time he had failed. He only had nine more jumps in the TFI, and he had sworn to make good use of them.

"I'm wasting this jump picking up this guy Mueller," Jason thought. At the same time something inside him kept reminding him of the DNA readout Dawn Phillips got on their last jump. It had shown some kind of direct link between Mueller and him. It was probably nothing, but he told himself maybe, just maybe.

T-Control had the authority to retrieve a suspect for arraignment once the World Court had issued a warrant. However, it was absolutely forbidden to apprehend suspects until they had died. The reason--preserve history and keep the retrieval team from changing the past. The actual grab or *arrest and retrieval* as the Prosecutor's Office preferred to call it was quite macabre.

A TFI team was provided an electronic arrest warrant to be served within 72 hours World Standard Time. Any warrant not executed within the 72 hour time limit was null and void. More than one defense lawyer had been successful in precluding prosecution based on this requirement.

A team would be sent through the Time Warp Continuum to a specific time and place vector to apprehend a suspect. Based on prior aura scanning, the team would have the exact time and place of the suspect's death.

Scientists had documented 14 distinct steps in the death process. At the precise moment the suspect began the first step, the TFI team would initiate apprehension procedures. It was an absolute requirement that the apprehension not be culminated until the suspect reached the fourteenth and last step in the death process, aura cusp disintegration. This was the moment when a person's aura would show irrevocable disintegration--the whisper of time when a person's body, mind, and spirit could no longer maintain its integrity. At that instant Big T would perform an aura data capture and beam it to the forensic team specialist assigned to the apprehension team. The team would immediately return to the Time Warp Continuum where the suspect's aura data was reintroduced without the element(s) that caused the suspect's death. Suspects were then placed under arrest and held in the Time Warp Continuum until their auras stabilized and they could be transported to face trial.

Once in present time, suspects manifested all of the normal biological traits of any human being although their aura analysis revealed an altered state of being. If suspects were returned to their time of death that process would continue as if it had never been interrupted.

The Prosecutor's Office had taken six months to prepare its case after Jason's team had marked Commander Mueller. Jason had received the arrest warrant only 12 hours before issuing the standard "Go" orders to the team--Dawn Phillips from the Forensic Lab and a first-timer named Mark Alexander. The three assembled in the briefing room and Jason went through the particulars of the warrant and the time vector where they would attempt to make the grab.

Jason reminded them, "Commander Mueller served a 12-year term for second degree murder on the collar we witnessed when we marked him on our last time jump. He died of an alcohol and drug overdose three weeks after his release from prison. His death occurred at 0307 hours, March 14, 2012, in a rundown hotel in Washington, D.C."

Jason also made sure each of the team members had read and re-read the evidence TFI had gathered on Commander Mueller's seven premeditated murders. The team would make the jump to March 14, 2012, 0305 hours, verify Mueller's status, and prepare for their return jump to the Continuum. At 0800 hours the team began their group "think" and attained corporate harmony at 1115 hours.

They were transported en masse to Space Command's electro-cyclotron in Colorado Springs, Colorado, and strapped into cocoon alpha. They reacquired harmony after reaching hyper-speed, and made their jump to the Continuum at 1237 hours. They moved through the Continuum and appeared in Mueller's hotel room at 0304:45--well within the plus or minus 30-second limit.

Mueller was passed out on his bed, his breathing labored, and his skin glistening with the cold sweat of a man dying. Dawn began feeding T-Control a video stream to document the team's mission while Alexander triangulated Mueller's position for aura apprehension. The fourteenth and final step in the death process was reached at 0307 hours. Mueller's aura data was scanned and transported to the Time Warp Continuum along with Jason and his team.

Chapter Four

TIME WARP CONTINUUM

Jack Mueller thought he must be dreaming. He was scared, more scared than he had ever been in his life. He felt cold and then suddenly warmer. He saw a bright, blinding light and said to himself, "They were right. All those crazies who talked about near-death experiences were right! I'm dying and moving to the other side."

The next words he heard were, "Commander Jack T. Mueller, you are under arrest for the premeditated murders of Mr. Lawrence C. Johnson, ..." Mueller didn't hear anything else until Jason Law asked him a second time, "Do you understand your rights? Do you wish representation in the Time Warp Continuum, or do you waive your right and agree to immediate transport to the World Court in the year 2314?"

Mueller wasn't sure any more if he were dreaming, had died, and gone to hell, or was still high on booze and pills and just needed to wait for the inevitable crash. In any event, he wasn't prepared to make a fight of it until his head had cleared, and he was in better shape to make a move.

"Sure, sure, whatever you say. Just let me rest for a minute. I've got to get my bearings." Mueller tried to focus, but he couldn't think straight.

Dawn Phillips was keeping a close eye on Detective Inspector Law as he read the suspect his rights. Jason was rushing through the process, and that made Forensic Specialist First Class Phillips especially anxious. Jason wanted to get this guy on TFI's turf ASAP. He wanted to make sure there was no connection between this sleaze ball and him so he could stop wasting his time worrying about it.

The law was very clear on the suspect being fully cognizant of his surroundings in the Time Warp Continuum before he could be read his right. Once a suspect's aura solidified, consciousness was verified through normal human vital signs. In this case Jason had pushed Dawn to perform an on-site aura scan without verifying the data with TFI Headquarters. It was within Dawn's authority but certainly not within her comfort zone on such a high-level grab.

Dawn made a note in her official diary: "Unilateral aura confirmation, per Detective Inspector Law's directive, one hour, 13.78 seconds mission duration. Suspect's vital signs follow: pulse 37 and weak, blood pressure 87/51 and rising. Breathing shallow. Eyes clouded but reactive." Dawn didn't like playing "Cover Your Ass" but Jason was very close to losing this case on a technicality, and she wasn't going to be part of that show. She was a trained scientist and this suspect was just as likely to believe he was on the sun as believe he was in something called the Time Warp Continuum.

Dawn was a team player, but she was also a survivor. Detective Inspector Law would be on his own if this one blew up in his face. She had warned him too many times--on and off the job. Jason pulled out the standard release form and Commander Mueller signed it. Detective Alexander signed the form as witness. Jason informed TFI Headquarters the team had apprehended Commander Mueller and that Mueller had signed an extradition waiver to the World Court's jurisdiction. The team, along with Mueller, immediately began the jump to present time.

Meanwhile, Space Command had been keeping a close eye on how much real time the team had to re-enter the cyclotron's cocoon and still be within the seven second hyper-speed window. Jason's team was cutting it close as usual.

They all had the standard cerebral microchips implanted in their brains. These microchips had become routine over the last half-century after 20 years of ethical and legal battles over a person's right to privacy. The issue had finally been settled to most people's satisfaction when the United Nations General Assembly approved a non-binding resolution making implantation voluntary at the age of consent (18 in most countries). The microchips could be programmed to receive, store, manipulate, and transmit almost

16

any conceivable data. They were especially helpful in the scientific and medical communities.

Although some governments used the chips to collect data on **very** personal subjects, for the most part, the microchips were seen as positive.

For military and police forces the microchips were anything but voluntary. That was certainly the case for the Time Force Investigations team. Each member was fitted with the latest microchip model after graduating from the academy. The chip's memory included the individual's personnel and medical data. It also contained the worldwide records of all convicted felons along with particulars on all open cases. Most importantly for TFI personnel on a mission, the microchips included special countdown alarms. The microchips provided subliminal messages every nanosecond on the time remaining in the seven second hyper-speed window.

Traveling to another time was almost instantaneous. When the team reached the desired time vector, a nanosecond in present time might translate to an hour, a day, a month or more on site. There had been a myriad of theories on how or if time moved within the Continuum itself, but scientists at Space Command's cyclotron had been unable to substantiate any measurable time changes within the Continuum. Transporting suspects required an even deeper "Group Think." The team and their prisoner appeared in cocoon alpha at 1237:063 (just within the seven second hyper-speed window). After the 53-second cool-down period, the cocoon came to a stop, and the team turned over Commander Mueller to the on-duty police team.

Jason had to wait on Mueller being processed and booked before he could get his hands on him. Law was not a patient man, but in a short while he would have Mueller in an interrogation room where he would find out about any connection between them.

Commander Mueller was transported by the police team to the United Nations Police Plaza where he was turned over for processing. The desk sergeant was a rather large Samoan who was coming up on 11 hours of a shift that was supposed to have ended three hours ago. He looked up from his scan screen and saw the escort team with Commander Mueller. "Name and disposition!"

Sergeant Siolo barked.

"He's a Time Transfer, Sarge," replied the escort team chief, a young two-striper. "His name is Mueller, Jack Theodore; time of death 0307 hours, 14 March 2012, Washington, D.C." Jack Mueller couldn't believe what he was hearing. He had a very foggy recollection of some guy reading him his rights and telling him to sign some form. He was sure he was hallucinating. He needed time to think and make some sense of what was happening.

Trying to put his present predicament in a real world context, however, was proving to be very difficult. The desk sergeant turned to the two-striper and said, "Empty Commander Mueller's pockets and place the contents on the desk for inventory."

Jack's pockets were empty except for a twenty-dollar bill, some small change, and a rather large pocketknife. Sergeant Siolo looked at the knife and immediately realized he had a problem. Detective Inspector Law's team should have confiscated the knife in the Time Warp Continuum. The police escort team should have patted the prisoner down before taking custody from the TFI team. Chain of custody was certainly going to be an issue now and this meant at least several more hours work time for Sergeant Siolo. The desk sergeant was not a happy man, and he let the prisoner, the escort team, and everyone within 200 meters know that it was going to be a very unhappy time for them as well. "Timmy, get over here and voucher this knife," he yelled to his duty officer. "I want that thing out of here and in Detective Inspector Law's hands now, and I mean now!"

Sergeant Siolo glared at the prisoner and read the pick-up sheet the police escort team had given him. These time transfers were always trouble. They were almost always loony, not legally of course, but still crazy. They were the worst of the worst -- serial killers, rapists, child molesters--who couldn't accept the fact that what was happening was real.

"It says here you are a retired Navy officer in the twenty-first century. Is that correct?" No answer. "I asked you a question, Mueller." Sergeant Siolo was usually not a man to anger quickly. He was the typical South Seas Islander with a demeanor perfect for the graveyard shift. If he was having a bad night, however, no one wanted to cross him. The prisoner still did not answer. "Okay,

Mueller, I'm going to read your rights again and then we'll let you enjoy our hospitality until the judge decides what happens to you."

Sergeant Siolo loved this part. It never failed to break through the "tough guy" shell. "Jack T. Mueller, you have been placed under arrest for seven counts of first degree murder in the twenty-first century. You have the right to remain silent. Anything you say may be used against you in a court of law.

"You have the right to an attorney that will be provided by the United Nations World Court Time Transfer Litigation Department. Do you understand these rights?"

Mueller still did not answer. He refused to believe what was happening. He felt somehow this was real, but he could not wrap his mind around the fact that he had been plucked from the jaws of death only to be charged for seven murders he had committed hundreds of years ago.

The desk sergeant wasn't wasting any more time on this guy. Sergeant Siolo had covered himself all the way. He had read Mueller his rights in front of witnesses and recorded everything using the Time Transfer Litigation Department's own holographic synthesis system.

"Take this guy to the Tombs. Lock him up and keep him on camera 24 hours a day."

"This isn't going to be such a bad night after all." Sergeant Siolo thought. If he was lucky he could be out of here in 45 minutes. Detective Inspector Law had screwed up not finding that knife, but that was his problem. The bad guy had been read his rights, and he was locked up on a 24/7 watch. Not a bad night at all.

Jack Mueller was in his cell. Everything was pink-- the ceiling, the walls, the floor. There were no bars, but when he got too close to the hallway, he got a nasty shock. It took twice for him to decide that wasn't a good idea. The guard manning the spy cam laughed and said, "Slow learner."

The lighting in the cell was subdued, almost soft. It was all part of a system to keep prisoners docile and easy to manage. Right now that was just fine with Mueller. He still couldn't get it through his head what was happening. He needed time to think and piece this mess together into something that made sense.

Mueller had been visited by his court-appointed lawyer

19

briefly after being brought to his cell. The news was bad. Jack was looking at seven consecutive life sentences. "To put it simply," his lawyer said, "at the moment of your death you will be revived in much the same manner as you were in the Continuum. After you serve your first life sentence the process will be repeated until you have completed all seven sentences. Before you ask, I am not aware of any successful suicide attempts by a Time Transfer prisoner."

Jack could simply not come to grips with what lay ahead of him. If he could rest, he might get his bearings and find a way out of what was obviously something much bigger than anything he had ever experienced. He closed his eyes and tried to calm down. He needed a drink but no way that was coming. Was he really being charged with all those killings? Was he really in a pink cell waiting for something, anything, to happen? Was he going crazy or was he already there?

"Go down and get Mueller," the on-duty desk sergeant said to Corrections Officer Mike Brown. This was a two-person job, so Mike grabbed his partner Kathy Lewis and together they went to retrieve Mueller for his arraignment. He would be shackled electronically and taken to the Lock-Up Holographic Section where he would be arraigned by a judge miles away in the World Court Magistrate's Division.

Mike and Kathy moved quickly to pick up Mueller. They only had minutes to get him to the Holographic Section. They went down the row of holding cells to Mueller's cell. Kathy yelled, "Get up, Mueller; it's party time!" She and Mike were about to shut down the force field to Mueller's cell when they both stopped dead in their tracks--Mueller had vanished!

Chapter Five

Mueller only had minutes before the guards would come to take him to his arraignment. Suddenly, Mueller's cell darkened, and a thick haze surrounded him. The next moment Mueller saw the now familiar bright light and felt the warmth cascade through him. All sense of time left him, and Mueller was strangely peaceful. His jail cell, the upcoming trial, and the indisputable outcome were fading away. Jack Mueller opened his eyes and instantly he realized that he was back in what his lawyer had called the Time Warp Continuum. He adjusted his eyesight and felt perfectly calm.

Meanwhile, Jason Law was standing before the chief prosecutor for the World Court's Greater American Federation Department headquartered in Washington, D.C. This was his first meeting with the lady, and it was unpleasant to say the least. "I have never been so embarrassed in over fifty years as a prosecutor. We have a madman who has supposedly disappeared from a holding cell with 24/7 monitoring and a foolproof lockdown system. There is absolutely, and I mean absolutely, no way an inmate could escape from that cell unless he had been beamed to another location. My people tell me that's even a long shot with the electronic jamming equipment the holding facility uses.

"Now I'm hearing that you cut corners bringing in this guy. Is it true you coerced Mueller into signing his Legal Representation Waiver and moved him out of the Continuum before he fully understood his rights?"

It wouldn't be a good idea to lie to Chief Prosecutor Jeanne Hastings. She had probably already read Dawn Phillips's report and had most likely grilled Detective Alexander. Jason hadn't even bothered to have Mueller patted down before he was transferred from the Continuum.

"I may have been a little hasty in bringing him in, but he's a bad guy. We needed to move him quickly. I've already checked with Forensics," Jason continued. "They have a full aura data array on Mueller, and they've fed it into the Inter-Agency Net. Mueller is not on this planet--at least not in this time vector. As crazy as it sounds, the most logical answer is Mueller had help and escaped to another time vector.

"I've spoken with our most respected consultant on paranormal time travel. He's the Himalayan monk, Do Chi. It was our first meeting, but I was very impressed with the old lama."

"Yes," the chief prosecutor responded. "I've met Do Chi. What did he say?"

"He thinks we're on the right track about Mueller being transported to another time vector," Jason said. "However, there's no record of any cyclotron activity. Do Chi believes Mueller had help, but he's not sure who or how." Jason took a deep breath before giving Hastings the rest of the bad news. "Forensics is scanning for Mueller, and if he's managed to make a jump back in time, we'll find him. Forensics tells me they're doing their best, but they had to reconstruct all of the aura data on Mueller. Specialist Phillips had only done an on-site aura scan when we grabbed him." Jason had said the wrong thing.

"Yes, and I know just whose idea it was to use the on-site scan. You know the rules. On-site scans are done in emergency cases only and not as a way to get around a suspect's rights. Detective Inspector Law, I made a fool of myself before the judge today. I got Mueller's arraignment delayed 48 hours. I'm not going to be embarrassed again. We must have Mueller before Judge Turner by 1000 Hours, the day after tomorrow. If not, I'll have no choice but to inform the judge that I've filed charges against you, Specialist Phillips, and Detective Alexander for felony one conspiracy to impede prosecution."

"Prosecutor Hastings, you know Specialist Phillips and Detective Alexander had absolutely nothing to do with this. Didn't you read Phillips's report? I forced her to do the on-site scan.

Alexander is so new he doesn't know which way is up." The chief prosecutor was in no mood to argue.

"First of all," she said, "Nothing in Specialist Phillips's report exonerates her. Alexander witnessed Mueller's signature waiving his rights. If you go down, they go down. You have 48 hours to bring back Mueller or turn yourselves in. Is that understood?" Jason made no reply. He simply turned around and walked out.

Jason called Dawn Phillips on his way to the office. "Phil, it's Jason. Find Alexander and get ready to make a jump to the Continuum. Mueller has escaped!"

"Yes, Sir, Detective Inspector Law," Dawn said sarcastically. Jason had never used his first name with Dawn before and she was less than impressed. "I already got the message. I've contacted Detective Alexander, and he should be here within the hour. I've processed the waiver paperwork for all three of us to make the second jump in a month. The Forensics Department has done a complete aura scan for Mueller, and they think they may have found him. The signal is weak --almost looks like it's being jammed. It keeps moving in and out of the Continuum from one time vector to another. By the time you arrive, we should have a better guess where Mueller is. Will there be anything else, Detective Inspector Law?"

"Phil, I'm sorry. You and I both know I screwed up. We'll get this guy and put him away. Then you and Alexander can do whatever you think you have to do. I won't stand in your way. For now, let's find Mueller!"

Chapter Six

TIME WARP CONTINUUM

Mueller rubbed his eyes to make sure he was seeing what he thought he was seeing--the outline of a man. The bright light surrounding the hooded shape made it impossible to really discern what or whom he was seeing, but there was no doubt where he was--the Time Warp Continuum. "Welcome, Commander Mueller. As you have already guessed, we are in the Time Warp Continuum. My name is not important so please don't waste your time or mine trying to guess my identity." The figure chuckled to himself and added, "Interesting that even with our ability to move through time, we still refer to it as something beyond our control. However, we must be wary of our enemies. Detective Inspector Law is making preparations to apprehend you and take you back to his time to stand trial. We both know you will be found guilty."

Mueller felt trapped and the other shoe was about to drop. "What do you want?" Mueller asked. "You didn't pull me out of that hole just to tell me I'm guilty. What do you want?"

The hooded figure chuckled again and said, "Very perceptive. You're correct. I do want something. I need your very professional services. In return, I'm ready to pay you in a way that is beyond your comprehension."

"Cut the crap. What do you want?"

"I want," the shadowy figure said, "No; I need you to kill Detective Inspector Law. Once you have completed your task, I will place you under my protection and reunite you with your beloved mother. The two of you will enjoy a long life uninterrupted by the authorities or anyone else. Do we have a deal?"

Mueller was caught off guard and for one of the few times in his life didn't know what to say. He wasn't sure the hooded stranger could pull off what he promised, but events lately had made Mueller believe almost anything was possible. "What do I have to do, and when do I get a look at the guy who hired me?" Mueller asked.

"I already told you--who I am is not important. Law and his team are almost here. Take this." The stranger handed Mueller his Turk Blade and Mueller accepted it quickly. "When Law and his crew appear, use that blade and make sure Law doesn't leave here alive. If you can get the other two, that's better, but you must kill Law. Understood?"

"Yes. Once I kill Law and the other two, what happens next?"

The stranger replied, "I'll be here, and I'll make all the necessary arrangements after you've completed your part of the bargain." Before Mueller could say anything else, the hooded figure had disappeared. Mueller was alone with his six inch Turk Blade. He inspected it quickly but expertly. It was still razor sharp and ready to do his bidding.

Jason Law, Dawn Phillips, and Mark Alexander had just made their jump to the Time Warp Continuum. T-Control kept getting readings on Mueller in the Continuum, but they were fluctuating erratically. Mueller had to be getting help. An escape to the Continuum was beyond his technical knowledge, let alone the massive logistical support it must have required.

"First things first," Jason reminded himself. Although there had been intermittent signals from at least one other contact, Mueller was the only viable target T-Control was scanning. Jason had to be ready for anything, but he didn't know what. He hated going into the Continuum without better intelligence, but he had no choice.

When Jason and the other two appeared in the Continuum Jason was savagely attacked and he felt cold steel slice through his left arm. "Good to see you, Detective Inspector. I was hoping you and I would meet again. This meeting will have to be quick."

Mueller raised his hand to finish Jason when Detective Alexander caught Mueller with a shot from his stun gun. Sophisticated replicas of the twentieth century's Tasers the stun guns of the future required no contact to unleash their debilitating electronic shocks. Mueller went down instantly but still had a tight grip on his Turk Blade. Somehow he rolled on his back and managed to get to his feet. "I'll see you dead, Law!" he shouted. Alexander began to fire again when Mueller made a quick jump forward and grabbed Dawn Phillips. He put his six inch, bladed knife to her throat and told Alexander, "Back off!"

Alexander complied, and before he could make another move, Mueller and Phillips disappeared before his eyes. Jason yelled at Alexander to contact T-Control to see if they could get a reading on Mueller and Phillips. Instead, Alexander moved to Jason's side and made a quick assessment of Jason's wound. The knife had cut deeply into his arm, slicing open the large artery that pumped life into his left hand. Alexander used his belt to fashion a tourniquet above the wound and asked Jason to hold the belt tightly with his right hand.

"T-Control, this is Alexander. Mueller is gone and he's taken Forensic Specialist Phillips with him. Detective Inspector Law was attacked by Mueller as we arrived. Law has a severe wound to his left arm that requires a tourniquet. Recommend Law and myself be returned to home base."

Jason was ready to pass out and was in no shape to argue with Alexander's assessment or recommendation. They were transported to home base. There Jason's wound was laser-graphed, and he received a much-needed blood transfusion. He was then immediately returned to duty status.

In the meantime, Detective Alexander had met with the Forensic Unit and T- Control staff. They had managed to get a general readout of Mueller and Dawn Phillips. The two had jumped to the year 2003, somewhere in Washington, D.C. T-Control thought it might be possible to narrow the search pattern once Jason's and Alexander's cerebral implants had given the Forensics Unit a more precise analysis of what the two of them had experienced in their confrontation with Mueller. For some reason Dawn's implant was not providing any data. T-Control estimated it could take up to three hours to get a more precise fix on Mueller and Phillips.

Immediately after Jason was cleared for duty, he went looking for Alexander. The young detective briefed Law on Mueller and Phillips's location. "What do you mean it will take another three hours to get a precise reading of their exact time and space vector?

We don't have three hours! Do you understand in three hours of our time, Mueller could kill Dawn a thousand times and still be able to hide himself forever?"

Detective Alexander was near the breaking point, but somehow he managed to look Jason directly in the eyes and speak. "I know you're concerned for Specialist Phillips's safety, but I had to make a decision, and I made one. If you think I screwed up, you do what you have to do."

Jason realized he had taken his frustration out on Alexander for no good reason. "All right, I'm sorry, but we need to move quickly if we're going to save Dawn. We need to know how Mueller got his hands on that knife he used on me."

Alexander responded, "I've already checked with the D.C. police. There's no record of the knife they confiscated from Mueller."

"No record? How did Mueller manage to get his hands on that thing? It just doesn't make sense." Jason decided to ask the Forensics Unit to do another scan of all of Mueller's records. The response was immediate. There was no entry showing that Mueller had ever owned a Turk Blade. Worse, there was nothing showing Mueller had ever committed any murders with such a knife!

Someone had altered Mueller's records in an attempt to hide his dark past. In addition, there was no record of any DNA/aura association between Mueller and Jason. However, T-Control had narrowed down its earlier estimates and now placed Mueller in Washington, D.C. on July 4, 2003. T-Control was unable to provide any more exact time or space vector coordinates.

Jason would have to go back in time to Washington, D.C. and hunt down Mueller. Heaven help Mueller if he had hurt Dawn! Detective Alexander needed no coaxing to make the jump with Jason. Somehow they had to find Dawn Phillips and stop Mueller before he killed again. That included stopping whoever was helping Mueller. Someone very powerful was behind Mueller, and they had to find out who it was. Why would anyone want to help Mueller, and what could be gained from Jason's death? Once Dawn was safe, there would be time to sort out the details.

Chapter Seven

TICK TOCK BAR,
2003

Mueller had grabbed Dawn Phillips more out of desperation than any thought-out plan. His only chance of saving himself was to keep her between him and the TFI detective and his stun gun. Mueller was about to warn Detective Alexander to stay away when he felt the unmistakable sensation that could only mean he was being transported through time again. He held tightly to Dawn Phillips, and in the next instant, he appeared behind his old haunt-- the Tick Tock Bar--with Dawn Phillips still tightly in his grip. It was late evening, and after he got his bearings, he realized he and Phillips were in a dark alley at the rear entrance of the bar.

Dawn began to shout, "Help, help!" Mueller took the butt of his Turk Blade and hit Dawn sharply at the base of her neck. She slumped over and made no more noise. Mueller found an old piece of rope lying in the alley and bound Dawn tightly. He used his handkerchief and belt as an effective gag and threw her behind several trash bins. He felt in his pockets--no money. He had to think and think quickly. He had botched his attempt to kill Law, and he had no idea how he had ended up in Washington, D.C. What day was it--let alone what year?

Mueller felt a shudder go through him. Out of the darkness he heard the voice of the stranger who had rescued him from prison. "You will be unhappy to know that Detective Inspector Law survived. He is searching for you frantically to rescue the young lady you have just rendered unconscious. I brought you here to give you one last chance to fulfill your part of our bargain. Law must die. You must return to the Continuum if you are to kill him.

28

"People of his time are unable to sustain themselves physically when they interact in another time vector. Ms Phillips's only connectivity to this time vector is you. Her cerebral implant is useless. If you were to die, she would return to the Continuum immediately. Since you made physical contact with her in the Continuum, she is bound to you as much as an alter ego. However, make no mistake. She has a mind of her own as she so vividly displayed in her attempt to escape when you appeared here.

"Before Law gets here, I want you to return to the Continuum with Ms Phillips. Law will follow. He has no choice. When you arrive in the Continuum, Ms Phillips will be with you but in an altered state. Think of her as a zombie, a member of the walking dead."

"All right, I'll do as you say. Once Law's dead though, and I get rid of Ms Phillips, you keep your end of the bargain!"

"Yes, yes, you and your mother together under my protection. How do you think you got here alive? If I hadn't interceded, you would be back in your cell still awaiting trial. Now, prepare yourself. Untie Ms Phillips and hold her in your arms." Mueller did as he was told and again felt the bright light surround him as he appeared in the Continuum with Dawn Phillips in his arms.

As Mueller and Dawn Phillips entered the Continuum, Jason and Detective Alexander were preparing to make their jump to Washington, D.C., July 4, 2003. They had appeared in the Time Warp Continuum thinking they would immediately be transported to D.C. Instead they received an urgent message from T-Control that Mueller and Dawn Phillips had disappeared from their July 4, 2003, time vector.

T-Control couldn't get a precise reading on where Mueller and his hostage were. The only conclusion--T-Control could draw was the two were most likely in the Continuum. That's exactly where T-Control was sending Jason and Alexander.

The Time Warp Continuum was amorphous--there were no physical boundaries and seemingly no form. However, up seemed up, and down seemed down. A person moved about and interacted the same as on earth. Color was a different matter. How a person perceived color in the Continuum depended on the person's aura. A myriad of forces--genetic makeup, age, gender, and a person's physical/psychological well-being all impacted his or her perception of the Continuum's color.

Generally, most people saw the Continuum in bright, ever-changing colors. People under stress saw the Continuum in darker, more subdued colors. For Jack Mueller the Continuum was very dark.

Jason felt Mueller's breath on the back of his neck as he and Alexander appeared in the Continuum. Jason only had one chance. He screamed at Alexander, "It's Mueller. Try to get a shot at him!"

Jason dropped to his knees and spun around to avoid Mueller's blade. He saw Dawn standing beside Mueller, making no attempt to escape or help. Jason had no time to think. He jumped to his feet and kicked Mueller in the groin as hard as he could. Mueller screamed, took a step back, and then became a madman.

He lunged at Jason, throwing his knife to the side. He was on top of Jason biting, kicking like a wounded animal. "You're a dead man!" he screamed.

Jason tried another kick to the groin but missed. He and Mueller were turning over and over, making a clean shot by Alexander highly unlikely. Jason grabbed Mueller's left arm and pulled it behind and above Mueller's shoulder blade. Jason heard Mueller's arm crack as it broke just above the elbow.

Mueller yelled in pain but turned quickly to face Jason. "Do you think you can finish me that easy?" He grabbed his Turk Blade and lunged at Jason. The next instant there was a bright flash as Alexander shot Mueller. Somehow the Navy pilot continued toward Jason.

Alexander shot again, and Mueller dropped on top of Jason, heaving a dying breath. Alexander ran to Jason, pushed Mueller off him, and checked Mueller for vital signs. Satisfied Mueller was dead, Alexander turned and saw Jason's body jerking uncontrollably after the fight. Alexander reported to T-Control to give Jason time to recover.

Alexander then ran to Dawn Phillips, who still stood motionless, her eyes transfixed in a glazed stare. Alexander had never seen anything like this before. He was over his head. He went back to Jason who was regaining his composure. Jason had faced death before but not in the never-never land of the Continuum. He wanted to make sense of everything, but first, and most important, he wanted to make sure Dawn was unharmed. He went to her and saw the same vacant stare that Alexander had seen. Jason took Dawn's hand and looked into her eyes. You're safe now, Dawn, and no one can hurt you. Mueller's dead. We're all safe. Come back to me."

At that instant, Mueller rolled over, his knife still in his right hand. He struck at Jason but missed. Alexander raised his gun again. "What does it take to kill this guy?" he screamed.

Mueller moved first. He threw his Turk Blade and hit Alexander in the chest. The knife was buried to the hilt in Alexander's heart. The detective was dead before he hit the ground.

Jason moved back in horror. He grabbed the gun from Alexander's hand and shot Mueller over and over. "Die, you freak, die!" Once he was sure Mueller was dead he shot him again between the eyes. It was wrong, but he didn't care.

Mueller had done something horrible to Dawn and killed Alexander. And Jason was sure Mueller was connected somehow to his mother's death. Mueller deserved to die.

Jason radioed to T-Control for back up, took Dawn by the hand, and cried harder than he had ever cried. A safe distance away, shielded from T-Control's curious eyes a shadowy figure watched Jason Law and swore Law would die. Somehow, Law would die.

Chapter Eight

Jason Law was at the breaking point. He had spent countless hours cursing God and then begging Him to save Dawn Phillips. He was in her hospital room waiting for her doctor. It had been over three weeks since Jason, Dawn, and Detective Mark Alexander's body had been returned from the Time Warp Continuum. Alexander was dead. Jason had to face it. There was no reprieve for those killed in the Continuum. Dead was dead.

"I'm begging you, God! You've already taken my father, and stood by while my mother was murdered. I can't handle this anymore. Not Dawn, not this time.

Please, God, please!" There was no answer, only silence.

Mueller's body had disappeared. When Jason and the others were transported from the Continuum, T-Control had good readings on everyone including Mueller. When they appeared in present time, Mueller's body was missing. T-Control did an immediate sweep of the Continuum and could find no trace of Mueller. In fact there were no indications he or the mysterious figure had been there in the first place. T-Control was continuing to look for both of them, but so far they had no idea how or what happened.

The past three weeks had been a blur. Prosecutor Hastings's threat to file charges against Jason, Dawn, and Alexander had become meaningless.

The doctor walked in the room flanked by two other men. "Detective Inspector Law, this is Doctor Shaw and Doctor Johnston. I've asked them here to examine Ms Phillips." Jason nodded his head but didn't even bother to get up or shake the doctors' hands. These two physicians were just two more in a long line of white coats that had made their way into Dawn's room.

The two of them went to work immediately. Earlier the data from Dawn's cerebral implant had been connected to the hospital's diagnostic computer system but the information had been little help to the two physicians. After about 20 minutes, the two stopped their examination and compared notes. They conferred with the first doctor and then left the room.

The first doctor then turned to Jason and spoke. "I'll be blunt, Detective Inspector Law. Ms Phillips, in our opinion, is not likely to recover. She is in a catatonic state that is beyond our reach. If this were trauma-driven we could help her. Something else has happened. You've heard the old saying, 'frightened to death'? Ms Phillips has been frightened into a sub-conscious state of mind I'm sorry but even in the twenty-fourth century there are some things beyond our reach. I'm sorry."

The doctor left the room, knowing he had failed. He walked down the hall and was about to make his way to the transport walk. Something was telling him to stop, to try again, but he was a pragmatic man and this patient was beyond medical science. Then he saw an old friend, Dr. Norma Bing, the daughter of the late Dr. Thomas Bing. Norma had continued her father's work in time travel and had become world-renowned herself.

She saw the doctor as she left the transport walk and instantly smiled. The doctor waited for Bing. After exchanging pleasantries, he told her about the Phillips case. "Norma, I don't know why I'm telling you this, but I don't know which way to turn. We've tried everything, and we still can't reach Ms Phillips. There's nothing physical that's keeping her in her catatonic state, and we can find nothing in our aura scans or psychiatric work ups. I just don't know what else to do."

Dr. Bing spoke softly, "Have you thought of the paranormal? My father was an absolute believer in the scientific method but he learned there are dimensions and truths that go beyond science. His good friend, Do Chi, is still alive and is perhaps the world's best authority in the ways of the spiritual mind. There are others, of course--Su Dahl, San Lo, Barbara Jeanel, but Do Chi is at the top of the list." The doctor had never met Do Chi but knew him by reputation and was willing to try anything to save Dawn Phillips.

"Do you think it's possible Do Chi would agree to do a virtual examination of Ms Phillips?"

"No," Dr. Bing replied, "but I think I can talk him into doing an on-site examination. He's here with me, attending a World Forum on Time Travel and the Future, and I know he will help."

Six hours later, Do Chi, Dr. Bing, and the doctor were standing in Dawn's room talking to Jason Law. Do Chi spoke, "I make no promises, but I will try".

"You don't have to worry," Jason said sarcastically. "Dawn's living will is in order, and you can't be touched." This was only Jason's second meeting with Do Chi, and it was getting off to a bad start.

"Don't be so presumptive, Detective Inspector Law. I wasn't speaking to you. I was talking to Ms Phillips. She hears and understands everything we say. She is in this world and in the next. If she wishes to return to this world, she will; if not, she won't."

Jason had been a jerk, and he apologized immediately. "Please, Your Eminence, I'm truly sorry, but if there is anything you can do, I will be in your debt forever." Do Chi said nothing but moved to the head of Dawn's bed. He bent over Dawn, put his right hand with its long, thin fingers behind her head and whispered in her ear.

The old lama spoke softly to Dawn, but no one could hear his words. Everyone stood for several seconds and stared at Dawn-- everyone except Do Chi. He backed away quietly, bowed, and left the room.

Jason stood next to Dawn's bed and looked deeply at her face. At first he saw nothing. Dawn continued to look as before. Then Jason thought he saw her right eyelid quiver. "Look, Doctor. Her eyelid moved."

"No, Detective Inspector Law, her vital signs remain constant. You only thought you saw movement. We sometimes see what we want to see."

"I'm telling you her eyelid moved!" Suddenly, Dawn gasped and seemed to take in a deep breath of air. The doctor moved to her side and looked up at the monitors. "You're right. She appears to be regaining consciousness." Moments later Dawn opened her eyes and looked directly at Jason. She could only manage one word, "Jason."

It took several minutes before Dawn Phillips regained full consciousness and was coherent enough to speak again. Jason looked through her eyes into her soul. They both realized they had moved far beyond a professional relationship since Jason and Mark Alexander had rescued Dawn in the Time Warp Continuum. Alexander's death could never be forgotten, but Jason's and Dawn's futures were inexorably entwined.

Dawn spoke to Jason, "I'm sorry I couldn't respond before. I've been aware of everything that's happened since Mueller grabbed me, but I felt as though I was in another world. No, that's not true. I felt as though I was in another dimension. It was as though I was seeing, hearing, feeling everything through some type of filter. I thought I could never come back. Then I felt the same warmth and saw the same intense light we see when we enter the Continuum. I heard a voice whispering to me to come back."

Jason tried to be gentle, but he had to know what Do Chi had whispered to Dawn. "What exactly did the voice say?"

"It was so simple," Dawn said. "The voice said, 'Open your eyes. There's more to be seen.' At first I thought it was God. I felt a hand guiding me from the other dimension to you."

The doctor spoke quietly, "I have never seen anything like this in my 60 years of medical practice. Ms Phillips has had all of the excitement she needs for one day. Detective Inspector Law, Dr. Bing, I'm sorry, but we need to let Ms Phillips rest."

"No, I'm rested enough. I need to speak to Jason. After Mueller grabbed me we made a jump in time and ended up in some dark alley. I have no idea when or where we were. Mueller knocked me out and then tied me up and gagged me. As my head was clearing, I saw a shadowy figure appear in the alley. I couldn't see his face but I know his voice. It was the same voice that whispered to me and brought me back to this world."

Jason couldn't believe what he was hearing. Do Chi, the man who saved Dawn and brought her back from the un-living, was the same person who had guided Mueller and put Dawn in her catatonic state in the first place. Why would Do Chi help Mueller? "What did he want?" Jason asked.

"He wanted you dead," Dawn replied. "I have no idea why, but he wanted you dead. As he was talking to Mueller, he raised his hand, and I could see he wore a beautiful blue sapphire ring with four feathers carved in the stone. He gave Mueller one last chance and told him that he was transporting us to the Continuum.

"He said you had to follow and that Mueller must kill you. He continued saying that once in the Continuum I would fall into an altered state of consciousness. When we appeared in the Continuum, I was aware of my surroundings but felt as though I was watching a movie on one of those old television screens. You know the rest."

"So that's why Mueller and I had a DNA/aura connection," Jason said. "It was Do Chi. We've got to find him no matter where or when he's gone."

Dr. Bing listened to Dawn and Jason intently and shook her head in disbelief. "I cannot believe that Do Chi is this sinister figure from the Time Warp Continuum. Do Chi and my father were inseparable. If it weren't for Do Chi, we most likely would not have Time Travel. I will not accept the word of a patient who has obviously been through an unparalleled trauma."

"Dr. Bing," Jason said trying to interrupt Thomas Bing's daughter.

She would have none of it. "We need to be sure before we accuse someone in Do Chi's position. He is not only a noted scientist but also the beloved leader of millions of people who believe their karma is tied directly to his. Detective Inspector Law, you simply cannot grab this man and tell the world he is the driving force behind a serial killer such as Mueller."

Dawn's doctor spoke quietly but firmly. "Ms. Phillips requires rest. Dr. Bing, Detective Inspector Law, you will both leave the room now."

"No, Jason," Dawn said. "I've got to go with you. He'll kill you--I'm sure of that. Our only hope is to face him together. You can't go without me, I won't let you."

"Dawn, the doctor's right. You need rest. I won't do anything without seeing you first. You rest. I need you with me, but you've got to be ready to go."

Jason took Dawn's hand and squeezed it. Then he turned around and motioned to Dr. Bing. They left the room with the doctor still flabbergasted at Dawn's recovery and Dawn obviously distraught over the circumstances that led her to the hospital.

Dr. Bing waited until Jason had caught up to her outside Dawn's hospital room. "I meant what I said, Detective Inspector Law. I will not stand by while a man of Do Chi's reputation is railroaded through the so-called justice system."

"Relax, Dr. Bing. I have no intention of trying to get a warrant on Do Chi. No judge in his right mind would issue a warrant based on the testimony of someone in Ms Phillips's condition."

"Good. Please don't misunderstand. If he has done anything wrong, I want him to face charges, but I will not believe Do Chi is capable of this until I see the evidence with my own eyes. Good-day, Detective Inspector Law."

As Dr. Bing left, Jason only had one hope. He had told Dr. Bing the truth. No judge would issue a warrant. That just meant he'd have to go after Do Chi without one.

Jason believed without a shadow of a doubt that the next few hours would mean life or death for Dawn, for him, and possibly millions of other people. Most importantly, he knew Do Chi was waiting.

Chapter Nine

THE CYCLOTRON
2314

Jason had pulled in all the favors people owed him and then some. Somehow the TFI Forensics Unit had gotten their hands on an old aura scan of Do Chi. They had matched up the data and performed an initial workup on the most likely whereabouts of the lama. The first and most obvious conclusion was Do Chi was not on Planet Earth or Near Space in present time.

They began scanning the Time Warp Continuum and Do Chi's last suspected time/space vector--the alley behind the Tick Tock Bar where he had supposedly encountered Mueller and Dawn.

There was a high probability Do Chi had been on-scene in the alley. However, after Jason's last encounter with Mueller in the Continuum, Do Chi's trail had bounced from one time vector to another, always returning to the Continuum. It was almost like he was taunting Jason. It seemed as though he was waiting for Jason to come and get him. Jason didn't need any encouragement. He needed Dawn, and he needed to get to the TFI's cyclotron.

It had been almost 12 hours since he had left Dawn's hospital room. It was 0300 hours, and the hospital was dark for the most part. Jason moved easily past the security and nurse stations and walked into Dawn's room unnoticed. She was asleep, or so Jason thought. "Jason, I've been waiting for you."

"Shh. How do you feel? What does the doctor say?" Jason asked.

"They're releasing me tomorrow morning. The doctor said he's never seen such a miraculous recovery. We can't wait for tomorrow morning. We need to find Do Chi. He's waiting for us. I don't know why, but I know he's waiting for us, and we have to find him as soon as we can."

"You're right, but I don't think he's just waiting for us. He's daring us to come after him. He knows that we can't all survive. Either we get him or he gets us. He's not some bad guy we have to bring back. It's either him or us--period!"

After leaving the hospital, Jason and Dawn made it to the TFI cyclotron. To make the jump to the Continuum, Jason and Dawn would need help--lots of help. Luckily, Jason could count on his friends who worked at the cyclotron. Once he and Dawn had told them how Detective Alexander had died and who was behind Mueller, they all agreed to help.

Jason and Dawn were strapped in to the cyclotron at 0515:30. Exactly at 0517:30 they made their jump to the Time Warp Continuum. Immediately they could feel something was different. They still felt the warm glow and saw the intense light as they entered the Continuum, but as their forms solidified, they both felt a cold breeze blow past their faces.

"You look so much like your mother, Jason," Do Chi said softly. I still remember your mother's lovely face and how timid her small son was." Do Chi raised his hand and gestured for Jason to come closer. Jason saw the older man's slender fingers and the large sapphire ring on the third finger of his right hand. Jason almost fell as he remembered those same long, thin fingers around his mother's throat.

The ring on that stranger's right hand had slipped as he had pressed harder, suffocating Jason's mother. The carved feathers in the blue stone pressed hard against his mother's neck as the stranger gripped harder and harder. His mother's face became ashen and then a deepening blue that seemed to match the outline of the stone that Jason could still see cutting into her skin.

Jason had tried. He had tried so hard to stop the madman. But he was too small and the old man too insane with rage to be stopped by the small boy. The man finished and dropped Jason's mother to the ground. She lay motionless with small rivulets of blood dripping from the wound the carved stone had made in her neck.

The coroner later commented in her autopsy report, "There

is a one sixteenth inch straight line cut on the back of the deceased's neck with three small cuts appearing at an angle from the straight line cut." When Jason had been questioned about the death of his mother and, in particular, about the cuts on his mother's neck, he had no memory of the event. Until this very moment, he had blocked that terrible episode from his memory.

Now, seeing his mother's killer, it had all come flooding back to him. "You killed my mother!"

"Yes, I killed her," Do Chi answered. "I had no choice. Millions of people support me with their prayers and offerings. I am a man sworn to celibacy, and yet I had to have your mother."

"Your oath meant nothing to you!" Jason hissed.

"Each monk knows he will face that moment of temptation--the moment when he will face carnal knowledge and decide where his heart lies. Your mother was my temptation. Your father had died when you were only four, and your mother was left raising you alone. She refused my advances and threatened to expose me to my followers and the world. I could not allow that to happen. I had only one choice--to eliminate her from my life--and yours."

"God used you when you killed my mother, and He is using you now. Damn you and damn God. I'll see you both in hell!" Jason yelled out to the shamed lama.

"You must look beyond the life of your mother, Jason. What lies before you is the very meaning of life. Time is a veil, a veil you can pass through. Today is yesterday and tomorrow. The key to the riddle is you. You can walk through time once you accept that you are one and you are all."

Jason had heard almost the same words years before during a ritual of manhood in a secret cave in the Outback. He tried to put the past out of his mind, and concentrate on Do Chi. Jason looked at Dawn. She was scanning Do Chi and feeding the data to T-Control, hoping they could lock on the lama's coordinates. T-Control was responding to Dawn through her cerebral implant. They were receiving no data on Do Chi. The only people showing up on their monitors were Jason and Dawn. Jason got the same message.

"What are you trying to say, Old Man? It's obvious you let us catch you. What do you want with us?"

"First, I want you to understand that you and your kind have no hold on me. I fear neither man nor his silly inventions. So many years ago I told Dr. Thomas Bing that time travel was a matter of the mind not machines. He understood so little, and yet he understood enough to use my talents to train the original time travelers from your civilization."

Jason couldn't help himself. He asked again, "What do you want from us?"

"I want you to see the possibilities that lie in front of you and that can be yours for so little in return. Close your eyes. You are five years old, and you have just fallen and cut yourself just below the chin."

Jason opened his eyes, and he was on his old playground. Not just remembering the playground but actually lying on his back with blood streaming down his shirt. His mother was running to his side. "It's okay Jason. We'll get you fixed up better than new. Don't worry. It won't hurt. I won't let it."

Do Chi spoke again, "Close your eyes--you are seven years old. It has only been three years since your father died, and you are watching your mother's death."

Jason opened his eyes and saw the strange man choking his mother to death. When it was over, the old man said to Jason, "You are to forget my face, forget my voice. You will remember nothing." Do Chi had been correct. Jason had forgotten everything, everything except those long, thin hands.

"I also took care to erase any forensic evidence. Not even your vaunted TFI could trace me," Do Chi chided.

"Why are we here now?" Jason asked the lama.

"Patience, you will know everything soon. First I want to take both of you on a trip to the future. Close your eyes." Jason and Dawn did as they were told and were almost afraid to open them. When they did, they were in a world they had never seen before. They were on a busy street walking among thousands of other people, people and other beings that could only be described as alien. Some could almost be copies of comic book characters. Others could easily be plant-based beings, and still others were beyond description. "You are in the year 2755 at an inter-galactic conference on time travel. I am to be a featured speaker." Do Chi chuckled as he gazed at the marquee with his name prominently featured.

"This is some kind of mind game you're playing!" Jason spat out. Or was it? He was afraid what he was seeing was the truth, and that truth was in the hands of a madman. Jason closed his eyes and opened them quickly. He, Dawn, and Do Chi were back in the Continuum. Jason acted without thinking. He had to stop Do Chi but he had no idea how. Jason grabbed Do Chi's right hand and felt for the sapphire ring. He ripped at the ring with all his power, but it wouldn't budge. Do Chi tried to fight, but as long as Jason held his ring finger, the old man seemed to be paralyzed.

Jason screamed at Dawn, "Use your laser. Cut his hand off. It's our only chance!" Dawn pulled her sidearm out as Jason held out Do Chi's hand. Dawn moved on instinct and sliced through Do Chi's wrist. The lama looked surprised but didn't say a word.

Jason looked down at Do Chi's hand and the sapphire ring. He looked up at Dawn and turned back to Do Chi. The strange man that haunted Jason's dreams was gone!

"Where did he go?" Dawn shouted.

Jason contacted T-Control and they still had no readings on Do Chi. However, the readings on Dawn and Jason had gone off the charts. They both had been through a severe trauma.

Later, as they were being debriefed by a group of TFI officials and members of the scientific community, Jason and Dawn both insisted on what they had seen and what had happened. Unfortunately for them, their only proof--Do Chi's right hand and his blue sapphire ring--hadn't survived transport from the Time Warp Continuum.

"Jason, I'm afraid," Dawn had whispered as the two were about to go into their first debriefing session. "They'll never believe us, Jason, never."

Chapter Ten

It took months of counseling for Jason and Dawn to accept that they had been hallucinating, and Do Chi had nothing to do with Mueller. Mueller's escape was most likely not an escape at all. Rather, when Jason rushed Mueller's processing in the Time Warp Continuum Mueller's aura had not totally solidified.

The TFI Forensics Department hypothesized that Mueller's aura had broken down once he had been transferred to present time. Mueller's aura decomposed in his holding cell, and he was returned to the Time Warp Continuum. Once there, Mueller began bouncing from one time vector to another like a dog chasing its tail. In the end, Mueller was doomed. If Jason hadn't killed Mueller in the Time Warp Continuum, he would have died from aura decomposition.

The Internal Affairs Division reviewed Jason's culpability in Mueller's aura breakdown and found Jason was negligent. The matter was referred to the Chief, Time Force Investigations, who promptly passed the buck and sent the case to Prosecutor Hastings.

It wasn't even a close call. Jason Law had crossed the line and could easily be charged, but if Hastings charged Law, it could bring down the TFI. Better to allow the TFI to handle the situation. She sent the case back to the TFI with no comment.

Internal Affairs recommended a reduction in rank and 12 months forfeiture of pay. The Chief, Time Force Investigations, waived the reduction in rank and placed Jason on three months unpaid leave to be served concurrently with his medical leave.

The question remained, how had Do Chi's DNA been tracked

to Mueller's space and time vector? Quite easily it turned out. When TFI Agents attempted to contact Do Chi at his United Nations office they were informed Do Chi was meditating at an unknown time vector, and he could be gone for some time. However, the agents found exactly what they were looking for in the sect's files.

On a disk marked "Consultations", Do Chi detailed his meeting with Jason about Mueller's disappearance from his holding cell. Obviously, or so the agents thought, Do Chi's aura and DNA data had been co-mingled with Jason's when they shook hands, and Do Chi offered his blessings during their meeting.

Dawn and Jason had grown even closer during their so-called rehabilitation. It started with longer and longer chats during counseling sessions. Then they started having lunch, then dinner and finally long walks on the beach. As they walked, Dawn saw a bright blue feather and picked it up. She started to hand it to Jason when they both realized they were about to take a giant step forward in their relationship. They looked at each other and Jason started to say something.

"No, Jason, don't say anything," Dawn whispered. Jason took her into his arms and they kissed the sweet kiss that can only be the first. They stood on the beach and held each other closely, neither saying a word.

Finally, Jason felt Dawn shiver and said, "Here, let me give you my jacket."

"No, Jason," Dawn said. "I'm not really cold. You're all I need to keep me warm tonight."

Years later the two would argue about who had actually kissed the other first, but it didn't matter. They had found each other and would be together forever.

Meanwhile, somewhere in the year 2993 in a small cave in the Himalayan Mountains, a man sat before a fire holding an identical feather to the one he had left on the beach for Jason and Dawn. He put the feather in his tunic and stirred the fire with his left hand--his right hand missing. He kept repeating the words, "Time is a veil, a veil you can pass through. Come to me, Jason. Come to me."

Chapter Eleven

THE CYCLOTRON,
2314

Jason saw the blinding light and felt the unmistakable rush as he began his transition to the Time Warp Continuum. He began to relax and let the euphoria engulf him. Then he saw it again--the bright blue feather! He couldn't get it out of his mind. He had seen several government shrinks who gave him varying opinions on what the feather meant.

He understood he was still deeply troubled by his mother's death, but he couldn't grasp the significance of the feather and what secret he was hiding from himself. Somehow it had crept into his mind and broke the intense concentration required to bond with his two teammates sitting beside him in the cyclotron's cocoon. Without that bond, the group would be unable to attain their corporate mind-set and make the simulated jump to the Continuum.

"We're bringing the cyclotron's speed down, Detective Inspector Law. Please report to the watch commander for debriefing once you've disembarked from the cocoon." This was Detective Inspector Law's third and final attempt in the TFI simulator to obtain a line of duty determination "fit for duty." It had ended in failure just like the other two.

"Why am I imagining that blue feather? It just didn't make sense," Jason said to himself. He reported to the watch commander who formally told him that he had failed in his final attempt to be certified for duty. The whole debriefing took less than fifteen minutes. Then the watch commander told Jason that Chief Prosecutor Hastings wanted to see him ASAP!

Jean Hastings had become close friends with both Jason and

Dawn during their rehabilitation. It had started at a chance meeting in a local restaurant and now all three were best friends. They all agreed it was better if their friendship remained secret within the TFI. The latest developments had proved them right.

"Jason, I'm sorry but regulations only give you two choices. You can accept a position in this office as Liaison Officer with the TFI or you'll be forced to retire."

"You've got to be kidding! I'm not sitting behind a desk. You know I'm not ready for retirement, Jeanne," Jason said too loudly.

"Jason, you and I both know your options are limited. You are officially not fit for duty in the TFI, and I can only do so much. Talk to Dawn. Think it over. I'll work with you, but I can't spin gold out of straw."

Jason hated it when Jeanne used those ancient colloquialisms, but she was on his side and she was right. He needed to talk to Dawn.

Jason and Dawn had been married in a small chapel in upper state New York while they were still on medical leave. Dawn was back at work on a limited duty status and was getting used to the daily grind.

She and Jason had talked about having a child, and Dawn was sure they could be happy together. If only Jason could shake those terrible dreams and his obsession with that bright blue feather. Jason had tried and tried to convince her that it meant more than just a pretty feather she had found on the beach. This was the one issue that kept their relationship from being perfect. It all stemmed from their last time in the Time Warp Continuum, but she was unsure how. Jason kept pushing her about the blue feather, and she didn't like it.

Jason walked into Dawn's lab and gave her the bad news. "I blew it again. I can't get that blue feather out of my mind. I've run out of chances with TFI, and they've given me my walking papers. Jeanne Hastings says I can work in her office, but I'd rather leave and start again. Phil, I'm going crazy. I know that feather is the key!" Dawn smiled when Jason called her Phil.

"I stopped and picked this up." He showed her the bright blue feather. Jason had found it in her personal items deep in the back of her antique bedroom chest. Dawn's smile dimmed. She was angry

46

and ready to snap at Jason. Then she looked into his eyes. He was desperate. "Dawn, I know I shouldn't have gone through your things, but I had to see this, touch it. I want you to run a full analysis on this feather. I want to know what it is, where it came from, who's touched it, everything!"

"Jason, you know I can't do that without authorization. This could mean my job."

"I know what I'm asking, but if we don't figure this out, it could mean a lot more than your job. It could mean our marriage, our lives."

"Jason, you're not making sense. You've got to get control of yourself." Dawn bit her lip. "I'm sorry. I'm sorry, Jason. I'll do it, but we both have to agree this is the end of it. No more!"

"All right, no more. I promise," Jason said. They looked at each other knowing that one way or the other their lives were about to change forever.

Chapter Twelve

TFI FORENSIC LABORATORY,
2314

Dawn took the feather from Jason. No use worrying about contamination now. No matter, once she had completed her testing, she could reason with Jason and show him he was chasing windmills.

Dawn went to the lab and set up the usual DNA profile protocols. She would conduct multi-layered, nuclear DNA extractions to determine the origin of the feather and who or what may have touched it. DNA analysis was not only much more sophisticated in the twenty-fourth century, it was also a much quicker process.

Within ten minutes Dawn returned from the lab. Her face was ashen, and she was visibly shaken. She kept reading the report over and over to make sure she hadn't made an error. She had already run the analysis twice, and there was no mistake.

The feather itself had come from a red-billed blue magpie, an extinct bird that had once flourished in altitudes up to 10,000 feet throughout the Himalayan Mountains. The bird had disappeared completely about 50 years ago. The bird's bright blue tail feathers were tipped in white and now were considered a gift from heaven by some sects. Dawn had found her own DNA on the feather along with Jason's--no surprise there, but the feather also contained DNA from Do Chi . That was impossible unless Do Chi had made direct contact with the feather.

Jason gasped after he read the report. "It's Do Chi!" As soon as the words left his mouth, he screamed in agony. Officials in the Department of Justice referred to his conditioned response as "induced behavioral modification." People on the receiving end of this technique simply called it BEHAVE and usually said it felt like a migraine on steroids.

BEHAVE was administered through cerebral implants and was an integral part of Jason's and Dawn's therapy. Saying no to the therapy meant automatic suspension without pay for government employees and endless administrative and court procedures that almost always ended in the government's favor.

"You're just having another memory lapse, Jason. Take a deep breath; it will pass in a moment."

"I'm not going to take this anymore!" Jason shouted. "I'm not going to take it." Jason cringed as the second BEHAVE shock went through his system.

Jason only had one more chance to comply. A subject was offered two opportunities to behave but the third time the incentive was much stronger--sometimes strong enough to render the subject unconscious. The government used a person's cerebral implant to administer the so-called therapy. The first two thought adjustments were automatically computer generated and no specific record kept of the events. The third time, however, the subject's unauthorized thought pattern was registered with the immediate supervisor and kept in the subject's permanent electronic personnel data record.

"Jason, you've got to snap out of this now! One more outburst and you'll be on report and me with you."

Dawn only had one option. She had already disconnected the uplink on her cerebral implant. Her lab's equipment provided too many chances for false negative reports being generated by her implant. TFI personnel working around such equipment were required to "unplug" while they were within five meters of electronic equipment linked to T Control's master computer system. However, they were also required to plug in every 90 minutes for quick scans.

Dawn had about 20 minutes before her next uplink. She had an override code that also allowed her to disconnect other employees' implants in emergencies. This was definitely an emergency although she doubted her boss would agree. She scanned Jason's head with her palm-sized monitor and entered "EIO-- electronic implant override. Jason took a deep breath and immediately fell to the floor.

Within two minutes Dawn would have to provide T-Control a text message explaining her action, but she had to check on Jason first. She bent over and scanned his vitals. He was shaken but all right. She forwarded a message to T-Control and her boss.

> *Subject recovering from second modification inducement. Third application could risk permanent brain damage. Will monitor subject locally and report back ASAP. END...*

Her boss and most of the people in T-Control knew Jason personally or by reputation. Dawn was betting they would be willing to give him some slack. She was about to find out that wasn't true.

Chapter Thirteen

Kevin Cross was a very precise man who made sure everything in his life was lined up perfectly and fitted into tidy boxes. He abhorred chaos and anyone who couldn't understand the necessity of planning every step ahead of time. As Director of T-Control, he was a man with immense power within the Time Force Investigations Unit. He was Dawn's immediate supervisor and was less than happy discovering she had disconnected her husband's cerebral implant. It was an obvious conflict of interest, and she had done it without consulting him.

Kevin liked Dawn in his own way, but he hated Detective Inspector Law. The man was obviously unbalanced and should never have been offered the opportunity to rejoin TFI's active force. What Kevin hated most about Jason Law was his disdain for doing anything by the book. If there was a rule, Law would find a way to break it with or without good cause.

Cross read Dawn's text message one more time. If Law had received two behavioral modifications with no success, there was something very serious going on in Law's mind.

Immediate action was required, and Cross didn't have time to plan his next move. He fell back to what was comfortable. He went to the Emergency Procedures Protocols and read them, knowing he would find what he needed. There it was--Rule 17, "Security Breach, Behavioral Modification Interruption." Cross had memorized Rule 17 just as he had memorized all of the other Protocol Rules, but he needed the security of reading the rule one more time before he acted. "Rule 17--Reconnect cerebral implant and notify Chief Prosecutor, World Court, immediately." Cross executed a reconnect command message to T-Control.

The "Action Complete" return message should have been instantaneous. Instead, the T-Control System was silent. Cross reissued the command message but still received no confirmation. Then Cross did what any good bureaucrat would do. He followed Rule 17 and pushed that problem upstairs. He sent a message to Chief Prosecutor Hastings.

> *Detective Inspector Jason Law was administered two BEHAVE modifications with no apparent attitudinal change. Forensic Specialist Law has performed an emergency electronic implant override. I have attempted two reconnects with no success. Recommend immediate TFI pounce team dispatch to arrest both subjects. END..*

There was a momentary pause and then Hastings's response.

> *DO NOT, repeat DO NOT dispatch pounce team. Report to this location immediately. END.............................*

Cross couldn't understand Hastings's reply. He had gone exactly by the book. There was no other authorized response. He had two choices--go over Hastings's head or report to her office as ordered. He grabbed his hat and headed for Hastings's office.

Jeanne Hastings read Edward's message one more time. No matter how hard she stared at the message, the words were the same. Something had gone terribly wrong, and she had to make some quick decisions. Cross would report as ordered; she had no doubt of that. He was a competent man, perhaps even gifted in his field of expertise, but he didn't know how to make a decision that wasn't covered by the book. He could be trouble unless she did something and did something fast.

Then Jeanne Hastings made a fateful decision. She would stall Kevin Cross and hope that somehow Jason and Dawn could find their way to safety.

At that moment, Kevin Cross burst into Hastings's office, and his contorted face showed that he had lost all control. "Ms Hastings, I don't understand. Why didn't you authorize a pounce team to apprehend Detective Inspector Law and his wife? Regulations are quite clear on this matter. We need to move quickly, or we may not catch them. We need to do something now!"

Jeanne Hastings put on her tough prosecutor's face and hoped Kevin Cross would buy it. "Mr. Cross, I understand your frustration, but we've been keeping tabs on Detective Inspector Law and his wife for some time," she lied. "You're the first person outside of the inquiry that I've told about this, and I must insist on your discretion. Don't bother trying to find a record of the investigation in the computer. There is none."

Jeanne was taking one of the biggest gambles of her career. If Cross didn't buy this, it would mean her job and possibly her freedom. "Don't ask any questions. I can't answer them, but I can tell you this: Jason Law is on borrowed time. He's been cutting too many corners and he's going to pay for it. When I declined to prosecute him for his negligence in the Mueller case, I was only giving him enough rope to hang himself. In days, at the most weeks, he'll be in solitary confinement, and his wife will be in the next cell."

Kevin Cross let Hastings's words flow over him as he envisioned Jason Law being brought in to the U. N. Lock-Up for booking. Cross didn't like Hastings ignoring all the rules, but he had faith she wouldn't do it without authority from the higher-ups. He'd go along but not before covering himself.

"Ms Hastings, I'll take your word. It was only a matter of time before Law found himself in jail. However, in accordance with TFI Regulation 357.3, I'm preparing a time dated memorandum of our conversation for the record and filing it in my cerebral implant. I trust you completely, but I must consider my own well-being in such a tenuous matter."

Jeanne Hastings chuckled to herself and replied, "Of course, I would expect nothing less." Cross left Hastings's office already dictating the memorandum to his implant with a note to follow up with Prosecutor Hastings in one week. Law was finished, and Cross wanted the credit.

Meanwhile, Jeanne Hastings was taking a deep breath and hoping she had bought some time. Her days were numbered at the

United Nations, and she had to make good use of them. But how?

Chapter Fourteen

Moments after Jeanne Hastings finished her conversation with Kevin Cross, she received a call from a Major General Michael Busby about an Operation Future Tense.

Some years ago the United States, Canada, and Mexico formed a confederation known as the Greater American Federation. The United States held a leadership role in the Federation's military and General Busby was Chief, Experimental Operations, Time Travel Directorate, United States Air and Space Staff, the Pentagon.

Busby had called Hastings on an ops-secure video hook-up and, after introducing himself, had given her devastating news. "Do Chi was behind the Mueller fiasco and somehow Do Chi has escaped to the future. Worse, Do Chi is threatening to destroy the world."

General Busby had been given the job of stopping Do Chi. The operation was code-named Future Tense, and he wanted Hastings's help. The general told Hastings that he needed someone intimately familiar with American and international law, and the Chief Justice of the American Federation Supreme Court had recommended her personally.

Jeanne Hastings could not believe what the general had said about Do Chi, but her eyes told her that this Two Star General had very little humor in his make-up and was deadly serious. This meant Jason Law had been correct about Do Chi all the time. Maybe she could use Operation Future Tense to save Jason, Dawn, and herself.

The general explained that a number of years ago the Greater American Federation had asked Dr. Norma Bing and some of her associates to continue her father's experiments with time travel.

One of Dr. Norma Bing's chief assistants was Dr. Juan Cortez, University of Applied Sciences, Rio de Janeiro, Brazil. Interestingly, he had also been in Dr. Thomas Bing's original group of students.

Dr. Cortez had been working with Dr. Norma Bing's team, pushing the envelope further and further to see if there was any limit on time travel to the past. He wanted to stretch the concept of infinity and turn time travel on its head. Rather than meditating to reach a specific time and place, a time traveler would leave all conscious thought behind. Embracing the concept of infinity itself, the traveler would be free to move along the Infinity Loop to the very beginnings of time.

Cortez had received his Master's Degree in advanced cryonics--now recognized by medical science as a legitimate way of maintaining people in a deep hibernation while they awaited advances in medical science. One of the side effects of cryonic hibernation was significant molecular changes in the cerebral cortex after patients were revived.

That portion of the cortex responsible for thought, reasoning, and memory became much more intense in its gray hue. There were striations along the cortex that almost shimmered. During routine debriefing sessions, patients who had been revived appeared much calmer, more reflective, and generally at peace with themselves and their surroundings. The change in brain molecular structure seemed to occur regardless of the length of the patient's hibernation period.

Cortez wanted to test the hypothesis that an individual could be placed in cryonic hibernation, immediately revived, and still display the same cerebral cortex molecular changes. His hypothesis was validated in a series of experiments with three volunteers at the Cryonics Center in Toronto, Canada. Each was placed in a momentary state of cryonic hibernation. Real-time, 3-D brain scans showed the anticipated molecular change in the cerebral cortex of each volunteer, and psychological tests confirmed what the volunteers already understood. They had shed their fear of the unknown and now embraced it with the calm certainty of a believer.

The three volunteers were placed in a six-month, total immersion study program reviewing the teachings of Do Chi on one hand and the Philosophy of Transparency on the other. First mentioned by Mid-Eastern philosophers in the first century and called Sublime Transparency, its objective was to allow the mind to become a void to accept God's will. The trick was to maintain transparency without lapsing into a permanent coma. Transparency was the opposite philosophy of Do Chi's teachings that relied on group dynamics to synergistically move a person along the Infinity Loop. Transparency allowed one to be lost in the void of nothingness. A person never understood transparency, rather one accepted that transparency was a complete surrender of self. After the three volunteers completed their six-month study program, they were beamed to the TFI Cyclotron in Denver, Colorado. Each one hoped he or she would be the one to race back in time to meet history.

Chapter Fifteen

THE CYCLOTRON,
2314

Juan Cortez had a very difficult decision to make: Which one of his three students would be the first to attempt a jump to the unknown beginning of time? All three of the students were more than qualified--advanced degrees in hard science, veteran time travelers, and eager to try Cortez's insane idea. However, one of the students, Lieutenant Commander Debe Jackson, stood out from the other two.

Commander Jackson was a team player but was never afraid to speak her own mind. During training exercises, she was always eager to be the first, and she never gave up. A graduate of the Greater American Federation Naval Academy, Commander Jackson had been the first of the three students to grasp the solitary nature of transparency. She was fluent in several languages and could read several others.

Dr. Cortez made the announcement two months before the time jump to nowhere was to take place. Commander Jackson spent the two months reviewing the protocols established for the attempt, reading ancient texts on the philosophy of transparency, and meditating on the meaning of oblivion. After undergoing a final battery of physical and psychological tests, Cortez told her she was ready. She would make her attempt the next day.

Commander Jackson was strapped into the cyclotron's cocoon at 0700 Hours. She was still constrained by the three-minute window that faced all time travelers. The cyclotron would take two minutes to attain hyper-speed, maintain the speed for seven seconds, and then use the remaining 53 seconds to slow down and make a safe stop. When time travelers jumped to specific time-space vector, physicists could calculate how long they could stay at that location--minutes, days, years--and still make it back safely within the seven-second window. The time depended on where and when they were going and the relationship of that time-space vector to present time on the Infinity Loop. This was different.

Commander Jackson was trying to reach an unknown target --the very beginning of time. Physicists' projections on how long ago that might be varied greatly and, in truth, were no more than educated guesses. Commander Jackson would have to rely on the automated feedback T-Control was going to give her through her cerebral implant. T- Control's master computer would monitor Jackson's present time's mission window and, hopefully, ensure she returned safely.

The mission was a crapshoot and Commander Jackson's odds were less than good. She was not normally a betting woman, but she wanted to find out for herself when time began.

Jackson heard the now familiar countdown as the cyclotron began its trip to hyper-speed. She cleared her mind and allowed herself to float above the stress of the moment. As she approached the speed of light, she began to feel the same tingle she experienced each time she entered the Time Warp Continuum.

She fought hard to remember the teachings of transparency and realized she was fighting too hard. She needed to allow the darkness to envelop her--to give herself to the experience rather than trying to control it.

Then it happened--no blinding light, no shared experience of moving through time with her team members. There was silence, deafening silence, and a frightful feeling of falling down a deep hole. She had visited caverns before and thought she understood what complete darkness was. However, what she was feeling now was the collapse of self as she tumbled into utter nothingness. She was about to panic but kept repeating the transparency mantra that had been drilled into her during her training--"to submit is to accept, to submit is to accept." She surrendered to her fate and embraced her future willingly.

Her mind began to drift. Then she saw a dim light that became more and more intense. Jackson didn't know where she was going, but she knew she was about to reach her destination.

She felt a sudden shudder as her surroundings began to solidify. She couldn't believe her eyes. There were no ancient remnants of mankind, no smoldering gases oozing life from the earth's mantle. Instead, there were people floating through a crystal cylinder in hushed silence. She was inside the tube and soon realized that, just as in all of her other time travels, the people around her were unaware of her presence. She reached out as a rather large man passed by her, dressed in the same light gray material as all the other people in the tube. She touched him on the shoulder, but he felt nothing.

She felt reassured that she had passed through the Time Warp Continuum and arrived at an undetermined time in the past, but where and when was she? These people definitely didn't look like anyone she had ever seen or studied before. She had not expected to see another human being let alone any living thing in her search for the beginning of time.

Two men were having a conversation as they passed her. The language was unfamiliar, and T-Control's communication module couldn't match it to any known dialects in the world of the present or the past. Commander Jackson received a short burst message asking her to make an on-site recording of the conversation in case it had become garbled in transmission to the T-Control master computer. In the meantime, T- Control was performing a complete scan of both men to gather as much information as possible.

Commander Jackson acknowledged the message and began to record the conversation. It was pure gibberish, and she was unable to make any direct or contextual sense of it. She fell back on her training as she closed her eyes, relaxed, and allowed herself to rise above the people in the tube. She was hanging above them with no effort.   Her mind seemed to be tuning into their conversations in the same way her antique short wave radio worked when she passed time in the basement of her condo unit. She began to pick up a word here and there, and, suddenly, she was listening to a conversation between the two men she had seen earlier. They were dressed in the same light gray material as the others. The only discernable difference were the striped epaulets they both wore on their shoulders--they were military!   Commander Jackson had to remain calm or she would lose touch with the two uniformed strangers. She allowed herself to relax again, and she heard the older man speak to the other. "We have months, not years, to complete the evacuation! I don't want to hear anymore of your excuses. We're behind as it is, and I will not be shamed in front of the Commission again! Do you understand? I will not be shamed again!"

The younger man looked directly into the older man's eyes and said the only two words available to him, "Yes, sir."

"Good," the older one continued as he rubbed his cloned right hand. It had taken him less than twenty years to find his way out of that abandoned cave in the Himalayas and establish his new identity as the Federation's Space Command Chief of Staff. "The evacuation must be complete by 0300 Hours on the 17th. I have given orders to the fleet, and, by 0400 Hours on the 17th, this planet will not exist.

"If the Commission had listened to me, we could have avoided this whole catastrophe, but they insisted that they could negotiate a truce. The only truce the East European Confederation understands is the truce that starts with their surrender. We've managed to evacuate over 90 percent of our population in less than six months. The planet was doomed anyway. This living "under glass" isn't human. Too many people and not enough space.

"I warned the Commission we must strike first, but they wouldn't listen. The fools! When we're off this planet, we'll make sure nobody else can use it.

"Life won't be pretty for us until we find another home, but at least we have hope for a future. We must have faith in the future and what it holds for us. When I'm done with the Confederation, it will only be a memory. History will record 17 May 3011 as the last day on earth. Now leave me." Do Chi felt a chill, and said, "I know you're there; I can feel you. I know who you are, Commander Jackson. Your future is my past. I can see into the past just as you can travel to the past.

"I allowed Jason Law to find me once so I could be rid of him. He escaped me then but it will not happen again. Go back and tell Jason Law that I'm waiting, waiting to complete our circle of fate.

Tell him!"

Commander Debe Jackson was trying to assimilate what she had just heard. She contacted T-Control to make sure they had recorded Do Chi's words. They had.

She was drawing her own conclusions when Dr. Cortez contacted her personally from T-Control. "Commander Jackson, I need you back here immediately so we can do a complete readout of all your equipment. Somehow, and I'm not sure how, you've jumped to the future. We need you here now! You're in grave danger."

"Doctor, we may never get this chance again. We've stumbled on something that will change life for all mankind. We need to learn more. How much time on my seven-second window have I used?"

"That's just it, you haven't used any time. Our instruments still show zero/zero on the hyper-speed indicator. Time in the future seems to have no correlation with time in the past. It appears that when you're in the future, your time in the cyclotron is not affected.

"Dr. Thomas Bing's theory that all time is simultaneous may be in jeopardy, but theories can wait. I need to know everything I can about the older man you were observing. We recorded the telepathic message he sent you. Did you notice anything special about him?"

"Yes," replied Commander Jackson. "He was obviously military and definitely in charge. He wore a similar uniform to the younger man, but I noticed the he had a bright blue feather embossed on his left breast pocket."

"Do Chi," Cortez muttered but tried to keep his composure. "The old man has made fools out of all of us," he said to himself. "We need you out of there now, Commander Jackson! Prepare for retrieval." The world was facing disaster, but Cortez needed Commander Jackson home if there was any hope of challenging the future.

Commander Jackson began her total release on the future and all of its unanswered questions. Her last thought before being transported to the Time Warp Continuum was, "This is the end of the world."

Chapter Sixteen

"General Busby, I've already told you I am a patriot and my country comes first, but we must go to the United Nations and tell them the truth. The end of the world now or 700 years from now is something we need to face as a global community. We can't keep this secret, trying to save earth without the rest of the world knowing."

This was Jeanne Hastings's second secure conversation in as many days with General Busby about Operation Future Tense. Jeanne Hastings was sure General Busby wasn't about to take her suggestion. The general saw this as a responsibility of the Federation only.

Jeanne kept trying to focus on what was obviously such a dire situation but she kept thinking about Jason and Dawn. She hadn't been able to find either of them since her conversation with Kevin Cross.

During their first conversation, General Busby had told Hastings of Commander Jackson's encounter in the future and Do Chi's plans to destroy the planet. Do Chi was aware he had been found and was challenging Jason Law to try to stop him. The purpose of today's secure video-con was to develop a strategic game plan on how best to advise the President, given Commander Jackson's inadvertent brush with the future.

"Ms Hastings, before we go any further, I need to introduce you to the other members of our group." Jeanne Hastings sank into her chair. She hadn't even checked her console before she had given her speech about the end of the world and America's responsibilities toward earth's other countries. Blinking in front of her were readouts showing three other video-con participants. Even during secure video-cons the readout would give the title, name and organization of each participant. This time it read simply, "Eyes Only--POTAF."

Jeanne Hastings was stunned. By direction of the President of the American Federation, the identities of everyone except General Busby would be revealed on a need-to-know basis. "I want you to know, Ms Hastings, that the other three could not hear or see our conversation, and they do not know your identity either, but it's time we get down to work," the general said flatly.

The general then spoke to the group as a whole in a very rapid, almost abrupt manner. "I have spoken to all four of you individually, and you have all agreed to be part of this commission. For the record, I have previously provided your resumes to the President who has agreed to your participation.

The general's voice rose as he said, "I am not exaggerating when I tell you that we are dealing with the very survival of our planet. I've briefed each of you individually on Commander Jackson's travel to the future. Our scientists are still unsure how Commander Jackson traveled to the future, but they do have a working hypothesis. Their original goal was to go back to the very beginning of time.

"Theoretically, they were concerned that they might disturb the Infinity Loop and, in turn, the fabric of Time. Unintended consequences are always a risk, and that is exactly what our scientists experienced when they sent Commander Jackson on her mission. According to Dr. Cortez, Commander Jackson traveled so far into the past along the Infinity Loop that she was hurled forward along the loop to a future time.

When our people travel to the past they can call up a specific time and space vector. However, since we cannot see into the future, we are unable to direct our travelers to a specific time or place. Dr. Cortez believes the chaos axiom controlled events, and Commander Jackson was drawn to Do Chi because of his heavy influence on our early experiments with time travel. The fact that Do Chi was cognizant he was being monitored is not surprising. As he so aptly put it, our future is his past."

General Busby paused and let everything sink in for a moment. The chaos axiom had long ago stopped being a theory, and Jeanne Hastings understood its basic thrust--seemingly unrelated data are actually connected through an underlying order.

She and the other commissioners would have to accept that, somehow, Commander Jackson had been drawn to Do Chi as she had made her journey to the future. Do Chi probably anticipated every move the Commission was considering before it came up for discussion. Hastings was used to thinking outside the box, but this was stretching credulity.

General Busby continued, "Why Commander Jackson happened upon Do Chi at that particular time in the future is unclear. What is clear is the absolute certainty that Commander Jackson did in fact observe Do Chi and an unknown male sometime in the year 3011. Our scan of Do Chi confirmed his identity by DNA and aura scan analysis. Our time readout showed 1247 Hours, 12 February 3011, but we can't be sure since our software was written to verify established dates in the past. The best we can say is Do Chi made a specific threat to destroy the earth between 0300 and 0400, 17 May 3011.

"There are credible arguments being made by our scientists that if Do Chi destroys the earth, there could be major ramifications at all time vectors within our solar system and possibly beyond. If Dr. Bing's Treatise on Linear Applications remains constant, then any large disruption at a past or future time vector along the Infinity Loop can impact all other time vectors.

"The bottom line is Do Chi's action in the future could seal the earth's doom, no matter what actions we take today. Our only real hope is to send someone to the future to stop Do Chi. Any questions?" There was silence from the other three commissioners. It was Hastings's chance.

"General Busby, there's only one man who can track down Do Chi and do what needs to be done--Jason Law." She had rolled the dice. If they came up seven, then perhaps she, Jason, and Dawn might keep their freedom and get a chance to stop Do Chi.

"Ms Hastings, according to my screen Jason Law is a fugitive and wanted on a serious charge. He will not be associated with this effort. Do I make myself clear?"

"Perfectly," Jeanne replied, but inside she had already made her decision to make her run for freedom. If she could find Jason and Dawn, there still might be a chance.

Chapter Seventeen

Dawn had never regretted for a moment the quick decisions she and Jason had been forced to make after she disconnected his cerebral implant in her lab. Her implant had already been disconnected while she was working with the lab's electronic equipment.

Their first job was to find a way out of town and out of the country, if possible. They left the lab quickly, hoping to evade any strike team that Cross might send to arrest them. They needed help now.

Jason and Dawn still had friends at TFI in Washington, D.C., and there were people at Space Command in Denver, Colorado, that would stick their necks out if needed.

Jason's name was probably already on the TFI's "grab list", so Dawn made a call to a trusted friend at a beaming station. They waited for a busy time when they were less likely to be noticed. Dawn's friend pushed them through a less than perfect security check, and within moments they had been beamed to a secondary beaming station just outside the Sydney, Australia's city limits.

They took a skycab to a small beach community and registered, using one of several assumed identities Jason maintained as a TFI agent. Unfortunately for the authorities, Jason had kept this particular moniker completely to himself. He slipped the desk clerk a fifty and didn't bother to register Dawn at all. Once in their room, they looked at each other and began to talk.

"Jason, what do we do next? I'm scared. You know Cross won't stop until he hunts us down. We need help now!"

Dawn was right, but there was someone in Sydney that might be able to help--Dr. Bob Francis. Doc was a world renowned psychoanalyst whose work in dream analysis techniques was cited in all the leading psychiatric and psychological curricula. He had taken "I'm Okay, You're Okay" to another level in his book on group dynamics entitled *Divergent Views of the Minority.*

Doc also happened to be Jason's father's best friend and Jason's godfather. In these times of ever-changing social mores, Doc took his title of godfather as a serious matter. He made it a point to be in Jason's life after Jason's father died. When Jason's mother was murdered by Do Chi, Doc was always there for the young boy.

Doc saw only two choices on how to care for Jason since the boy had no other living relatives. Either Jason would become a ward of the state or Doc could adopt him. It was an easy decision for both of them. Jason had moved in, and they mutually agreed that Jason would call his new step-dad Doc.

Growing up, Jason learned to trust Doc, and Doc never betrayed that trust. If there was a problem, Doc was there. If there was a special occasion, Doc was there. So it was only natural that Doc received the first call when Jason and Dawn married.

After he congratulated the newlyweds, the first words out of Doc's mouth were, "Son, life's short. Make the most out of it." Doc's credo--life's short--stuck with Jason. He had seared those words in his brain and promised himself that he'd never look back.

That's about all he had been doing, however, since he had that terrible flashback about Do Chi in Dawn's lab. As soon as he had mentioned Do Chi's name, the memories came flooding back to both Jason and Dawn. They had made it here safely, at least for the moment, but they needed to do something fast to cover their tracks. Jason was taking a chance, but their only hope was Doc.

"I'm calling Doc. Maybe he can get me straightened out. Besides, he knows everyone in Sydney, and he should be able to hide us." Jason didn't like putting Doc at risk, but he didn't have any choice. Doc would help. He had to help, or Jason and Dawn were both bound for very small cells in a very remote Federation prison. Before he called Doc, Jason took all of the standard precautions, filtering his signal through numerous satellite systems. When he finally placed the call, he made it "voice only."

Doc answered saying, "Doctor Francis. May I help you?"

"Doc, this is Jason. I can't talk long, but I need to see you. I'll meet you at the usual time and place." Before Doc could answer, Jason broke the connection and scanned for intercepts. None.

Jason turned to Dawn and said, "Doc will be at the Oceanside Wharf at six P.M." When Jason had been a small boy, the wharf had been their favorite fishing spot and the place where Jason had made his first catch. Doc had office hours until five P.M. and had made six to seven their hour.

Jason and Dawn reached the wharf about five minutes before six. They waited in a secluded grove of trees just off the wharf. Then Jason saw him. Doc was walking onto the wharf with a small bag of popcorn, throwing it into the air to attract sea gulls.

Jason moved out of the trees quickly before Doc could move too far down the wharf. "Doc, Doc," Jason watched him turn around and move toward the trees. He looked the same: thick, salt and pepper hair, a ruddy face that had seen too much trouble, and clothes that were completely black--shirt, pants, and shoes. Jason had never understood how he could stand the Sydney heat dressed like that, but it was Doc's trademark.

Doc saw Jason almost immediately. He walked nonchalantly toward the trees making several stops to pick up stones and throw them toward the water. He walked into the trees and was pulled down to the ground immediately by Jason. "Whoa, what's gotten into you, Jason? You look like you've seen a ghost. What's going on?"

"Doc, we're in trouble, big trouble. I'm about to tell you something that sounds like a terrible nightmare. But, it's true, and I don't know what to do." Jason told Doc the whole story of his encounter with Do Chi--how Do Chi had used Dawn as his pawn to lure Jason to the Time Warp Continuum and how Do Chi had confessed to killing Jason's mother.

It was too much for Doc. Several tears ran down his face and he sighed. Jason had never seen Doc like this before. He has always been Jason's anchor. Now he looked like an old man who had finally given up on life. He cried for several minutes and then took a deep breath, pulled out an overused handkerchief and blew his nose hard. He dabbed his eyes and took another deep breath. He seemed to change in front of Jason's and Dawn's eyes.

Jason looked into Doc's eyes and immediately understood what Doc was doing. He was self-talking. It was a centuries old trick shrinks taught many of their patients, a trick used to deal with internal demons. Basically, self-talking was giving yourself a pep talk. It was particularly effective in periods of intense stress. You gave yourself a moment to experience the panic and then gradually allowed yourself to unwind using muscle relaxation techniques. Jason saw Doc's eyes flutter as he went through the process and quietly mouth the words, "relax, relax."

Doc had regained his composure and looked at Jason and then Dawn. "We're in this together. We stand or we fall together, agreed?" Jason and Dawn both nodded their heads and the three of them hugged each other until they thought their ribs would break.

Jason was the first to speak. "Doc, I've got to find Do Chi. I'm not sure how I'll find him or what I'll do when I see him, but he and I have unfinished business." Dawn was about to protest when Jason grabbed his head with both of his hands.

He looked like he was having a stroke. Jason would pass out in a matter of seconds if the pain didn't stop. Then the pain passed, and Jason began receiving a coded message through his cerebral implant. Someone had obviously performed an emergency reconnect on his implant and he was plugged into T-Control's Master Computer.

Emergency reconnects were dangerous, sometimes fatal, and not even used to track fugitives such as Jason. Jeanne Hastings was among a handful of people who knew Jason's unique, ops immediate code name to be used only in times of imminent disaster. His implant allowed Jason to receive coded messages from Hastings that only he and she could understand. The implant also allowed Hastings to verify Jason's location. To maintain security, messages had to be sent in short microbursts and begin with a random color and number combination.

Jason heard Jeanne Hastings's voice using his ops immediate code name. "Boomerang, stand by for message in four parts. Do not, repeat, do not reply. Take independent action. Out." Over the next 30 seconds Jason's implant received four messages in a random order.

Once the last message was received, his implant collated all four of the messages in the right order, and Jason heard Jeanne

Hastings's voice as she relayed the story of Commander Jackson's encounter with Do Chi. Dawn breathed more easily as she saw Jason's face regain its color and Jason begin to relax.

She became concerned again as she saw Jason's face contort when he heard the terrible news. Jason could hardly speak as he retold the story to Dawn and Doc. The three of them stared at each other, hoping the others would know what to do.

Doc was the first to speak. "Jason, there's no way you can go back to TFI and go after this Do Chi. We've got to come up with a plan and come up with it fast."

Jason cringed and replied, "Right, Doc," but inside he was asking himself how he could get back in the game.

Chapter Eighteen

Jeanne Hastings was sitting at her desk in her office. She was worried and had a right to be. Reconnecting Jason Law's cerebral implant had put his life at risk and just as surely her own freedom. Jeanne took a deep breath and was about to let herself relax when her office door blew open and four men rushed in with side arms drawn. They were in Pentagon Special Security uniforms and were obviously sent by General Busby. Her message to Jason had been intercepted.

Jeanne Hastings pushed the hidden panic button under her desk with her right foot and prayed the TFI Agent on duty would have the guts to answer her call. "What's the meaning of this? Who are you and how dare you enter my office without permission?"

The man in charge of the Pentagon Special Security team said, "Jeanne Hastings, you are under arrest for treason. You have the right to..."

"I have the right to what? Do you know whom you are addressing? I am the Chief Prosecutor for the World Court's Greater American Federation Department. Once again, I demand to know who you are, who you represent, and under what authority you are supposedly arresting me?" Jeanne Hastings was bluffing--she had no choice.

At that instant the TFI agent on duty and two uniformed cops ran into her office with weapons ready. The agent had his side arm drawn and the two policemen were pointing their shoulder-fired laser guns directly at the four intruders. "Agent Gaines, these people are trespassing and attempting to execute an illegal arrest warrant. Arrest them and take them down to Isolation. No one is to know anything about this until I get a chance to speak to Justice Swearingen. Do you understand?"

"Yes, ma'am!"

Jeanne Hastings looked directly at the ill-fated patrol attempting to arrest her and said, "Drop your weapons!"

The arrest team had been outflanked. All four team members had been facing Prosecutor Hastings when the TFI agents had entered. Now they had three very deadly weapons pointing at their backs, and had to surrender.

The arrest team chief spoke with a small smile on his face, "We do not recognize your authority, Prosecutor Hastings, but we do recognize the weapons your men have pointed at us. Let me be clear. We are here under a legal arrest warrant signed personally by the President of the Greater American Federation. You are charged with treason and, in due course, you will face the justice you deserve." The team chief motioned for the other three to drop their weapons and they complied.

Jeanne Hastings smiled back at the team chief and said, "Agent Gaines, take these four to Isolation. I have no idea who they are or why they're here, but I'm going to get to the bottom of this immediately. Read them their rights but hold them incognito for 48 hours. I'll clear it with Justice Swearingen, ASAP. Don't let them communicate with anyone--understood?"

"Understood."

As soon as Gaines and his men led the four security officers out of her office, Jeanne Hastings made a decision. She was heading for Australia to help Jason and Dawn. There was no turning back. She dictated a short note to T-Control's Master Computer absolving Agent Gaines and the police officers. She marked it "Eyes Only-- Justice Swearingen" and put a dispatch code for no earlier than 48 hours.

Jeanne Hastings took a deep breath, walked out of her office and into the unknown of the future. She was scared, more afraid than she had ever been, but strangely she felt more alive than she had in her entire life.

Two hours later, she was being beamed to Sydney under an assumed identity that she had prepared before she had made the emergency reconnect on Jason's implant. Ten minutes after leaving the retrieval station in Sydney, Jeanne Hastings hailed a skycab and gave the driver the only address she had in Sydney--the home of a Dr. Robert Francis listed as next of kin on Jason Law's TFI application.

Chapter Nineteen

Jason Law could not believe his eyes. Standing in Doc's front bay entry was Jeanne Hastings. She looked tired, even scared, but she smiled when she saw Jason and Dawn in the living quarters. "It's okay, Doc, we know her. She's the one who sent the message about Do Chi. Jeanne, what are you doing here?"

Jeanne stumbled past Doc and grabbed Jason and Dawn. "I'm sorry. I know you must think I'm crazy, but I barely made it out of the U.N. alive."

She released her grip on Jason and Dawn and was introduced to Doc. She sat down with all three of them and filled them in with the details of her encounter with Kevin Cross, her run-in with General Busby, and her escape after the Federation soldiers tried to arrest her.

"You mean the President signed the warrant himself?" Jason asked.

"Yes, and I'm afraid I've put all of you in harm's way."

Jason was about to console Jeanne when Doc broke in, "Ms Hastings, you're welcome here, but you're right. None of us are safe. We need to move and move now! We'll go to James's place in the Outback. It's only about four hours from here in the hovercraft."

"Taking a skycab would be too risky. I'll call him and ask if we can visit his hut for a few days--at least long enough so we can decide what our next move will be."

Jason looked at Dawn, and she nodded her head. "Right, Doc."

Dr. Pirramuar James was an Australian archeologist who just

75

happened to be one of the few full-blooded Aborigines left in Australia. Doc had introduced Jason to Pirramuar when Jason was still a young boy. On their first meeting Jason had tried his best to sound out the Aborigine's name, but the best Jason could manage was "PIRMER."

Even at such a young age Jason was aware that an Aborigine's name was something held sacred. Pirramuar felt Jason's embarrassment and diffused the situation quickly saying, "Jason, in my people's language my name means "the shield." A shield is what a warrior uses to protect himself from those that might harm him.

"Hundreds of years ago, an ancestor of mine was also named Pirramuar. He was a great man who was captured by outsiders and forced to live as a slave. But he persevered and returned to our people to lead them again. Each day when I awake, I tell myself I must live up to the name that such an honored man of our people held.

"Outside my tribe, I have taken the last name James. Why don't you call me James? Does that sound all right?" That was more than fine with Jason. From that moment on, next to Doc, James became Jason's best friend, his protector, his shield.

On school holidays and an occasional weekend, Doc would take Jason to James's hut where the three of them would take long walkabouts, sit by a camp fire looking at the stars, and listen to the sounds of the night.

One special night, when Jason was about ten, the two men and he were in the Outback staring at the stars, doing their best to ponder the Universe. "Doc," Jason asked, "where do you really think we came from--humans, I mean? I know what we learned in Sunday school and I know what my school taught us about evolution, but what do you think?"

"Well, Jason, I think the church and the schools are both right. God's too smart to let a little thing like evolution stand in the way. So the bottom line is I believe that the Earth and everything on it is constantly evolving, but in my heart, I know Someone a lot smarter than us had a hand in how it all works out. Maybe you should ask James. After all, he's got dual citizenship--not only is he a top notch archeology professor, he's his people's holy man."

Jason jumped at the chance. "James, what do you think?"

"As Doc said, I'm a professor of archeology not theology, but let's give it a go. You've had physical science classes, right?" Jason nodded his head and James continued, "Early in the life of the Universe, it was full of only hydrogen, helium, and the simple particles--protons, neutrons and electrons. There was no other matter--no carbon, oxygen, neon, or anything else.

"The hydrogen and helium condensed into gas clouds and when they were dense enough they became stars. The stars are powered by nuclear fusion, turning hydrogen into helium then later helium into carbon and oxygen. Later stages of a star's life produce even heavier elements such as sodium, calcium and even iron.

"Finally, when some stars die, they do so in a spectacular explosion that produces still heavier elements such as platinum and uranium. Every atom that makes up our bodies, animals, plants, the Earth and other planets was once part of a star. How does that sound?"

"I'm still confused."

"Don't worry, we all are, but I agree with Doc. There's no reason why science and the spiritual world can't both be right. We are in a universe where we are all evolving, but in the beginning, God's hand scooped a handful of stardust and molded us for the future. Got it?"

"Yes," Jason replied. But inside the young boy was thinking, "It's a sin to kill, and God killed mum. God sinned!"

On Jason's twelfth birthday, Doc asked him if he would like to visit James. The Aborigine was going to offer Jason a chance to go through a special ceremony celebrating Jason's passage into manhood. Jason jumped at the chance to see James again but wasn't quite sure about a special ceremony. Doc assured him that the ceremony was strictly voluntary, but the weekend was sure to be fun with or without it.

Jason counted the days before his newest adventure and was waiting at the door when Doc picked him up that Friday night. They made the four-hour trip in Doc's ancient hydrogen-powered hovercraft. They skimmed the surface at over 400 clicks per hour as they moved out of the city and headed for the desert of the Outback. Thanks to the onboard avionics and the automatic pilot, the hovercraft had no problems in negotiating the rough terrain.

When they arrived at James's hut, Jason could see it hadn't changed--still more hut and less weekend getaway. There was no front door, only a kangaroo hide over the low, crawl-through entrance. The structure was built against a rock outcropping and made of reeds from some unknown river. Shaped like an egg on its side, the hut had a hole in the ceiling to allow the smoke from the campfire to escape.

Doc and Jason pulled up to the hut about eleven. James was standing in front of the entrance and waved as Doc shut off the hovercraft's engine. As usual, when James was in the bush, he dressed in his native garb--a loincloth. This time he had also painted himself using traditional dot painting. Jason had studied the ancient art in school but had retained little.

James was covered head to toe in the pale yellow and reddish-brown paints Aborigines made from the iron oxide they mined from ochre rock. Jason was unsure of most of the symbols covering James' body with one exception. Covering his chest was a large vertical oval painted in deep reddish-brown. This was the Aboriginal symbol for the shield, James's Aboriginal name.

When Doc and Jason got out of the hovercraft, James met them with a smile and a firm, almost formal handshake. "Jason, you have come of age, and it is time that you receive the name that was given to you in the Dreaming."

This was a great honor. James was offering him a chance to undergo a rite of passage to manhood and be given an adult Aboriginal name. This was a rare opportunity and one that Jason was not going to miss. The fear left him, and Jason looked directly at James and said, "Pirramuar. I am ready."

"Good, you are to come with me into my hut. What you are about to see, to hear, to feel can never be revealed, even to Doc. Do you understand?"

"I understand."

Doc and James had been talking about the possibility of offering this chance to Jason for some time. As a therapist, Doc was very aware Jason needed structure in his life and a safe place he could retreat to in times of stress. Doc had done everything he could to give Jason a normal life, but there would always be a void that couldn't be filled.

He had finally talked to his old friend James about the problem, and James had suggested the manhood ritual. Although certainly not normal by modern standards, James was sure the experience would provide Jason with a greater understanding of who he was and why he had to keep moving forward in his life.

Doc asked question after question, and James answered each one as truthfully and completely as he could. "What does the ritual mean? Will it conflict with the spiritual teaching he's received in church?

"Every since Jason's mother was murdered the youngster's been struggling with his faith. It was hard enough when his father died. It's almost impossible now."

"I understand, Doc."

Before James could say anything Doc asked two more questions, "No drugs, right? Why can't I be with Jason during the ceremony?"

"Relax, Doc. Before the ceremony, I will explain my people's oral tradition on creation or, as we call it, the Dreaming, to Jason. That through music, dance, and meditation, it is possible to become one with the Dreaming where time does not exist. I will also tell Jason that nothing he sees, hears, or feels during the ceremony is meant to discourage what he has learned in church.

"You know that I do not believe in using hallucinogens and that I would not allow Jason to become wrapped up in an unsavory experience. Jason has you first and last in his life. Still, he needs structure, something to hold on to when he's alone and needs to be strong. I can give that to him if he's willing to accept it. Perhaps this ceremony will give Jason a second chance at finding God.

"You must trust me. I cannot allow you to be with us during the ceremony because you have not gone through the ceremony yourself. Doc, you and I are both educated men, but only one of us has knowledge of the Dreaming. Let me give that gift to Jason." Doc agreed, and the two of them made plans to offer Jason this unique experience.

Chapter Twenty

James's Hut,
2268

James took Jason by the hand and led him into the hut. Jason had been in the hut many times, but this time was much different. James had allowed the fire to become embers that glowed in the dark, giving off waves of heat. The hole in the top of the hut was much larger, allowing the stars in the clear night to show brightly. In the rear of the hut along the rock outcropping, Jason could see light coming from an entrance to a cave. The entrance had been hidden by a large boulder that had been moved. Thousands of years ago, some ingenious soul had found a way to balance the boulder against the rock outcropping in such a way that a single person could move it with relative ease if one knew exactly where to push. Press at any other point, and the task was hopeless. The entrance was only opened for special occasions, and only members of Pirramuar's tribe had ever seen its secrets. Jason was about to become a member of that select group.

Pirramuar motioned for Jason to take off his shirt and sit before the burning coals. He poured water on the coals and steam rose to the top of the hut. "Breathe deeply, young Jason, and prepare yourself to become a man. Breathe in the freedom that comes to those that know the Dreaming and breathe out all that you fear. Breathe in the knowledge of the People and breathe out your cares. Within the cave are secrets that only a few have known. Before you may share those secrets, you must take the name of a man. Stare at the sky and look upon the stars. I have told you before that we are molded from stardust. In the stars you will find your name. Look, Jason. Look!"

Jason did as he was told and stared into the clear, starlit sky. He looked for what seemed hours but, in truth, was about 15 minutes. Then he saw it, the constellation that would bring him his new name. Now he understood why James had been spending so much time showing him the stars in his past trips to the Outback.

"I have found it, Pirramuar--the Southern Cross."

"Pirramuar smiled and replied, "You have done well. One ancient story says the Southern Cross is the left hand of Tagai, the Warrior. You are Tagai, the Warrior. I am Pirramuar, your shield. Trust me. I will keep you safe. There are other stories about the Southern Cross that you will learn later, but tonight you have taken the name of Tagai, the Warrior."

Jason nodded and said, "I trust you."

"You have done well. Now it is time to become one with the Dreaming." Pirramuar took Tagai by the hand and led him through the cave entrance to a world of wonder.

The entrance to the cave was even lower than the hut's, large enough for only one person at a time. The cave held the secrets Pirramuar's people had kept for thousands of years.

Aborigines numbered about a million before the Europeans began settling Australia in the eighteenth century. By the twenty-first century there were fewer than a quarter million Aborigines, and the number was even less in Jason's time.

Pirramuar stood up in the cave and motioned for Tagai to follow him. Tagai could not believe his eyes. The room was rounded and approximately 100 meters in circumference. The ceiling was over 150 meters high, and there was a hole in the dome. The hole allowed the starlight to shine brightly on Tagai the Warrior and Pirramuar the Shield. Huge stalactites and stalagmites filled the cavern, but the center of the cave had been cleared centuries ago to make room for a large fire pit and a dancing floor where the ancient rituals were performed.

To the rear of the cave along its wall were hundreds of cave paintings depicting the Dreaming or creation of the world. The history of the People was spelled out on the wall from the People's migration to the land surrounding the cave to its wars with other Aborigine tribes, to the sighting of the first white man. The shame of the white man's exploitation of the Aborigines was there, too, along with the white man's shock at coming face to face with intelligent beings from another planet for the first time. Even Dr. Thomas Bing's discovery of time travel was spelled out on the wall with a whimsical picture of an Aborigine holy man obviously saying, "I told you so."

Underlying everything on the wall was the People's continuing connection to the Dreaming and its spirits. Pirramuar looked at Tagai and said, "When you enter this place, you are no longer a white man. You are Tagai, a warrior of the People. Do you understand?"

"Yes, Pirramuar."

"In this cavern are the secrets of the People, and only the People may know those secrets. Do you understand?"

"I understand."

"Come with me," Pirramuar said as he led Tagai to a large stalagmite in the center of the dancing floor. Pirramuar took out the rock-cutting tool he had fashioned years before. It was razor sharp, and Pirramuar held it expertly in his right hand. "I am the Holy Man of the People. When it is time, all men and women are brought to this place to mingle their blood with all who have come before them. Once your blood flows with theirs, you are one with the People forever. Today is tomorrow and tomorrow is yesterday. It is all the same in the Dreaming. Do you understand?"

Tagai was not sure how, but he was sure he understood. "I understand."

"Give me your right wrist." Pirramuar made a cut along Tagai's wrist and pressed it on the stalagmite. "Repeat after me. I am Tagai, I am the People." Tagai repeated the words and let them engulf him as he felt a joy he had never felt before. There was no pain, only joy. "It is done. Follow me to the outside world but remember you are one with the People and the People are one with you."

Pirramuar led Tagai out of the cave and back into the hut. They both stood up, and Pirramuar embraced the young Warrior. "In the outside world, you are Jason, but you are always Tagai. Let there be no confusion in your heart. Doc is your link to your mother and, therefore, you must always hold him close to your heart. I am your shaman, your Shield. We are both one with the People. Do you understand?"

"I understand," Tagai said, and somehow for that one moment he forgot the cruel joke God had played on him.

Jason and James walked out of the hut, and Jason went over to Doc and hugged him. "Doc, thank you for bringing me tonight. I'm ready to go home now." Doc looked at James, who nodded and then went back into his hut. Traveling back, Jason swore that someday Tagai the Warrior would challenge the evil man who had killed his mother. And he knew that, at that moment, Pirramuar the Shield would protect him.

Chapter Twenty-One

THE PENTAGON,
2314

Major General Michael Busby was more than a little concerned. Somehow Hastings had slipped out of his dragnet, and the man Cross was no help at all. During intense questioning, Cross kept repeating, "I have a self-dictated memorandum proving I had no knowledge of Prosecutor Hastings's intentions or whereabouts. I swear, I had nothing to do with Ms Hastings's escape. I swear!"

The Office of Special Investigations (OSI) assured General Busby that Cross appeared to know little or nothing. However, just to be safe, Busby had ordered Cross's confinement.

In less than 24 hours General Busby was scheduled to brief the President on what Do Chi and Operation Future Tense. But, the operation had blown up in the general's face.

Earlier, Busby had spoken to Dr. Leo Lehman, Chief Scientist for the Pentagon's National Review Board, who gave the general nothing but bad news. "Operation Future Tense is simply beyond the scientific community's expertise, general. I'm sorry but there's nothing we can do."

Mike Busby wanted to keep the two stars on his shoulder, and he certainly wasn't ready to face the President. The general had only met him twice, and both times the man had not been in a good mood. For the first time in his military career, Busby could taste the acrid bile of failure. He feared the next 24 hours might decide not just his future but quite possibly the future of mankind.

Chapter Twenty-Two

PIRRAMUAR'S HUT,
2314

The videophone beeped, and Pirramuar James took a quick look at the console. The videophone wasn't registering any return phone number, and that could mean only one thing. Whoever was calling him was using a throwaway videophone. A person could buy them at any of the discount stores, and their numbers were untraceable. Australia was one of the few remaining countries where individuality was fostered and the throwaways allowed.

"Professor James, may I help you?"

"Professor James, I was told you were an authority on Aborigine artifacts. A close friend of mine, a Mr. Tagai, recommended I call you."

James was stunned. It was Doc and he was using Jason's Aborigine name. That could only mean the two of them were in trouble. "Of course, what do you need?"

"Mr. Tagai told me you're familiar with a particular Aborigine archeological site where we might find some interesting cave wall paintings on the Dreaming. Is that correct?"

"Yes, I believe I know such a place. Would you like to see it?"

"The sooner the better."

"Is Mr. Tagai with you?"

"Yes."

"Good. Mr. Tagai knows the location. Let's meet there in the morning, say 10:00 A.M.?

"Fine, we'll be there, and thanks for your help."

"No trouble at all," James responded, but he knew there was something wrong, very wrong.

Doc turned around and spoke to Jason. "James will meet us at 1000 hours tomorrow morning at his hut."

"Good, at least we can keep low there," Jason responded.

Doc tried to appear calm but inside he was churning. "We'll have to leave no later than six to get there by ten tomorrow morning. Jason, you remember my old hovercraft. It's parked in the back. I'll make a few calls and see if we can find someone to fuel it and not record the sale.

"We'll need water and provisions for four or five days. James can still live off the land but the delicacies he serves aren't on my top ten list. Dawn, you and Jeanne start packing. All of my camping gear is in the shed by the hovercraft. Any questions?" Doc asked. No one had any, and Doc motioned for them to get to their jobs.

Doc looked at each of them as they left the room. Jason maintained his stoic glare, Dawn kept looking at Jason as if she needed to draw on his strength to endure what was coming, and Jeanne seemed mysteriously calm. "Funny," Doc thought, "how one person reacts to stress so differently than another person." Doc was at the breaking point, but he was determined to see this thing through to the end. He had promised Jason's mother that he would keep Jason safe, and if that meant giving up his own life, so be it.

Three hours later the team had completed their preparations for the trip and tried in vain to get a few hours sleep. At 6 A.M. they pulled out in Doc's hovercraft, heading for James's hut. There was little chance of being followed. Doc's hovercraft required no flight plan, and such an old transporter would most likely not raise any suspicion. Doc had recorded a message saying he had decided to take a short holiday and would return in a week.

The ride across the Outback took four hours. The hovercraft pulled up in front of James's hut where James was standing in front of the hut in his traditional loincloth. He raised his right hand but made no attempt to smile as Doc and his passengers arrived. Jason was the first to speak. "Pirramuar, we are in trouble. We need your protection." Jason had used James's Aborigine name without thinking.

"You have it," the Aborigine replied. Dawn was awestruck as she saw Pirramuar and Jason look at each other. It was as though they had mind-melded and were speaking with one voice.

Something was about to happen that she couldn't understand and that frightened her. She took Jason's hand and squeezed it. He looked away from James for a moment and smiled at her. Then he turned his eyes to Jeanne Hastings and finally Doc. His fate and the fate of those with him would be decided tonight in the cave hidden behind James's hut. James had built a small fire in front of the hut and asked everyone to sit around it. Doc filled Pirramuar in on what was facing them and the Aborigine nodded his head knowingly.

Pirramuar looked at Tagai and hoped that he was ready for the test that awaited them both. Since his twelfth birthday, Tagai had learned much about the People and the secrets of the cavern's paintings. Tonight, however, Tagai would hold the earth on his shoulders and feel the weight of the centuries. He had been preparing Tagai for this moment, but only the Wise One understood if Tagai was ready.

James spoke to the group. "Jason is no more. Tagai the Warrior sits before you." Jason had told the two women about James during their trip from Sydney. He explained James's profound impact on his life, but neither Dawn nor Jeanne Hastings was prepared for the next few hours.

"We must find this man you call Do Chi. Our path to this evil man lies through the Dreaming. Tagai, prepare yourself for the ordeal." Jason stood and went into the hut. Minutes later he reappeared dressed only in a loincloth, holding a rough-hewn stone cup filled with blood-red paint in his left hand and a bright blue feather in his right. He had taken the feather from Dawn as they escaped her lab and began their run for freedom. Tagai stood in front of the group as Pirramuar took the stone cup from him. Pirramuar painted Tagai's face and body with the secret symbols of the People and chanted blessings in his own language. Dawn looked on as she saw her husband transformed from Jason Law to Tagai the Warrior and couldn't help herself. She began sobbing, wishing she would wake up and everything would be a dreadful dream.

Doc came over to comfort her, but he realized that it was much too late for comforting. Instead, he sat down beside her and prayed as he had never prayed before. Jeanne Hastings was dumbfounded. But rather than being afraid or put off, she was drawn to the white Aborigine warrior that stood before her and the holy man that attended him.

Pirramuar took the feather from Tagai and tied it to a spear lying next to him. "Take this spear and know that you are the warrior that will strike down the one who killed your mother." Tagai took the spear, and his eyes burned with the fire of a warrior.

Then Pirramuar spoke to the group. "It is time. Tagai and I must cleanse our bodies and our souls for the confrontation that awaits us. You will all wait here until we return. No matter what you hear, no matter what you see, you must stay here and keep the fire burning. The fire is our guide to return. Without it, we are lost. Be vigilant." All three nodded their heads in agreement.

"If we do not return by midnight, you must leave. We will never return." Pirramuar turned and went into the hut. Tagai followed him without a word to anyone.

Chapter Twenty-Three

THE DREAMING

Pirramuar and Tagai walked through the hut directly to the hidden entrance to the cavern. Pirramuar motioned to Tagai who put his shoulder against the boulder that hid the entrance to the secret world of the People. It moved with relative ease, and Pirramuar and Tagai entered the world of the People.

Pirramuar turned to Tagai and said, "Before we can make the journey to the Dreaming, we must prepare ourselves. We must fast and meditate for seven days and seven nights. Only then will we be able to move from this world to the world of the Dreaming. Only then will you completely shed the cloak of civilization that still holds on to your soul.

"Even before we enter the Dreaming, we can make time stand still in this sacred cavern. The seven days and nights here will only be moments in the outside world. Our loved ones who tend the fire for us will not wait long."

Tagai nodded his head in acknowledgement, and the two men built a fire with wood that Pirramuar had already gathered. The flames of the fire cast shadows on the walls of the cavern, and the figures drawn on the cave's rear wall danced in harmony.

For seven days and seven nights the two men ate nothing and drank only water dripping from the cave's stalactites. Its taste was bitter, but it sustained them through the ordeal.

After three days, Tagai began to hallucinate, replaying the scene of his mother's death over and over. He would see her pleading with the old man with the long, thin fingers and the blue sapphire ring with the feathers carved in its stone. The old man pressed his fingers around his mother's throat and squeezed harder and harder until she was dead. Blood dripped along the back of her neck from the impression of the sapphire. Tagai saw himself throwing his small weight against the old man, trying to stop what had already happened.

Time after time Tagai would see the old man creeping into his mother's bedroom, and, time after time, he would try in vain to stop the unstoppable.

On the fourth day, the hallucinations about his mother stopped. There was darkness, total darkness. On the fifth and sixth days, Tagai began to see a faint light coming from the rear of the cave.

During this whole time, Tagai kept repeating what he had been taught by Pirramuar. "I am Tagai the Warrior. I come in truth. I come in humility. I am Tagai the Warrior. I come in truth. I come in humility."

The Aborigine warrior's words were true. He bore no doubts about the righteousness of God or the quest the two Aborigines were undertaking. Tagai had left Jason Law and his thoughts in the outside world. Tagai was now ready to take the next step in his journey to the Dreaming.

On the seventh day, Pirramuar allowed the fire to go out, and the two men spread the coals along a path to the light in the rear of the cave. The light grew in intensity. The time had come to enter the Dreaming.

Both men walked toward the light on the hot coals, feeling no pain. As they approached the light, it became brighter and brighter. Tagai felt a familiar warmth as the light covered him and became one with him.

Pirramuar took his hand and guided Tagai to a place where they were surrounded by light. "This is the Dreaming, the Creation. From here we can travel to any place, any time. Within the Dreaming, time stands still. We can move from the past to the future and back. Fear not. The man you seek does not know we are coming. You are no longer Jason Law. Your genes are no longer Jason Law's genes. You are Tagai the Warrior, and I am your shield."

"Pirramuar, how will we find the evil one who calls himself Do Chi?"

"We do not have to find him. The path has already been

made clear for us. Look through the light, and you will find what you seek."

Tagai strained but still could not see through the bright light blinding his eyes. Then suddenly the light softened, and he was peering down at two figures in a glass tube. Both were dressed in military uniforms and the older had a bright blue feather embossed on his left breast pocket. "Do Chi," Tagai muttered to himself.

He still held the spear in his right hand but somehow knew he could not strike Do Chi here. He looked behind him and Pirramuar was still looking at him from the Dreaming. Without speaking, Pirramuar was telling him that Do Chi was not vulnerable until he reached the Dreaming.

Pirramuar took a fishing net from a bag strapped to his waist. The net was made of spun gold and shimmered in the never-ending light of the Dreaming. Pirramuar took the net in his hands and cast it toward the old man with the feather embossed on his uniform. An instant later, Tagai was in the Dreaming, and the old man was lying before him, wrapped in the golden netting. Do Chi struggled to his feet and glared at the two Aborigines.

He spoke first to the older of the two. "Who are you and why have you brought me here? Speak before it is too late! Do you know who I am? Do you dare pit your powers against mine?"

Neither of the two Aborigines spoke, but the younger one drew back his spear preparing to kill the old man. Suddenly the old man vanished, and the net fell empty. Tagai looked at Pirramuar who looked back at the net.

"I told you I wanted your names. Who are you and why did you bring me here?" The old man's voice was strong, but he was nowhere to be seen.

Tagai spoke, "I am Tagai the Warrior, and I have come to kill you. Step out of the shadows Do Chi and face me."

The old man chuckled, "I am known by that name only in the past. There is only one man who would have the strength to find me, and yet you are not that man. Why would you kill me, Tagai the Warrior?"

"Because you killed my mother!"

Do Chi laughed and almost contemptuously showed himself. Somehow Jason Law had bathed himself in the identity of another man, but he was still Jason Law, and that made him vulnerable. "Jason, why can't you face me as a man? Why do you hide yourself in the cloak of another?"

Tagai said nothing but turned to face the lama from the past who had disgraced himself with the blood of Jason's mother. "I have come to kill you, Old Man." Tagai stepped forward and hurled his spear at Do Chi.

The spear hit Do Chi squarely in the chest, piercing his heart. Do Chi's body slumped over as the blood oozed from the gaping wound. The old man's chest heaved in a tortuous effort to suck in the air of life, but it was too late. Do Chi was dead.

Tagai bent over the body and ripped the sapphire ring from Do Chi's finger. Tagai was trembling uncontrollably, and he screamed a blood-curdling yell that shook the Dreaming itself. Then the impossible happened.

Tagai heard the voice of Do Chi repeating his threat, "Do you know who I am? The body you killed was only a shell I found useful. Do Chi was a good man, a man of faith, but how quickly he fell under my spell. That pitiful man, Mueller, was even more easily subdued. They both have finally begun to realize they will be with me forever. You may have stopped me temporarily from ridding the Universe of the puny rock you call Earth, but in the end you are doomed to fail.

"How many times have you asked yourself my true identity? I have been with you since early in your life on earth. I am the One who helped you open the door to your parents' bedroom and steal the dollar bill from your father's wallet. I am the One who showed you how easy it would be to cheat on your college entrance exams. Remember when you were a local detective in Sydney? I am the One who held the door open as you walked into an apartment and beat a suspect senseless just because he mouthed off to you. I am the One who put my hand in yours as we slowly pulled the trigger and shot Mueller one last time after he was already dead.

"Remember how the cold went through your body as you realized what you had done but felt no shame? Remember how I wrapped you in my veil of darkness and how you relished the moment?"

"No, no, it's not true. I was doing my job. I was defending my team," Tagai stammered, but the spirit behind the voice was right.

Tagai felt the doubts of Jason begin to fill his being. Jason had enjoyed shooting Mueller one last time, and he had to admit it if he had any chance of surviving this encounter. "You're right. I did enjoy it, and I'd do it all over again! Now I have no place in my heart for you. I'm done with you!"

"Done with me? It is not your choice! My voice makes mankind shake in fear. I will see you burn in hell Tagai or Jason or whatever you call yourself. You will die as easily as your mother."

Tagai dropped the sapphire ring and it fell into the brightness of the Dreaming. He felt two unseen hands stretch around his neck and begin to squeeze harder and harder. He fought back with all of his strength but he was growing weaker and weaker and would soon be unable to continue. He flailed at the nothingness that was choking out his life's breath and tried to stop from passing out. He could hear the chuckling of the spirit's voice and feel the unseen fingers grew stronger and stronger. There was no hope.

But somehow the Aborigine warrior threw off the weight of Jason's guilt, and heard Pirramuar's voice calling to him. "Break away from the Evil One's grip. Take the feather from the spear that still penetrates Do Chi's body. You have the strength of all mankind. Fight for your life, Tagai, for your soul."

Tagai tore away from the unseen grip and raced toward Do Chi's body. He grabbed the feather and held it tightly in his hands. There was silence--deep, deep silence. Then suddenly Pirramuar was at his side.

Together they had stopped the one behind Do Chi's plan to destroy the earth and with it the Dreaming. The future was safe. Jeanne Hastings could return to the Greater American Federation without fear of prosecution. Jason and Dawn could take the time they needed to heal from the terrible wounds they suffered to head, to heart, to soul. Tagai embraced Pirramuar, and they both sighed a deep breath. Tagai finally let himself relax. He had beaten the Evil One, and he could take the path back to Dawn, to life.

Pirramuar relaxed his grip on Tagai and began to whisper a prayer to himself. Suddenly, his face became contorted and he was violently thrown to his knees. The two hands Tagai had felt around his own neck were now choking the life out of Pirramuar. The holy man fought back with all his strength, but couldn't loosen the Evil

One's death grip. Pirramuar was being thrown about like a rag doll and his strength was ebbing.

"Run, Tagai. Run! The monster's grip is too strong. I am dying. Run!"

"I will never leave you, Pirramuar. I have defeated this demon once, and I will do it again." Tagai threw himself on Pirramuar's body and began wrestling with the unseen hands of death. For a moment Tagai could feel the Evil One's grip beginning to loosen, and then he heard a voice from hell whispering to him.

"Did you think it was so simple to be rid of me, Jason?" Jason looked at his body, and he realized it was true. Somehow, he had resumed his existence as Jason Law again. "I will make you a bargain," the voice continued, 'but you must think quickly. The one you call Pirramuar will be dead in moments. I will trade his life for yours. Submit to my will, and he will walk the path to the cave of his people. Fight me, and he dies!"

"I submit. Just release him," Jason whispered. Pirramuar took a deep breath and the color began returning to his face.

Suddenly, Jason felt his body shudder, and he was being jerked downward. He was being forced further and further down a never-ending darkness, and he cried out in terror. "Kill me. Kill me! Be done with it. If I am to die, so be it." Jason was sure he was doomed.

Jason lost consciousness, and his mind drifted back to his childhood. He could see his mother in the distance, and she was screaming at him to run, to escape from the madman who had ended her life. It was too late. He was a little boy, watching his mother's murder again. The old man finished with Jason's mother and then walked slowly toward Jason. The youngster turned and tried to run, but his movements seemed like slow motion, and each time he looked back the old man with the long, thin hands was getting closer and closer. Then Jason turned to face the old man. Even as a small boy he realized he had to make a choice. He could stand and fight, or he would be running the rest of his life. He chose to fight. He looked at the old man squarely in the eyes. "I am not afraid of you. I am ready to die."

"Die? Do you think I will permit you to close your eyes and sleep the silence of the dead. No, Jason. You are to spend eternity with me! You will die a thousand times and then a thousand times again. Your pain will never stop!" Jason adjusted his eyes and realized that he was no longer the seven-year-old who watched his mother's murder. He was crossing over from this life to another and there was no hope. He whispered goodbye to Dawn and turned to face his tormenter, but there was no one there.

"Show yourself! If I am to spend eternity with you, surely you can show yourself to me."

"You don't make the rules here, Jason, I do. However, to amuse myself, I will do as you ask." Do Chi appeared and the old man seemed to be glowing with anticipation. "I have taken Do Chi's appearance because that is how you know me, but I have been many people, in many places in many times. You have been an interesting subject, Jason, but now I must attend to other matters. I have decided to assign you to one of my trusted agents who will supervise your stay with us. I believe you've already met."

Jason turned and, standing behind him, was Commander Jack Mueller holding his Turk Blade. "I've been waiting to see you again. Come with me."

Jason began moving toward Mueller obediently when Mueller screamed at him, "Duck!" Jason dove to the ground and Mueller hurled his knife at Do Chi's heart. The old man dropped to his knees and fell lifeless. "Hurry, you only have seconds," Mueller shouted at Jason.

"How did you kill him? I thought he was beyond death."

"He is," Mueller gasped, but when he takes on the shape of another he can be wounded if only for a few moments. I learned too late what my sins have cost me. You may still have a chance. Get back to the Dreaming and return to your holy man. Hell's ruler will stay to finish with me, and that will allow you and the holy man to escape to your loved ones. Stay on guard, Jason. The Evil One will return someday to finish what he has started with you.

"Go with God. I must stay and pay for my sins. Your mother is in another place where there is love and peace, and there is still hope for you. Now go quickly!"

Jason sensed a tremendous weight leave him as he felt himself moving up. Faster and faster he moved away from the Evil One's power, and toward the Dreaming. For now he was safe, and he had to find Pirramuar.

Instead, Pirramuar found him. "What has happened?," the holy man asked Jason. "I have been looking for Tagai, but Jason stands before me." Jason explained his confrontation with the Darkness and how Mueller had sacrificed himself to allow Jason to escape.

"Commander Mueller will pay a heavy price," Pirramuar told Jason, "but he has given us time to return to the cavern."

Pirramuar led Jason back through the cavern to the fire still tended by Dawn, Doc, and Jeanne Hastings. They all hugged, laughed, cried, and hugged again. Pirramuar told Doc and Jeanne about the unbelievable events that had occurred while Jason took Dawn by the hand and led her into the darkness outside. "I know my mother's soul smiles down on us, Dawn. I love you. I love you."

"I love you Jason--now, in the future, forever. I love you."

EPILOGUE

In a cold, stark cell Thaddeus P. Nichols, the Confederate Senator who had been Jason's first arrest, was pacing back and forth. He had been in the same small cell for what seemed an eternity. Once he was found guilty, his aura decomposition was placed in remission, and he was sentenced to 13 consecutive life sentences.

His future for the next millennium seemed bleak, but somehow he was chuckling to himself. "So you believe this prison system is foolproof Detective Inspector Law. I will find the secret to my freedom and hunt you down. My hands tremble when I think of forcing you to watch as I wrap them around your beautiful wife's slender throat. If I can believe the stranger in my dreams, there may still be a way I can save myself and return to my own time. Have patience, Jason. Someday I will find you!"

A few meters away from Nichols' cell, Correction Officer Judy Nichols-Mason sat at her station. She had followed custom and kept her maiden name after marrying. The C.O. was reading the genealogy report her husband had given her for her birthday. She had read it over and over before she had approached the prisoner in Cell H700.

She showed the report to the prisoner who merely smiled and told her that a report could only show so much. So they talked for several minutes before the next scheduled electronic bio-sweep. The senator assured Judy her ancestors had indeed been the senator's close relatives. They were members of an elite Southern family who owned several thousand acres in the South before Union soldiers stole the land and gave it to carpetbaggers.

Judy was breaking all the rules, talking to the prisoner. Still, she couldn't help talking with this man from the past who knew so much about her family's heritage and the fortune that should have been theirs. Judy had crossed over the line. She was about to free this madman from the past and threaten the very heart of the nation.

BOOK TWO

~ SOUTHERN CROSS ~

Chapter One

SYDNEY, AUSTRALIA,
1829

Thad Nichols thought he was one of the most fortunate boys in the South. The year was 1829 and his father, Samuel Nichols, had decided to mix business with pleasure and take his family to Australia with him. "Thaddeus, it's time you learned something about the family business," his father had said to him.

"The third largest cotton plantation below the Mason-Dixon Line," Samuel Nichols often bragged. It had taken over 300 slaves working the cotton fields to bring in last year's bumper crop, and this year was going to be even better. "We need more field hands, Thaddeus, but I'm tired of all the complaining I hear in the fields," the father had said to the son. Samuel had always relied on his own breeding program and the slave markets along the Eastern seaboard to maintain his field-hand slave population, but he was looking for a better supply.

A friend seemed to have the perfect answer. "Samuel, I hear there's a place half-way around the world called 'Australia,' and they got blacks called Aborigines. Most of them are supposed to be so wild you can't catch 'em. They live out in something called the 'bush.' They say the place is so hot and so barren it's the work of the Devil. I hear the blacks can survive out there for weeks with little or no provisions. Sounds too good to be true to me, but you never know."

Even bigger profits were in Samuel's future if he could cross-breed his own stock with a number of Australian Aborigines. His goal was to cut down on the tremendous room, board, and upkeep he was forced to provide his current slave population. He might even be able to branch out and develop a breed that he could sell throughout America.

"First things first," he said to his son. "We need those Aborigines." Samuel smiled at Thad, and, for one of the few times in the boy's life, he felt the gentle touch of his father's hand. It would be the last.

Nichols and his family arrived in Sydney, Australia, on September 8, 1829. Within two days, Samuel had left his wife Anne and their three children to fend for themselves. He had barely spoken to Anne on the trip and saw no reason to do so now. "I'll be back in three weeks," he told her. Anne nodded and motioned for her two daughters and her son to come with her to their room.

His father grabbed Thaddeus and roughly held him up so they were eye to eye. "Mind your mother. When I return with our new stock of slaves, you and I will have work to do." Thad was completely confused, but he knew better than to question his father. He merely nodded as he had seen his mother do countless times, and his father put him down.

During the first three weeks he was gone, Samuel hired a local guide to find 20 Aborigines--10 men and 10 women. This stock would be bred with a like number of slaves from his farm. Within 15 years he hoped to learn if his grand experiment was a success. However, his first task was to find those 20 Aborigines. His guide, a weathered man in his early 50s, had warned him before they left, "You're not in the States anymore, mate. People here are an odd lot. We don't much care for a gentleman of your kind coming over here trying to push us around. Do you catch my drift, mate?"

"Yes, yes, I understand," Samuel replied. However, he soon found out it was much easier to buy slaves at American slave markets than it was to find them in the Australian bush. Samuel tried to buy them from local farmers and to barter for them with an alcoholic Aborigine clan leader. The farmers wanted far too much money, and the Aborigine still had enough dignity to refuse Samuel's offer of rum.

Finally, Samuel's guide led him to a constabulary outpost on the edge of the bush. There the guide bribed the commander to lead his men on several raids of local Aborigine tribes to find Samuel's 20 slaves. He was forced to settle for two men and three women. Samuel was more than a little upset, but he had no alternative. The three weeks had turned into three months, and Samuel had to return to Sydney for his wife and children.

When Samuel arrived in Sydney, he made arrangements to have his slaves shipped to America and then went to the hotel to tell his family of his adventure. "I'm taking you all down to the ship to see my new breeding stock."

His wife would have none of it. "I have no intention of dragging our two daughters down to that ship so you can parade those wretched creatures in front of them," she almost shouted.

"Fine," Samuel said, grabbed Thaddeus, and stormed out of the hotel. When they walked up the ship's gangplank, Samuel's heart began to pound. Once they reached the ship's hold he could smell the fear in the air. Samuel had absolute power over these five Aborigines and he loved it. He looked into Thad's eyes and saw the same fear as he saw in the Aborigines' eyes. All except the one the constabulary told him was the Aborigines' shaman or holy man.

Samuel talked quietly to Thad and asked, "Are you frightened, Thaddeus? It's all right--but never let a slave know you fear him. He will see it as a sign of weakness and he will not respect you. The next thing you know, your slaves are asking for more food and rest. Before long you've lost control. **Never** lose control, Thaddeus! Do you understand? Never!"

"Yes, Father," Thad replied without looking in his father's eyes, "but the big one is staring at me, and I'm afraid of him."

Samuel looked at the five captives and saw the Aborigine staring back at him. Shackled next to him was the woman the constabulary commander had said was the Aborigine's wife. Samuel made an instantaneous decision. He held Thad by the arm and dragged him towards the Aborigines' leader.

Samuel smiled as he looked into the man's face. "What is your name?" Samuel was about to teach Thad a lesson in the cruelty of man, and he needed the Aborigines to make his point.

The holy man sat staring back at Samuel but made no reply. When the five Aborigines had been captured, the constabulary commander assured Samuel their leader spoke English when it suited him. Obviously, it didn't suit him at this moment.

The shaman wore a hand-fashioned cross made of bone around his neck. Samuel had noticed it when the Aborigines were captured and had asked a constabulary sergeant if the Aborigines were Christian. "No," the sergeant replied, "but the cross is very sacred to some of the tribes. Has something to do with their idea of paradise. That's all I know."

That wasn't enough for Samuel. When the constabulary detachment brought the Aborigines back to the outpost that night, Samuel asked the commander for more details. "The cross the Aborigines wear is a symbol of a group of stars that form the outline of a cross that can only be seen in the Southern Hemisphere," the commander began. "It's called the Southern Cross. One legend has it the stars form the left hand of Tagai the Warrior.

Another says the four stars are the four daughters of a famous Aborigine leader. Before he died, he had a medicine man weave a rope out of the medicine man's beard. When the father died, the daughters went to the medicine man who showed the girls the rope stretched all the way to heaven. The girls climbed the rope to be in the evening sky with their father. Come out, and I'll show you." The commander pointed to the group of stars and said, "That bright star next to the cross is supposed to be their father."

"Very interesting," Samuel had replied.

Now his new slaves were on the ship, in chains and under his complete control. It was time to let them know their place in the world of the white man. "No slave of mine will be wearing a cross unless he's bathed in the blood of our Savior," Samuel said to his son.

The father went to the Aborigine leader and ripped the cross from his neck. "Blasphemy! You'll not wear the holy cross until you come to our Savior on your knees." Samuel gathered his composure and looked at Thad. "Take this and keep it. We control these savages' lives. We decide if they live or die. Do you understand?"

"Yes, Father," the small boy replied.

"Good. Now watch." Samuel smiled and then turned to the holy man's wife. "Does your husband have a name? Certainly he must have a name. I need to know his name so I might keep an accurate accounting. **What is his name?**"

The woman was whimpering and would not return Samuel's

gaze. Samuel turned to Thad and said, "You must never show fear, Thaddeus, never!" Samuel grabbed the woman's throat and began tightening his grip on her. She tried to scream but Samuel had cut off her air. Samuel looked at the shaman and repeated his question, "What's your name?"

The Aborigine sighed and replied, "My name is Pirramuar."

Samuel released his grip on the woman and turned to the husband. "I understand you are your clan's holy man. Is that true?"

"Yes."

"Good. I am interested in the power you hold over your people. Do you hold the lives of your people in your hands?"

"What do you mean?"

"Simple. I say I have the power of life and death over you, your wife, and the other three. Stop me if you can." With that, Samuel began to slowly choke the woman. At first she struggled, heaving her head back and forth, but her contortions began to slow and her eyes rolled up into her head. Samuel looked at the woman's husband and then Thad. The shaman closed his eyes and began to chant.

Samuel called to Thad, "Come here, Thaddeus. See the life leaving this woman? Slaves cost too much money to waste good flesh, but we cannot afford an uppity field hand. Do you understand?"

Thad had no idea what his father was saying but he dutifully replied, "Yes, Father."

Samuel looked at Thad. He had to go on with the lesson or the boy would have no chance of succeeding him. Samuel had killed his first slave when he was nine years old. His son would only be seven. "Come here, son. Give me your hand."

Thad stuck out his right hand, still gripping the holy man's cross. His father placed his hand on the woman's throat. The young boy's hand was just beneath his father's.

The holy man continued his chant, and the small boy shook as he felt the woman's pulse beating in her throat. Thad was horrified. How could his father be so cruel? How could he choke the life out of this woman from the bush?

Then the woman's eyes popped open, and she tried to cry out. Her husband struggled to break free from his shackles, but it was useless.

The shaman screamed, "Stop. I will do whatever you say. Stop!" It was no use. Samuel Nichols had no intention of stopping. He received no joy from it. It was strictly business. He had to teach his son the awesome power he would have some day.

Thad felt the sweat running down the woman's throat over his hand. Then something strange happened. He stopped being afraid. An excitement began to grow inside him like nothing he had ever felt. He began to breathe quickly and couldn't wait for the woman to die. He squeezed the woman's throat just as he saw his father doing. He squeezed and squeezed until the woman slumped in death.

Thaddeus Nichols lost the precious control his father had told him he should never lose, and he felt a passion no other seven-year-old had ever felt. He released his grip and saw the deep impression the cross had made on the woman's throat.

Then Thad spoke to the woman's body in a way that frightened even his father. "Your death has been an honor for you," Thad said out loud. He shot a quick look at his father to see if he had pleased him. "We are doing the Lord's work, Father. Look, the Lord has put His sign on the woman's neck."

Samuel Nichols had gone too far. A young boy's innocence had died and a monster had been born.

Chapter Two

Judy Nichols-Mason was screaming for her life. "You're killing me! I can't breathe!   Stop, please stop..." The young corrections officer felt the man's fingers tighten around her neck and she only had seconds before she would pass out. Her eyes began to bulge out of their sockets as the vessels in her eyes popped and bright red blood oozed down her face. How could this have happened?

Judy had committed an unpardonable sin--she had dropped the force field for Cell H700 to talk to the prisoner, and this wasn't the first time. She had begun talking to the prisoner, a Confederate senator from the 1800s, almost immediately after he was assigned to her cell block. His name was Thaddeus P. Nichols, and he was serving 13 consecutive life sentences for killing 13 war brides while their husbands were away fighting for the South. Judy had hung on his every word as they discussed the past and their common family name.

Senator Nichols had played Judy from the start. "May I call you Judy? Your ancestors were most certainly part of the South's landed gentry, and you are entitled to the riches the Union stole from your family."

The prison authorities insisted on a top-level security check to make sure there was no possibility of any bloodline ties. It was just Judy's bad luck that had given this madman the chance to kill her. The DNA sample taken from Nichols during his in-processing at an overworked lab, had been lost and no one had followed up on the mistake.

But Judy was smart enough to ask, "How could all of the computer checks have missed our ties to each other? It's hard to believe."

Senator Nichols told her, "Many of the records from my time were lost or destroyed during the war, and it's not only possible but likely that we are of the same blood." Judy had bought the con completely and spent more and more time talking to what she thought was her famous ancestor in Cell H700.

Senator Nichols had promised her they could find a way to return to the time of the Confederacy. Together we can ensure you take your rightful place among our people and help foster a free, sovereign Confederate States of America." Judy was about to join her ancestors all right but not in the way she hoped.

Judy was slipping in and out of consciousness as her arms and legs flayed and her heart pounded. She could feel Thaddeus Nichols's breath on her neck, and she began to hallucinate. She felt the passionate touch of her husband as he wrapped his hands around her neck as he had done so many times before. Tighter and tighter he squeezed. "Honey, don't be so rough, you're hurting me. Stop, stop!" Then it ended.

The Senator released his death grip on the young woman and cursed himself for acting so foolishly. He had been planning his escape attempt for several years, and he needed CO Nichols to have any chance at all, but as Judy had entered Thaddeus Nichols's cell, the man from the past had gone crazy. He wanted to feel the power of life and death in his hands again, and he was willing to do anything to make that happen.

Nichols only had two or three minutes at the most to do something to cover his tracks. Judy had cut short their conversations many times to make her quarterly hour status reports, and her next report was due any second now. Thaddeus moved on instinct. Judy had shut down the automated scanning system when she went into his cell. It was the only way she could safely enter the cell without being picked up by the auto-scanner. Judy had called in and told the cell monitor, "I'm rebooting the auto-scanner manually. I'll have it up and running within the required seven-minute window."

"Roger," the bored monitor replied. He filed the standard Systems Error Report and immediately forgot what had happened.

Thaddeus Nichols was on a short leash. He pulled Judy out of his cell and grabbed the electronic cell key and stun gun from her belt. Thaddeus ran to the next cell and used the electronic cell key he had seen Judy use so many times to drop the force field down for Cell H701. He had no idea who was in the cell and didn't care. When he entered, he saw a young Oriental woman sleeping. She jumped from her bed and looked almost happy as Thaddeus Nichols aimed the stun gun at her. He had set it on maximum stun and pulled the trigger. The senator ran over to the female prisoner's body and began choking her--just enough to leave marks. Now she and Judy Nichols both showed the signs of a terrific struggle where they each tried to choke the other to death.

Nichols set the gun on kill and released the prisoner from her never-ending agony. She gave out a short whimper and died almost peacefully. She was now beyond even this future world's touch.

Nichols ran to Judy's body, picked it up, and threw her into the other cell on top of the dead female prisoner. He placed the stun gun in Judy's hand and took a second to check the scene he had set. It was almost perfect, all except for the forensic evidence he had learned so much about since arriving in the twenty-fourth century. He didn't have time to do anything about it. Nichols dialed back the stun gun to a non-lethal level, shot himself while it was in Judy's hand and crawled back to his own cell. The auto-scan system came back on-line almost immediately--and the force field went up in both cells.

It was only moments before the crash squad came running down the cell block, scanning each cell as they went. Thaddeus could hear them screaming, and he understood the next few moments would decide his future. A helmeted, two-man squad ran into his cell and saw him writhing in obvious pain. They asked no questions and quickly ran out of his cell. Thaddeus could hear their lieutenant asking, "What did you see?"

"Both cells are locked up tight, Lieutenant. The prisoner in 701 is dead and the one in 700 has been stunned and probably wishes he were dead."

"Play back the last five minutes of the auto-scan in 701. I want to see what happened."

"No can do, Lieutenant. We already tried, but the auto-scanner's been out of operation for the last few minutes." The lieutenant was not happy. There was no record of what had happened in Nichols's cell or to the prisoner in Cell H701. Lieutenant Jack Dawson was in trouble. No matter he had just pulled a double shift. No matter his team was undermanned, and he was forced to use two green pencil pushers for prisoner control. So Lieutenant Dawson did what any unseasoned, junior officer would do. He asked his senior sergeant.

Lieutenant Dawson pulled Sergeant Nathaniel Pope to one side and said, "What do you think, Sergeant? I need a way out of this, and I need it now!"

The old sergeant had been in the system more years than he cared to remember, and was an old hand at hiding his dirty laundry. "Well, Lieutenant, the way I see it, you've got two choices. You can call the captain and ask him to come down to bail you out, or you can make the best of a bad situation on your own. The prerogative of command, Sir, the prerogative of command." Sergeant Pope was giving the young lieutenant enough rope to hang himself, and the lieutenant bit.

"What do you mean?" the lieutenant asked.

"Simple, boss" It was the first time Sergeant Pope had been so loose with Lieutenant Dawson, but he knew the lieutenant needed him now more than ever. This was going to cost Lieutenant Dawson big time.

"You only have one way out if you hope to keep your lieutenant bars. I'll wipe both bodies clean--the forensic geeks won't find a thing.

"What about those bruise marks on both of their necks? Something's going on, and I don't understand it. I don't like this; I don't like it at all."

"Me either, Lieutenant, but your career is on the line. You've got to do something fast. With the auto-scanner down and no electronic record, you get to write the report. I'll make sure none of the guys say anything. Leave it to me, Lieutenant."

That's exactly what the lieutenant did. He wrote the report, drawing the obvious conclusion that Correction Officer Nichols had been forced to use her stun gun to bring the prisoner in H700 under control and then was forced to kill the prisoner in H701. The female prisoner had most likely tried to jump the correction officer when she entered the cell to quiet the prisoner. Young Nichols had obviously grabbed her stun gun while she was still in the prisoner's clutches and killed the inmate before dying herself.

Three levels of command reviewed the report and a letter of reprimand was placed in Lieutenant Dawson's personnel file. With the help of Sergeant Pope, however, he was sure he could get back on the fast track to promotion to captain.

As for Sergeant Pope--well, suddenly he was allowed to come in a little late and get the occasional afternoon off. Things were going to be fine for Sergeant Pope, just fine.

Chapter Three

It had been eight years since Jason Law had faced his worst nightmares and put an end to Do Chi's hold over him. Meanwhile, the diplomatic niceties were attended to, and Jeanne Hastings returned to her old job.

Hastings was a workaholic and instantly threw herself back into her work. She tried to stay in contact with Jason, Dawn, and the others but, inevitably, they drifted apart. Then Jeanne's world came apart at the seams. She had been working on a very rare appeal case. The World Court had agreed to hear an appeal from a condemned time transfer prisoner--Thaddeus P. Nichols. He had been placed on suicide watch after a terrible incident where a female prisoner had killed a corrections officer. The Confederate senator from the past was monitored continuously but had been a model prisoner. He spent 14 to 18 hours a day researching case law to find a way to appeal his case.

Jeanne could only find two other time transfer appeals that had actually been heard by the Court. Both appeals had been very technical in nature and had only resulted in the defendants getting a few breaths of fresh air before they were returned to their cells to face one life sentence after another. Jeanne had been briefed on the Nichols's case by an associate prosecutor but wanted to know everything before entering the courtroom.

She opened the case file and read the executive summary to get a better feel for the legal arguments the defense would make. The case centered on the defendant's contention that Senator Nichols was the legal representative of a sovereign nation. The appeal asserted the Time Force Investigations Unit had no authority to arrest Senator Nichols without the expressed permission of the Confederate States of America, and such permission required a Writ of Extradition.

The next morning, Court was called to order with Jeanne Hastings representing the United Nations and a court-appointed public defender representing the defendant. The senator had requested he be allowed to dress in the same clothing he had been wearing in his own time, and the Court had granted his petition.

Thaddeus Nichols walked into the courtroom in the clothes of a Southern gentleman circa 1863. He wore a deep red tailcoat and dark gray pants. His tie was a matching gray against his off-white shirt. Senator Nichols waited patiently as he was released from his electronic shackles, and then he bowed to Jeanne Hastings. His public defender motioned for him to sit at the defense table and the senator obliged.

"All rise," the bailiff commanded as Justice Andrew T. Goodwin made his entrance to the courtroom.

"Be seated," the justice ordered as he gazed out into his courtroom. "I don't believe what I'm seeing," he quipped to himself as he stared directly at the defendant. As the most junior of the seven justices on the World Court, Justice Goodwin was stuck hearing pretrial motions for this particular case. Usually these motion hearings were very necessary but very boring, and that was just the way Justice Goodwin liked it. He would make sure today was no exception. He had to admit to himself though, that he had been taken aback not only by the way the defendant was dressed but by his general demeanor. It was obvious Senator Nichols was used to being in control despite the years he had spent in prison. When Justice Goodwin had entered the courtroom, Senator Nichols waited until everyone else had risen. Only then did he rise from his chair, bow slightly to the justice, and sit back down without waiting for Justice Goodwin's perfunctory, "You may be seated."

"I note for the record the Government has complied with the Court's Standing Orders and has filed all the necessary administrative motions relative to these proceedings. Does the government have anything further?"

"Not at this time, Your Honor, although we reserve the right to amend our motions as authorized under the Court's Standing Orders."

"Very well," the Justice replied in his monotone, matter-of-fact, official voice. "Does the defense have any motions other than those administrative motions previously submitted?"

"Yes, Your Honor, a special proceedings motion," the public defender replied as he stood. His name was Paul Garrett and he was a career public defender. Not once had he filed a special proceedings motion. In fact, no one in his office had ever heard of a special proceedings motion ever being filed. It was clear neither the prosecutor nor Justice Goodwin had ever been involved with one either.

"Your Honor, the government has had no notice of any special motions. Standing Order 676 clearly states that any such motions must be filed with the Court's office, and a copy provided to the prosecutor's office at least 10 working days before the proceedings."

Jeanne Hastings was hopping mad, and she was not about to allow the public defender to pull this fast one. "The government insists that any discussion of the motion be held in abeyance until the Court and the prosecutor have had sufficient time to review this matter."

Justice Goodwin was in no mood for something so irregular, and he was about to put a stop to it. "Mr. Garrett, what do you have to say for yourself? The government is correct. Standing Order 676 does require such notice."

"May it please, Your Honor. There is one notable exception-- a defendant's petition to represent himself may be made at any time during the proceedings with no such filing. The defendant is so petitioning." Paul Garrett was almost as surprised as Justice Goodwin and Jeanne Hastings.

He had spoken to Senator Nichols only twice. The first time was after he had been informed that Senator Nichols was seeking a retrial. The second time was about an hour before these proceedings commenced. Garrett had tried his best to dissuade Senator Nichols from such a foolhardy exercise. Garrett explained to Senator Nichols that too much had changed since Senator Nichols graduated from law school in 1844, but the senator would have none of it and insisted Garrett present his petition.

"Mr. Nichols, do you understand what a gamble you are taking in representing yourself *pro se*?" Justice Goodwin asked the defendant directly.

"I understand, Your Honor, that it is my right to represent myself even in this so-called Court of Law," Senator Nichols snapped. Thaddeus Nichols was gambling with his life, but he had to make his point early. He was not someone to be bullied, and he thought he might have a chance of winning two legal arguments at once. He was a senator of the Confederate States of America, and he would demand that distinction. "Your Honor, please accept my apology, but I have been held in solitary confinement from the moment I was taken prisoner of war by the government's agents. Since my trial ended, I have seen only two human faces--my previous lawyer and the guard in my cell block. I apologize again for my outburst, but I must insist that I be treated with the due respect expected for a senator and special envoy of the Confederate States of America. Under the World Court's decision on *Moore vs. the Greater American Federation*, 2289, the majority opinion states that I am to be offered the same customs and courtesies I was afforded in my own time."

Senator Nichols was laying down his marker. If his ploy worked, he might just have a chance at pulling off his scheme. If not, he'd be back in his cell wishing he had held his tongue.

This was Senator Nichols's lucky day. Once Justice Goodwin found the computer record of the Moore case, he only took a few seconds to make his decision. Unfortunately for Prosecutor Hastings, this so-called senator from the past had been researching case law from his cell. Under the Moore decision, Nichols was entitled to all of the customs and courtesies of a representative of a Sovereign State during his first trial. Justice Goodwin made an immediate ruling from the bench that during the appeal process, Senator Nichols was to be moved from solitary confinement to a VIP Detention Holding Area. There he would have access to the outside world under the continuing scrutiny of the prison's guards. "Does the Government have any objections?"

Jeanne Hastings had been scanning the computerized Moore trial record and realized she didn't have a chance at stopping

Senator Nichols, but she wanted to make a record of her disagreement in seeing Nichols moved from solitary confinement. "Your Honor, the Government has very strong objections to allowing this serial murderer the luxury of being moved from solitary confinement. Request a 48-hour adjournment to give us sufficient time to research this obvious miscarriage of justice. This amounts to a second motion certainly not covered under Standing Order 676."

"You are correct, Ms Hastings. It does amount to a second motion. Still, under the circumstances, I see no way to deny the defendant the rights he was so obviously denied during his trial. Senator Nichols, your motion is approved. Don't abuse it."

"No, Your Honor." Senator Nichols had risen to his feet this time and bowed deeply to Justice Goodwin and Jeanne Hastings in turn. He sat back down and couldn't help himself as he smirked at Jeanne Hastings.

"Senator Nichols, we also need to address your original motion that you be allowed to act on your own behalf while in this Court. Your request is granted, and you will be allowed to represent yourself during these proceedings. But I warn you, I will hold you to the same rigorous standards I hold any other lawyer in my Court. Do I make myself clear?"

"Very, Your Honor," Nichols replied as a broad smile began to form on his face.

Jeanne Hastings was more than exasperated with the Court's ruling, but she maintained her composure. Justice Goodwin and Jeanne Hastings both understood now that trying Nichols was not going to be such an easy task. This crazy man from the past might not be so crazy after all.

Thaddeus Nichols had begun a trip that would turn this world of the future on its head. While somewhere in Sydney, Australia, Jason Law was oblivious to what was happening--but not for long.

Chapter Four

Jason Law was having the time of his life and actually getting paid to do it. Two years ago the Sydney police department's Chief of Detectives had called Jason at home and asked, "Jason, I know you're retired, but I was hoping I could talk you into helping us out a few hours a week in homicide. Your run-in with the TFI is old news. I can put you on a consultant's contract and pay you top dollar. I'd only need you 15 to 20 hours a week. What do you think?"

It took Jason all of about five seconds to think it over and say, "Sure, Chief. I could use the money, and, to be honest, I'm a little restless. I've got too much time on my hands." They both laughed at Jason's obvious pun. His one-year consulting contract called for him to act as a Special Assistant to the Chief of Detectives. Jason lost his official title as Detective and the chief made it clear Jason's real job was to whip the Homicide Department back in shape. Jason was in his element and couldn't wait to go to work.

The 15 to 20 hours per week quickly became 40, then 50. After that, Jason's wife Dawn stopped counting. She was too busy looking after their seven-year-old son Joseph--Jody for short. Jason was happy, and thankfully he was not involved in any apprehensions, or so he told her. Generally, it was the perfect life for a couple that more than deserved it, but that would all change when Jason received a call that would plunge him back into the world of darkness.

Chapter Five

Senator Thaddeus Nichols was enjoying himself after spending his first night in his new quarters. Sure, he was being monitored 24/7. That meant full spectrum cameras were monitoring him and a tracking chip had been inserted under the skin on his left lower arm. "At least now I'm being treated in the way a senator of the Confederate States of America should be treated," he said out loud.

His court-appointed lawyer had also intervened when the police attempted to have him forcefully undergo a cerebral implant procedure. The Court had issued an Emergency Stay to Desist, and the senator had been spared his every thought being monitored by the authorities.

Thaddeus needed rest before he could attempt his escape. He was tired after spending so much time in that lonely cell, and he had only begun his eternity of hell these people from the future called justice. He held the cross his father had stripped from the Aborigine holy man so many years ago. The police had returned it to him when he was released from his cell.

Perhaps he should have been more careful in how he had approached his 13 victims. Thirteen, no that wasn't right--14 if he counted the young corrections officer. "God must have been on my side, he thought. Why else would He give me such an opportunity! I am the Almighty's hand of death."

Nichols didn't even bother to count the female prisoner in cell H701. She was merely an obstacle to his freedom. "God has set me to the task of bringing victory to the Confederacy," Nichols thought. "I need to know what is God's plan? Who will show me the way?"

The next second Nichols' room went completely dark, and he felt a cold shudder go through his body. Nichols took a deep breath and tried to regain his composure, but he was losing control--not just of his body and his mind but his very soul. This was the same force that had overtaken him when he was a boy of seven in the hold of a ship in Sydney, Australia. He didn't have the power or the will to stop what was happening. He didn't want it to stop. He longed for more. In the deepest part of his being he had been overcome by the Lord of Darkness himself.

The Gehenna's ruler would use Thaddeus Nichols as long as it suited his plans. Those plans went far beyond this little man who would be Hell's tool to strike down Jason Law. The Great Deceiver roared, "Jason, it is time. You and those who sided against me will meet the same fate as all who have tried to stop me. Enjoy these next fleeting moments--they are your last on earth. You will cry for mercy just as Do Chi and Mueller beg me to end their torment, but the torture never stops. It never stops, Jason, it never stops!"

Chapter Six

Thaddeus heard the disconcerting digitalized voice of his computerized baby-sitter. "Visitor at the entrance. Visitor at the entrance." He saw a rather tall man dressed in the formal courtroom dress of a lawyer--white wig, long black robe, and dark circles under the eyes. Yes, this was a busy man who hadn't been getting the sleep he needed.

"Visitor at the entrance. Visitor at the entrance." Nichols felt strangely different, more powerful but at the same time submissive to whatever had taken over his psyche. He decided not to concern himself with the momentary lapse. He liked the way he felt, and that was all that was important.

Nichols went to the entrance and waited for the man to be scanned and the force field dropped. "Senator Nichols, I'm Jerry Evans from Evans, Scott, and Wheaton. My law firm specializes in World Court appeal cases. We've been contacted by someone who wishes to remain anonymous but has asked us to represent you in your appeal."

I've read the transcript of your first hearing, and I believe you may have a reasonable chance of getting a retrial. However, we're a long way from seeing that happen and before I spend more of my time and your benefactor's money, I wanted to get your consent to represent you."

Nichols was more curious than shocked. He had learned a long time ago to expect the unexpected. God was obviously at work here and he needed to let this scene play out to divine God's will. "Mr. Evans, I seldom take good news on its face value, but I believe this may be an exception. However, I'll need a little more information before I accept your generous offer."

"I understand, but, honestly, I know nothing more than I've already told you. A woman called me two days ago. She said she had a client who was willing to spend whatever it took to make sure you received a second trial. As I've already said, I believe you have a fair chance for a retrial, but I think your best option is to stretch out these appeal proceedings as long as possible.

"Once you win your appeal and go to trial, I fear the outcome will be the same as the first trial. My staff has researched the law and the facts of your case. The evidence against you is incontrovertible. As I said, your best option is to stretch out these appeal proceedings and live in this relatively luxurious setting as long as possible."

Lawyer Evans was right but Nichols needed to play Evans if he was going to have any chance of escaping. "Mr. Evans, I appreciate your candor, but I pledge to you I had nothing to do with any of those unfortunate deaths. Yes, it's true I knew several of the 13 ladies in passing. They had asked for my help in finding their husbands who had been listed as missing-in-action during our great struggle against the Union. I was there when they needed comfort, nothing else."

Evans wasn't buying any of it. "Certainly, Senator, certainly. If you want me to represent you I need your written request to withdraw your petition to act *pro se* and for me to replace your court-appointed lawyer."

"Yes, yes, of course. I take it as a great honor that someone has seen the injustice I have suffered and is willing to help me in my time of need." There was that word again. Time had become much more important to Senator Nichols since he was taken from his own time and banished to Isolation Cell H700. He was never going back to that cell he promised himself--never!

"Where do I sign?" he asked as the lawyer handed him a computer pad. Nichols signed two electronic forms--the first withdrawing his request to act *pro se* and the second appointing Evans as his lawyer. He and Evans talked for several more hours and agreed to meet again.

Chapter Seven

EVANS, SCOTT AND WHEATON LAW OFFICE,
2322

Jerry Evans sat in his office going over the private investigator's report. Jerry was not a man who waited for answers to come to him. He was a pusher, and he was pushing hard to find out who exactly had retained him to represent that kook, Senator Thaddeus Nichols.

Jerry was more than a little upset about representing someone who was so obviously guilty, but he believed in the right to counsel and this certainly wasn't the first time his client had turned out to be a creep. But Thaddeus Nichols was different. Sure, he was smart, but most of the serial killers Jerry represented were of above-average intelligence. Since his firm only took Time Transfer cases he had seen the worst of what history could conceive.

From the moment he met Senator Thaddeus Nichols, Evans realized he was staring in the face of evil. Not just some nut who had gone completely off his rocker, but the absolute epitome of everything that was bad in the world--past, present, or future.

Jerry had used his best private investigator to track down Nichols' benefactor but to no avail. Every time his man got close to a name, he'd be sandbagged or run into a stone wall. Jerry Evans was in no mood to accept some lame excuse from a retired police detective who was getting far too much money just to say, "Sorry, Boss, but we can't trace the money that was used to pay your retainer."

All banking was done electronically in the twenty-fourth century, and a smart banker or accountant could make it very difficult to trace transactions. The authorities could do the trace instantaneously with a warrant but Evans was in no position to get the court to issue a warrant just to soothe his curiosity.

"I want you to keep after this. Do you understand?" he said to his investigator. "I want you working on this 24/7, and I don't care what it costs. Got it?"

"Sure, Boss, sure, but this could take a few days--maybe even weeks. Are you sure it's worth it? You've got your money. Why push it?"

"I want to know. No, I **need** to know. Now get out of here and find out who's paying the bills." With that, Jerry Evans went back to work trying to find a way to win the appeal and get the guy a new trial. Heck, if he was really lucky he might have a slim chance of getting Nichols off, despite what he told him. "What a way to make a living," he muttered to himself as he turned to his computer screen and read another legal opinion.

If he could pull this off, he'd be only the second lawyer in history to spring a time transfer. The first had been his father 65 years ago, and Jerry was going to show the world he was even a better lawyer than his old man.

Jerry never called him that to his face. It was always "Father" or "Sir" even when his father was on his deathbed. Jerry spent his life trying to please his father, and when he died Jerry just tried harder. Now Jerry saw his chance. "I'll get this crazy man off, and I'll be free from this obsession," he cried. However, time has a way of changing a man's future, as Jerry was about to learn.

Chapter Eight

COLONIAL HEIGHTS SUB-DIVISION, SYDNEY, AUSTRALIA, 2322

Dawn Law tiptoed into her son Jody's bedroom. It was 7:30 in the morning and she had already let Jody sleep longer than usual. Jason had left an hour and a half before after they argued about Jody. However, it was past time to get Jody ready for school.

Dawn walked quietly to Jody's bedside and began to hum an ancient tune that Jason had taught her. The song was hundreds of years old and was the same one his mother had sung to him each morning as she gently awakened him. Jason couldn't remember the words, but Dawn noticed the smile on his face each time he hummed the tune. Jody had the same smile on his face as he began to open his eyes, and Dawn started humming. The young boy giggled and said, "Good morning, Mum. I love you."

Dawn still smiled when Jody called her "Mum." He was growing up a true Australian just like his father. "I love you, too, but it's time to get up. You'll be late for school. Gramps will be here any minute to take you."

Jason and Dawn had never asked Doc Francis if it was all right if Jody called him Gramps. It was understood by all three as soon as Dawn found out she was pregnant. The three of them had told Jody together that Doc was not his biological grandfather and how that made his relationship with Jody even more special.

Dawn gave Jody his "last chance" as she left his room. "Jody, it's time to get up now."

"Okay, Mum," Jody replied and slowly stretched and got out of bed. Dawn smiled and headed to the kitchen to prepare his breakfast.

The phone began to ring before Dawn got to the kitchen. She answered on the first ring. The call had been instantly screened and fed into her cerebral implant. It was the latest model implant and included a vast array of data. The call was from an old friend, Jeanne Hastings, Chief Prosecutor for the World Court. "Jeanne, how great to see you. How have you. . .

Jeanne Hastings cut Dawn off in mid-sentence. "Dawn, it's good to see you again, too, but I have something I've got to tell Jason. I called Metro Police, but they gave me the runaround. Dawn, I don't have time to find someone up the food chain who will get me in touch with Jason. I need to talk to Jason right **now**. Please, Dawn, please!"

Chapter Nine

Jason had given strict orders to anyone and everyone who would listen in the Metro Police Station. "No calls, no exceptions! Everyone got it?," he shouted as he left his office. He had turned off the communications system in his hovercraft because he needed to be alone. He was outside the station preparing to go to the Outback to clear his head.

He and Dawn had argued just before he had left for work that morning. Jason couldn't remember the last time they had talked crossly to each other. The argument started after Jason insisted Jody begin his Aborigine spiritual upbringing.

It would be five years before Jody could go through the same ceremony Jason had gone through celebrating his passage into manhood. Jason wanted Jody to have an early understanding of what it meant to become one of the People, as Pirramuar's tribe referred to itself. Dawn was just as determined to wait on Jody's indoctrination into the ways of the Aborigine spiritual world until he had a grasp of their church's spiritual beliefs.

Jason's private communicator rang. It had a level four security shield which meant this had to be a true emergency.

He looked at the screen and saw Jeanne Hastings' number appear. The next second Jeanne Hastings's face was on the screen staring intently at him. He could see the fear in her eyes. "Jeanne, what's wrong? How did you get this number? It's not Dawn or Jody, is it?"

"No, Jason. They're both fine. Jody's on his way to school with Doc. I just talked to Dawn. She gave me your number."

Jason sighed with relief, but the other shoe was about to drop. "What is it, Jeanne? You look terrified. Take a deep breath and tell me what's wrong." Jason was almost smiling. His wife, son, and Doc were all safe, and he had just talked to Pirramuar James. Jason had told him about the argument with Dawn. As usual James counseled patience and dialogue.

"Take a few hours off and head for the Outback," James had said to Jason."Jody's spiritual upbringing is not an either-or proposition, Jason. Perhaps it would be good for all of us to sit down and talk about it, but first get your head cleared. Then buy the largest bouquet of flowers you can find and go back and talk this out with Dawn." Jason had promised himself he'd make things right with Dawn when he returned from the Outback. For now, however, he needed to focus on what Jeanne Hastings had to say.

"What is it, Jeanne? Surely there's nothing so bad we can't work out a solution."

"Jason, he's back!"

"Who's back? What are you talking about? Settle down, Jeanne. I've never seen you like this. What's the problem?"

Jeanne Hastings tried to get control of herself, but she was past the breaking point. She looked at Jason's face on the screen, and feared he was her only hope. How could she explain the unexplainable? "Jason, I've seen the eyes of Evil. I've heard its voice. I thought I must be hallucinating, but in my heart I know it was real. I'm not a religious woman, but I know I've stared into the eyes of the Devil. He's back, Jason. He's back. I need to see you right away."

"Where and when?," Jason asked.

"How quickly can you be in my office?," Jeanne asked.

"Jeanne, I'm *persona non grata* in the American Federation. There are a lot of people in your country who want to see me locked up or worse."

"Yes, I know. All right, I'll come to you. I can be at your home in three hours. Can you have Dawn, Doc, and Pirramuar James there? This involves all of us. I've said too much. Can you have everyone at your home in three hours?"

"We'll all be there. Be careful, Jeanne. Whether we're dealing with the Devil or someone from the past who thinks he's the Devil, we still all need to be very careful. Get here as quickly as you can." With that Jason turned his hovercraft around and headed for home.

On the way, he called the Metro Police and arranged for

around-the-clock protection for Doc, James, and his own home. Next he called Dawn. He told her he loved her, apologized for being stupid, and asked her to tell Doc to turn around and bring Jody back home. Jody would have to miss today's school session. Finally, Jason called Pirramuar James and told him what Jeanne had said. James agreed to drop everything and meet the others at Jason's home.

Jason kept going over what Jeanne had said. She was not easily rattled but still, the Devil? Satan, if he existed, didn't spend his time dropping in on World Court prosecutors just to rain on their parade.

Jason couldn't help letting his mind drift back to a panicked call from Jeanne Hastings eight years ago. She had warned him of Do Chi's threat from the future to destroy the world. Jason's ordeal had ended with a confrontation with pure Evil in the Dreaming. Perhaps the struggle had been in his own head, in Pirramuar's psyche. Perhaps there was no Satan or Evil One as Pirramuar had called the force that confronted them in the Dreaming. Perhaps there was no God.

"Maybe," Jason said to himself, "I was just outsmarted by an old lama who wanted to scare me one more time before returning to the future."

And this time? What had so rattled a seasoned prosecutor that would force her to go to these lengths? Jason needed answers, and the only way to get them was from Jeanne Hastings.

Chapter Ten

COLONIAL HEIGHTS GRAMMAR SCHOOL,
2322

Doc and Jody turned the corner and saw Jody's school. "Well, buddy, we're almost there. Make sure you've got everything. We don't want your teacher thinking you're not prepared, do we?"

"No, Gramps."

Just as Doc was stopping at the school's drop-off area, his hovercraft's communicator popped on, and Dawn's face appeared on the screen.

"Doc, I need you to bring Jody back. I can't explain, but you and Jody need to get here as soon as you can."

"What's wrong, Dawn? Is Jason all right? What's going on?"

"Doc, I really can't explain on the communicator. Jason's fine, but you need to bring Jody home now. That's all I can say."

"We'll be there as soon as we can," Doc said. Something was wrong, very wrong, but it was no use pushing Dawn for an answer. He turned the hovercraft and headed back.

Doc began rubbing the back of his neck. He wouldn't be able to relax until he heard a full explanation about what was happening. Jody kept staring at his Gramps but somehow he understood this wasn't the time for questions. Doc patted him on the back and said, "It's all right, Jody. Everything's fine, just fine."

Jody held on to his Grandfather's leg and held back tears he couldn't explain. Intuitively, he understood everything wasn't fine. The young boy's world was about to change drastically, and there was nothing Jody Law could do about it.

Chapter Eleven

COLONIAL HEIGHTS SUB-DIVISION,
2322

Doc made it back in record time. He helped Jody out, and they both ran to the house. When they opened the door, Dawn was waiting for them. "What's wrong, Dawn?" Doc asked trying not sound too anxious in front of Jody.

"Mum, what's wrong?" Jody asked, looking more curious than worried.

"Nothing, dear. A friend of ours is coming to visit and I thought you both would like to be here. Her name is Jeanne Hastings."

"Why is she coming?" Doc asked. As soon as the words were out of his mouth, he knew that he had asked a very stupid question. Obviously, Dawn was holding something back. Jeanne would only be coming if it was important. The three of them waited together until James, Jason, and finally Jeanne arrived.

"Doc, it's good to see you," Jeanne said when she walked in the door. She quickly went over to hug him. Then Jeanne smiled and got down on one knee in front of Jody. "Hello there. Who are you?"

"Gramps says I'm his buddy, but my real name is Jody," the young boy replied and everyone chuckled.

"Well, Jody, it's nice to meet you. My name is Jeanne and that's what you should call me. I hope we'll have time to get to know each other, but right now..."

"I know. I know. Grown-up business, right?"

"Right," Jeanne replied, and everyone laughed again.

Dawn took Jody to his room while the others gathered in the home's safe room. It provided the latest in communications security and the peace of mind to speak without fear. In a few minutes Dawn was back wiping tears from her face.

"Jody kept asking me why we all looked so funny, and all I could say was everything would be all right. Will everything be all right?" she asked no one in particular, and everyone turned to Jeanne.

Jason was the first to speak. "Jeanne, what's so important that we all needed to drop everything? What's all this business about Satan or whatever you supposedly experienced? Isn't that a little over the top?" The other three couldn't help but stare at Jeanne.

Dawn was at the point of panicking. Jason had to grab hold of the situation before it got completely out of control. "Everyone take a deep breath." Jason went over to Dawn and sat beside her. He took her hand and gave it a quick squeeze. "We've all been through hell together. Nothing can be worse than what we've already experienced."

"You're wrong, Jason." Jeanne said. This could be much worse. You remember Senator Thaddeus Nichols, don't you?"

Jason nodded his head, but the name had obviously not registered with the other three. "Yes, he was my first arrest after I joined the Time Force Investigations Unit. He made some idle threat at his trial, but almost every Time Transfer does. What's the story on Nichols?"

Jeanne looked down at the floor and began to speak, "Senator Nichols was a Confederate senator during the American Civil War. During that time he killed a number of war brides who had been left alone by their husbands who were fighting for the Confederacy.

"He won an appeal for a second trial, but the trial itself was not going well for him. Once Nichols won his appeal his defense lawyers delayed the trial as long as possible. Nichols was in the VIP Prisoner Holding Area enjoying relative luxury. His chance of acquittal was practically nonexistent. Eventually his defense lawyers ran out of motions and the trial began.

"Senator Nichol's team had tried to argue that common law required him to be tried under the laws in effect at the time of the alleged murders. That would have meant that he would have been allowed to face his accusers--those husbands not killed in the Civil

War.

"The judge in the trial had actually taken several days to consider that motion but in the end ruled against Nichols. His team had also argued that forcing a condemned murderer to serve successive life sentences for each of the murders was cruel and unusual punishment. The judge had deferred that argument until the penalty phase of the trial. "The trial itself took eight days. On the final day, the judge had given each side three hours for closing arguments. As usual the defense went first, and that's when my world turned upside down.

"Senator Nichols rose and looked directly at me. He smiled and then turned to the judge. 'Your Honor, I renew my request to act *pro se* and act as my own lawyer.'

"The judge was not amused. 'Senator Nichols, you have waived your right to represent yourself. You cannot keep flip-flopping any time it suits you. This is a court of law and we follow the rules of law. Do I make myself clear?'

"Yes, Your Honor." Senator Nichols said, but his face turned red and then a deep purple. He stared at the judge as his color returned to normal and he sat down. Then something extraordinary happened.

"The courtroom turned dark, darker than I've ever experienced. I've been in caves and I know what it feels like not to be able to see your hand in front of your face, but this was different. It wasn't just dark, it was beyond dark. I was frightened, terrified. "I reached out to touch my assistant, but I was alone. I felt for my chair, and it was gone. I needed to sit down, so I slowly went to my knees and felt for the floor. There was no floor. There was no courtroom. There was no judge. I was floating in a terrible blackness, and, for the first time in my life, I understood what it was like to be alone with no hope.

"I screamed, but no one answered. I cried like a terrified child, and then I was a child. I screamed for my father to rescue me, but he never came. I cried out for my mother, but she never answered.

"I felt someone's hands gently squeezing my neck. The hands began to squeeze harder and harder. I thought I was going to pass out when I felt someone's breath on my neck. The breathing was fast and getting faster as the hands squeezed harder and harder. I begged for mercy, knowing there would be no mercy.

"Then I was no longer a child, and I felt the hands release me. I heard Senator Nichols. 'If it were my choice, you would be dead, but the one I follow wants you to carry a message to someone--Jason Law.

"'Your prison can no longer hold me. Tell Jason Law my master is waiting for him. When or where he will strike will be his choosing. Tell Jason Law he is a dead man.'

"Suddenly the darkness vanished, and I had returned to the courtroom. Everything was as it had been. The judge had granted the defense a recess until the next morning and advised everyone we would start promptly at 9:00 a.m. The proceedings ended, and my assistant was asking me if I needed him the rest of the afternoon.

"As the lead defense attorney and Nichols began to leave the courtroom, the Senator paused and looked directly at me. His eyes were burning like hot coals. I felt light-headed, and Senator Nichols grabbed me. 'Ms Hastings you must be more careful. Are you all right? Perhaps you've caught some type of bug. Here, let me help you.'

Nichols took both of my hands and gently lifted me to my chair.

"He bent over me and whispered, 'Tell Jason Law I'll see him in Hell before I'm done with him.' My assistant brought me a glass of water, and I looked around for Senator Nichols. He was already gone, but I could still see his burning eyes. It felt like Satan himself had whispered his warning to me.

"The next morning I was awakened at five by a court bailiff who told me Senator Nichols had escaped. I couldn't comprehend what I was hearing, but, suddenly I was back in the black nothingness with those hands choking the life out of me. I ran to my bathroom and looked at my neck in the mirror. What I saw made me shudder--a black and blue bruise mark in the shape of a cross.

"I cried for what seemed hours before I pulled myself together and contacted Dawn. Later I looked at my neck again, and the bruise was gone."

No one spoke for what seemed an eternity. Finally, Jason cleared his throat and started speaking very slowly. "I'm not sure how to begin," he said. "Jeanne, I know right now you believe everything you have said, but I can tell you from my own experience that time has a way of changing what we believe.

"Ever since James and I went through that ordeal in the cave, I've tried to reconcile my thoughts. I'm not sure what happened in that cave, but I think it's an even bet that what James and I experienced wasn't real.

"I began hallucinating about my mother's death, replaying time after time the last moments of her life. James, I've never said this to you before, but I no longer believe we traveled to the Dreaming to encounter Do Chi or some ruler of the underworld or anyone else. It doesn't make sense; it just doesn't make sense."

Jason stood up and began to leave the room when Dawn pulled him back. "Sit down, Jason. You don't get to say your piece and then run off like a puppy dog. We all need a chance to say what's on our minds. I'm a scientist, and I can tell you that in the forensics lab, hard evidence is all that counts--not hopes, not feelings--evidence."

"I understand your point, Dawn, and you too, Jason," Doc said. "Many parts of the mind are still a mystery to us, but I'm not so sure we can dismiss Jeanne's story out of hand. We need to..."

James sighed heavily and looked at each of the others before he began to speak. "Doc's correct. Don't be so quick to discount the spiritual world. I'm a scientist too, Dawn. As an archeologist I look for hard evidence to open the past but I am also my people's holy man. I tell you there are truths that cannot be found through science.

"Jason, what we saw was true; what we felt was real. I am as sure of that as I am that Jody is standing outside the door."

Jody, I told you I would come get you as soon as we were done," Dawn said.

"I know, Mummy, but the man said I should come get you."

"Man, what man?" Dawn said as she jumped up to make sure Jody was all right.

"The man in the funny clothes."

"What kind of funny clothes?" Jason asked his son.

"Well, he had on a funny dark red coat with tails, just like we see in our history lessons. He said his name was Thad and that he'd come back and play with me sometime."

"Where did he say he was going, Jody?"

"He didn't tell me, Daddy, but he'll be back. He promised."

Chapter Twelve

JODY'S BEDROOM,
2322

Jason ran to Jody's bedroom with the others right behind him. There were no signs of an intruder being in his son's bedroom. "Show me where the man was in the funny clothes, Jody. What did he look like? Did he say anything else to you?"

"He said he was a friend of Jeanne's. Did I do something wrong, Daddy? Am I in trouble? I'm scared, Daddy. What's wrong?"

"You don't have to be scared, Jody, but the man you saw is a bad man that shouldn't be in your bedroom." Jason was beginning to think there might be something in what Jeanne Hastings said after all. "If you ever see him again **anywhere,** you need to run away quickly and tell a grown-up. Do you understand, Jody? This is important. Do you understand?"

"Yes, Daddy."

"Jason, we need to do a scrub of Jody's bedroom just to make sure," Dawn said. "If Nichols was here, he had to leave some trace evidence. Even when Do Chi was moving from one time vector to another he left a trail.

"You need to get your forensics crew out here to see if they can find anything. Call Dan Brady. I know he's not your favorite guy, but he's the best crime scene analyst in the Metro Police Department."

Dawn was right on both counts--Dan Brady was definitely not Jason's choice for man of the year, but he knew his business better than anyone else in the department. "All right," Jason said. "I'll call him, but I want you on the team, too. I know your specialty is time transfer case analysis and..."

"Don't say another word," Dawn answered. "You couldn't keep me off this case. Can you clear it with the chief, or do I have to sweet-talk him?"

"I'll call him. You just concentrate on the case," Jason chuckled. They both smiled. Even under this terrible stress, they could count on each other and would both die before they allowed anyone or anything to harm their son. Dawn picked up Jody and comforted him the way only a mother could as Jason punched in the chief's number.

By the next morning, it would be clear that a life force of some kind had indeed been in Jody's room. Brady and his team spent all night collecting forensic data from Jody's room, and Dawn was there every step of the way. They sent the data to the World Wide Law Enforcement Data Collection Center in Paris, France, with no success. Luckily, Jeanne Hastings had asked the Time Force Investigations (TFI) Unit forensics team to send Dan Brady all of the data they had collected on Senator Nichols. The results were mixed. Whoever or whatever had been in Jody's room had indeed shared some aura DNA characteristics with the Confederate senator from the past. Someone had gone to a great deal of trouble to leave such tantalizing clues. Dan Brady was only able to say that whoever had been in Jody's room had a number of common DNA factors with Nichols. Any information beyond that was beyond Brady's expertise, and he made the rather obvious suggestion that any more information would have to come from TFI.

"Dawn, what do you think? Is there any way to get the data we need without showing our faces back in the American Federation? Is there something you can do if I can get you into the Metro Police Department's forensics lab?"

"Jason, I'm sorry, but Dan Brady has done everything that can be done. I'd need to do an aura photo-cellular analysis to have any chance to find out what we're facing. The only computer in the world capable of doing that is the main frame at TFI Headquarters. I'm afraid neither one of us are welcome there anymore."

"Don't be so sure," Jeanne Hastings blurted out. "Justice Goodwin presided over Nichols's appeal. He's been absolutely beside himself ever since Nichols escaped. Let me make some calls." Twenty-four hours later, Dawn Law was in the TFI forensics lab and

Jason had been reinstated as a TFI Agent. Doc and Jody were receiving police protection 24/7 in Sydney, and Pirramuar James promised he was only a call away.

But Senator Thaddeus Nichols had already made his first move, and he was being helped by a very powerful woman--Dorothy Rhoades.

Chapter Thirteen

Thaddeus Nichols met Dorothy Rhoades for the first time during a court recess. They had chatted for a few minutes, and Thaddeus had been instantly hooked.

Ms Rhoades spoke quietly of her plan to reconstitute the United States with priority given to states rights. "There can be a place of prominence for you in the new United States, Senator Nichols. You can become the country's folk hero and more."

Dorothy saw Jerry Evans leaving the court room so she turned to Nichols and spoke quickly. "We'll talk soon, Senator. I know I can count on your discretion until then, and that means you don't talk about this to anyone, including your lawyer.

Nichols smiled and said, "I look forward to our next discussion, Ms Rhoades. You may count on my discretion. Our conversation is between us."

Later, after Nichols was found guilty he realized even more how important his meeting with Rhoades had been. After the verdict Jerry Evans accompanied him to his V.I.P. quarters but left quickly saying only, "I did my best."

Seconds later Dorothy Rhoades arrived with a short, rotund man. The first words out of Dorothy's mouth were, "I was in the gallery. I'm sorry about your conviction, Senator, although I must say I wasn't surprised. How long will you stay here?"

"I haven't talked to my lawyer in detail yet, but I believe during post-trial motions I will remain here. Later, I'll be thrown back into that hellhole of a cell."

The man with Rhoades suddenly pulled a small device out of

his pocket, and a blue haze engulfed the room. "Don't worry, Senator Nichols," Dorothy said. "Paul is performing a security sweep of your quarters. That little toy in his hands can't be detected and the guards have no idea what's happening. They're watching a pre-programmed video showing a virtual benign visit from a friend and her companion.

"Now let's get down to work. I want you to hold a special position in the new United States of America. How does 'Senator for Life' sound? In your capacity, you will act as presiding officer in the Senate and cast the deciding vote when required."

Dorothy continued, "You will light the way for the nation with the motto 'Freedom through Service'." When Nichols heard those words from Dorothy Rhoades, he was unsure what they meant.

Dorothy was quick to explain. "Everyone must understand the greater good must be the goal of all Americans. Restrictions on free speech, the right to vote, and the right to bear arms may be needed from time to time, but, as I said, only for the greater good of the United States. Such restrictions will be proposed by the President and ratified by the Senate.

"States' rights will be the lynch pin of our newly re-established country. Only state governors will be eligible to run for President, and only citizens of the Twenty Families will be eligible to run for governor of a given state."

"What do you mean 'Twenty Families'? Which twenty families? Who decides which twenty families?" Nichols asked.

The Twenty Families will be chosen by the American States' Rights Association Board of Governors. Before you ask, I submit the names for all members of the Board of Governors. Any other questions?"

"Only one. You can't be offering all this to me without wanting something in return. Just what do you want me to do for you?"

"Nothing for the moment, Senator, but someday, perhaps in the near future, I'll be asking you to do something very special for me. In the meantime, I can hide you. Agreed?"

The Confederate senator smiled and said, "Agreed." Thaddeus would let Dorothy Rhoades believe she was in control for now, but when the time came, he would do his master's bidding, no one else's.

Dorothy Rhoades made several quick calls and then said, "Sit tight, Senator. I'll have you out of here soon, very soon." She didn't say another word and Thaddeus Nichols was left to ponder his future.

The Confederate senator from the past and one of the most powerful women in the world had just struck a deal that would shake the very foundation of the Federation. Before that could happen, however, Dorothy Rhoades would have to take care of another pressing issue, and his name was Jerry Evans.

Chapter Fourteen

Jerry Evans was beside himself. Senator Thaddeus Nichols had escaped and was on the run. The good news--Jerry had a lead. His private investigator had finally tracked down the mysterious benefactor who had funded Senator Nichols's defense. It was no other than Ms Dorothy Rhodes--chair of the board for the ultra-conservative American States' Rights (ASR) Association.

Evans almost dropped the report when he read Dorothy Rhodes's name. "That old broad hijacked the ASR 50 years ago when the organization was on its last legs and desperate for money," he chuckled to himself.

Rhoades was a wealthy wind power tycoon who was more than happy to spend all it took to gain control of the floundering organization. Over the last half-century, she had overseen an almost miraculous turn-around in membership and lobbying clout for the ASR. She had even wrangled special envoy status at the United Nations for the Association's second vice president.

Behind all the public hype for states' rights was Rhodes's devious plot to split the American Federation and restore the United States of America. "It took decades for the United States, Canada, and Mexico to form a cohesive, functioning federation," Jerry reminded himself, "and centuries to ease the obvious tensions among the peoples of the three countries." It had only been within the last hundred years that most of the Federation's one billion citizens finally accepted the Federation as legitimate.

For a significant minority, however, there could be no true freedom until the United States became a truly independent nation, again leading the world. Most of the people who felt this way were well-intentioned, patriotic citizens who worked within the system. Dorothy Rhoades and a small number of radicals, however, wanted much more--the reinstitution of the Confederate States of America.

Jerry Evans had read his investigator's report over and over, and Jerry was stumped. What was Dorothy Rhoades trying to do? The report's final line read, "Our contact within the ASR was unable to provide any more details on D. Rhoades's plan to reinstate the United States of America. Our contact fears for his life and has broken off any further communications. REPORT ENDS."

Jerry was more than curious. He was absolutely beyond himself. He had met Dorothy Rhoades several times and had even attended one of the ASR's formal dinners honoring Federation politicians who favored increased states' rights. It had been a favor to his personal secretary who was a card-carrying member of the ASR. He didn't really know Ms Rhoades well enough to get the information from her directly, but Jerry was a man of action, and he decided to make a bold move.

"Ms Foster, could you come into my office for a moment?" Jerry asked his personal secretary. **No one** got through Ann Foster unless Jerry wanted it that way and all calls were screened by Ms Foster before Jerry was bothered. Of course, he kept a personal communicator, but when it came to business, Ms Foster was the gatekeeper from hell.

"Yes, Mr. Evans."

"I need you to do a special favor for me. You're still a member of the ASR, aren't you?"

"Yes, sir."

"You know Ms Rhoades's Administrative Assistant, don't you?"

"Yes, sir. Why?" Ms Foster was becoming very uncomfortable.

"See if you can set up an appointment for me to see Ms Rhoades, preferably this afternoon."

"This afternoon? Sir, I don't know if that's possible. Ms Rhoades is a very busy woman, and she'll almost certainly be booked for the whole day. I don't even know if she's in her office today."

"Let's give it a try. If anyone can do it, you can. I really need to see Ms Rhoades as soon as possible. Give it a try, okay?"

"Yes, sir." Ann Foster walked out of her boss's office, sat down at her desk, and made the call. "Del, it's Ann Foster. You're not going to believe this, but my boss wants an appointment with your boss this afternoon.

"I know, I know, but can't you do something? My bonus is due next month--I need to get Mr. Evans in to see Ms Rhoades today.

"Great! I owe you. Next week's lunch is on me. Thanks!" Ann Foster smiled. She'd done it, but she wouldn't let Mr. Evans know until after lunch. In the meantime she'd clear his calendar for the afternoon and let him stew for an hour or so. "What could be so important that Mr. Evans needed to see Ms Rhoades today?" Ann wondered to herself. "What was it?"

Chapter Fifteen

Del McCrady was more than a little nervous. Ms Rhoades hadn't had a moment all morning to talk to her between appointments. Del heard the familiar buzz on her computer as Ms Rhoades's face popped up on the screen. "Del, I'm leaving for lunch. I should be back in about 45 minutes. What do I have left today? Thank heavens, I don't have any more boring people to see. I think I'll..."

"Ms Rhoades, I'm sorry but I didn't have a chance to tell you. Mr. Jerry Evans's office called and said he needed to see you this afternoon. His office said it was an emergency. I'm sorry, Ms Rhoades, but I thought you'd want to see him. If you wish, I can cancel the appointment."

Dorothy Rhoades thought for a moment and tried to recall who Jerry Evans was. She recognized the name but couldn't pin him down exactly. "Del, I'm not sure I know this Mr. Evans, do I?"

Del was scrambling. She pulled up the video and background information on Evans and forwarded it to Ms Rhoades's screen. "There you go, Ms Rhoades. Mr. Evans is a very important lawyer known throughout the Federation. As you can see, you've met Mr. Evans twice, and he attended one of the ASR's dinners. His office did say it was very important, Ms Rhoades."

"All right, all right. What time is the appointment?"

"Two-thirty, Ms Rhoades. I've scheduled him for 30 minutes."

"Fine, but I want him out of my office in 30 minutes, got it?"

"Yes, Ms Rhoades. Thank you." Del had put her head on the chopping block. She only hoped Ms Rhoades wouldn't decide to separate her head from her body once she saw Mr. Evans.

At 2:20 Jerry Evans walked into the ASR headquarters and walked to the reception area. "Mr. Evans to see Ms Rhoades. I have an appointment for 2:30."

The pretty blonde, twenty-something young lady scanned her computer screen, smiled and looked up at Jerry Evans. "Yes, Mr. Evans, her office is expecting you. Take tube number five. It goes directly to Ms Rhoades's office."

"Thank you," Jerry answered as he gave the young woman his best smile. She smiled, and returned to her screen. Jerry walked to tube five and waited. He hated jump tubes, but they were efficient and extremely fast. They had taken the place of elevators and escalators in the late twenty-second century and came in a number of shapes and sizes. Tube five was a single occupant jump tube reserved for Ms Rhoades and special guests. Jerry was getting the royal treatment. He just hoped he could turn the information from his investigator's report into something useful.

Could Dorothy Rhoades be implicated in Nichols's escape? The ASR was always looking for heroes, but aiding and abetting a fugitive?

"Good afternoon, Mr. Evans, so good to see you again," Dorothy Rhoades said as she walked around her desk and shook Jerry's hand.

"Good to see you, too, Ms Rhoades. It's been a while."

"Oh, I hate formalities. Call me Dorothy, Jerry."

"All right, Dorothy."

"What can I do for you, Jerry?"

"I hate to sound so trite, Dorothy, but it's not what you can do for me; it's what I can do for you," Jerry lied.

"Do for me? What do you mean?"

"I'm going to get right to the bottom line, Dorothy. Senator Thaddeus Nichols has escaped. I know that you're the person who paid for his defense. I also know you're behind some crazy idea to restore the Confederate States of America. You're playing in the big league now, Dorothy, and I'm not sure you know what that means. Do you really think you could use Nichols to bring back the Confederacy?"

"I don't know what you're talking about," Dorothy snapped.

"I have no idea who this Nichols is, and I certainly had nothing to do with funding his defense. I could care less if he's alive or dead.

"I'm afraid you'll have to leave now, Mr. Evans. My time is valuable, and I'm wasting it with you. Good day." Dorothy stood up and began to walk around her desk towards her office door.

"Dorothy. Dorothy! You don't have any choice. I can prove what I've just said, and you're better off dealing with me than the press or the government. Sit down and hear me out. We can both come out on the winning side if you'll just listen to me." Dorothy turned around, walked to her desk and sat down. "That's better. Now tell me what you're trying to do and I'll tell you how we can both profit from this little enterprise."

Dorothy Rhoades was not easily shaken, but she was in a corner. "All right, Jerry. I'll tell you what you want to know." Dorothy buzzed Del and told her to hold all of her calls and then shut off her personal communicator.

She turned to face Jerry Evans directly and calmly pulled out her stun gun. Dorothy pointed it at Jerry's heart, smiled, and said, "Jerry, you're not that different from your client once you strip away your veneer. From what I've read in Senator Nichols's case file and the dossier I had prepared on you, I'd say you're very much alike-- both men who grew up under the heavy hand of overbearing fathers. Both men who would do anything to show their fathers they were just as talented, just as fierce, just as willing to do whatever it takes to win.

"Yes, I'd say you're both very much alike, but there's one big difference. Senator Nichols will go on to greater heights; you won't. Good night, Jerry. We'll talk later." Dorothy pulled the trigger and Jerry crumpled to the floor.

Dorothy had the stun gun set in mid-range--high enough to keep Evans incapacitated for several hours. She buzzed Del and said, "Mr. Evans and I are leaving in my private tube, Del. I should be back in about two hours. Call Frank and tell him to have my hovercraft ready." Dorothy pulled a touch-syringe from her desk and gave Evans a "zombie" shot. His eyes were open. He could walk and he could respond to simple commands, but he remained unconscious and would have no memory of his movements.

Dorothy and Jerry were in her hovercraft heading for her

home outside the city. They arrived in less than 15 minutes, and Dorothy pulled the hovercraft into her underground garage. She helped Jerry out and walked him into the basement level of her house where they were greeted by Paul Radford--the same short, squat man who had security swept Senator Nichols's VIP quarters. "Paul, take Mr. Evans to the Cryonic Laboratory. I don't want him bothered in any way, do you understand?"

"Yes, Ms Rhoades."

"In fact, tell the lab to prepare Mr. Evans for cryonic deep sleep. I don't want him put all the way under. We don't need him in a state of hibernation. I just want him in a deep sleep so he is susceptible to suggestions. Got it?"

"Yes, Ms Rhoades."

"Senator Nichols giving you any problems?"

"No, Ms Rhoades. He's studying the Civil War. He's going over each battle minute by minute at the warehouse."

Dorothy had spent a lot of her money and compromised several of her best agents to ensure Nichols's escape was successful. The key had been Sergeant Nathaniel Pope who had successfully covered up Nichols's murder of Correctional Officer Judy Nichols-Mason and the female prisoner.

Pope loved money and was a card carrying member of the American States Rights Association. He personally escorted Thaddeus Nichols out of the prison supposedly for questioning. The last time anyone at the prison saw Nichols or Pope was leaving the prison grounds in a bogus police vehicle.

"Have you removed the tracking chip in Nichols's arm?", Dorothy asked?

"Pope did it on the way over from the prison. I've also had Pope's cerebral implant disconnected."

"Good, now I need to talk to General Busby. Give me his private number." Thirty seconds later Dorothy Rhoades was seeing General Michael Busby on her screen. "General Busby, this is Dorothy Rhoades. It's time to settle your debt, time for you to earn those four stars I put on your shoulders. We're going to make our move!"

Dorothy Rhoades was calling in an old marker, and the man in uniform was going to pay up or face a court martial for treason.

Chapter Sixteen

THE PENTAGON,
2322

General Mike Busby had always known he'd get another call from Dorothy Rhoades. She was a woman of her word, and Busby had to face an unpleasant truth. He had sold his soul for his fourth star. He earned the other three.

The first he earned as a wing commander and the second as the first Chief of Experimental Operations in the Air and Space Time Travel Directorate in the Pentagon. It was Busby who had pushed and pushed until he convinced everyone up to the President that the Pentagon needed to at least start using time travel for intelligence gathering. The President had made it very clear, however, that the military would not develop war strategies and tactics using time travel.

General Busby had quickly proved that he understood the world of time travel and that he could make the hard decisions. He was moved to a four star position in the office of the Chairman, Joint Chiefs of Staff, before he had even pinned on his third star. It had taken a waiver by the Secretary of Defense, but Mike Busby had proved he was worth it.

Then Busby ran in to a buzz saw. His boss, a four star Navy admiral had come up the hard way, and he didn't want any hot-shot breathing down his neck. Two times Mike was put up for his fourth star and both times the admiral gave his heartiest official recommendation for Mike's promotion. On both occasions, however, the admiral made sure Busby's promotion was blackballed by a senator who owed the admiral a favor.

The last time Dorothy Rhoades had spoken to Mike Busby

had been four years ago. A friend of a friend had told Dorothy that there was a three-star named Busby who was being blocked for his fourth star by Senator Clay Sheen (I, KS).

Dorothy and the senator had grown up in the same county in Missouri and had even dated for a short while. On several occasions Dorothy had been forced to slap Clay's face while in the back seat of his hovercraft. Once during his first term as senator, they had even spent a night together. It was certainly less than fulfilling for Dorothy but well worth the price she had paid to make sure Clay was more than ready to do her a favor.

Dorothy had called Lieutenant General Busby within days of hearing about his predicament. After a few pleasantries, she got right down to business. "General Busby, I understand you've been up for your fourth star twice, and both times it's been blocked in the Senate."

"That's correct."

"General, how would you like to make your fourth star this time?"

"I'm not sure what you mean, Ms Rhoades."

"Simple. You were born in the South. You do support my organization's push for a free United States of America, right?"

"Yes, that's right, but I never let my politics interfere with my duty."

"Of course, General Busby, but I always try to support those who believe the same way I do, and I'm sure I can clear your path to putting on that fourth star."

"But?" the General snapped. Mike Busby was not easily swayed by people with power, and he wasn't about to let this woman get the better of him.

"There is no 'but.' I'm going to do this favor for you because you deserve your fourth star. Of course, if you'd like to do me a favor someday, I'd always appreciate it. For now, let's just say this is one hand shaking the other. You leave everything to me. Good bye, General Busby."

With that Dorothy Rhoades had disconnected without another word. In the meantime, she had done everything in her power to make General Busby look like a card-carrying ASR member in good standing.

Busby had received his lifetime membership card within days of speaking to Dorothy Rhoades. The letter accompanying the card made it clear that General Busby was being singled out as a VIP within the association and that his loyal years of military service were the only payment needed for his membership card.

Mike should have returned the card, but he didn't, and that was the beginning of his downfall. Over the next few years he received several awards from the ASR, and he allowed his name to be used in soliciting members for the association. It was a close call, but his legal staff told him he could get away with it.

One year later the ASR's Membership Committee Chairman asked General Busby to sit on an advisory board for the association. Once again Busby's legal department said there was no problem. Finally, six months later, Busby received a video cube at his apartment. A private mail service had delivered the cube with a note from Dorothy Rhoades. It read, "Mike, what a naughty boy you've become. We'll keep this between you and me **for the time being.**"

Mike tore open the cube and placed it on the player. The cube began spinning and the images appeared on the player's holographic screen. The video had been recorded in Mike Busby's bedroom. Brigadier General Audrey Cain and Mike were locked in an embrace and the action skyrocketed from there. Audrey Cain worked on Mike Busby's staff, and any intimate contact was not only unwise but specifically prohibited by law.

It had happened after Busby's promotion party to four star general at his apartment. Everyone had drunk too much and stayed too late. Audrey Cain had been too tipsy to drive herself home, and Mike had offered her his second bedroom to sleep off the booze. "I'm afraid you've had too much to drink, Audrey. You can bed down in the guest bedroom."

"Yes, sir," Audrey managed to say as she stumbled toward the guest bedroom.

By the time Mike had cleaned up his apartment, it was almost 3 A.M. He headed for his bedroom and dropped into bed. When he rolled over, he saw Audrey Cain on top of his covers wearing nothing but her earrings.

Mike started to protest but said, "The hell with it," and gave

Audrey a passionate kiss. They spent the night together, and Audrey only left after she had made him breakfast. She had talked incessantly about her love of the United States and how much she cherished her membership in the American States Rights Association. There and then Mike Busby accepted the fact he had been seduced--not by Audrey Cain but Dorothy Rhoades. Mike Busby had been sure a time would come when he would have to pay too high a price for his fourth star, and that time was now.

Chapter Seventeen

JOINT EXPERIMENTAL TIME TRAVEL OPERATIONS (JETTO), DENVER, CO, 2322

Jason Law was not a patient man. He and Dawn had been waiting at JETTO for over six hours, and Jason didn't like it one bit. JETTO was a separate and distinct headquarters jointly manned by elite TFI and military personnel. Their mission was to pool their expertise and develop new time travel systems and operational procedures that could be used by both organizations. At least that was the official mission. In the real world neither side trusted the other and they both guarded their secrets jealously.

When Jason and Dawn left Australia their first stop had been the TFI headquarters. There, Harry Friedman, the TFI Chief, had ensured all of the normal bureaucratic in-processing was waived with one big exception. Jason and Dawn would both be required to have their cerebral implants reconnected. Both of them were unhappy about the tethers they would have to endure but they had both accepted their fate.

With the administrative requirements out of the way Jason and Dawn were able to concentrate on their main objective--to be re-certified for time travel. Neither was sure where Thaddeus Nichols's trail would lead but there was no doubt he was still alive. Dead men's spirits just didn't pop into a young boy's bedroom. Something even more sinister was afoot, and they had to be ready to meet it in this time or another.

For some reason, their final check ride at the TFI Simulator had been postponed, and they had been asked to attend a briefing at JETTO. Harry Friedman had called Jason personally to extend the invitation. "Jason, I called to ask you and Dawn to a briefing on something called Operation Live Wire. I can't say anything else even on a secure line. I need both of you at the briefing, no excuses."

Of course, it wasn't an invitation at all; it was a command performance and Friedman left no doubt about it. If Jason and Dawn wanted to keep their temporary jobs at TFI, they'd cooperate.

Jason kept pacing back and forth as he and Dawn waited for the briefing to start. "I still can't get used to all the military uniforms around here," Dawn said. "Why did the TFI ever agree to sharing this headquarters with the Federation's military?"

Jason nodded his head and said, "Good question. I can't get anybody to open up on what's really happening. I know one thing, though, it sure looks like the military is running this show."

"You're right." What can we do about it?"

"Nothing, but that doesn't mean we have to like it," Jason said emphatically. "Harry Friedman says the TFI is an equal partner but I doubt it."

While Jason and Dawn were talking, a military officer walked over and said, "Sorry to bother you, but General Busby just beamed in from D.C. He should be in the briefing room in about ten minutes. You need to be there before him. Protocol, you know."

"Protocol, my foot!" Jason growled.

"Jason, take a deep breath," Dawn chided. "You know he's right. Let's go."

Jason and Dawn made it to the briefing room with two minutes to spare. They had barely sat down when the general's aide announced, "Ladies and gentlemen, General Busby." Every one of the ten people in the room rose to their feet except Harry Friedman.

Dawn nudged Jason and whispered, "What's Harry up to and why does that general look so worried?"

"That's what we're about to find out," Jason said quietly.

Jason had no idea how prophetic his words would be and how the next few moments would push the world to the edge of chaos.

Chapter Eighteen

"You may be seated," the general said as he sat at the front of the large meeting table. Three other Federation military personnel were at the table--Major General William Leary, who commanded JETTO, and two colonels. General Leary's aide stood at the door. There were also four civilians at the table. Two were physicists working at JETTO. One was a female medical ethicist from the Surgeon General's Office and the fourth was Harry Friedman. He remained seated to let everyone know he was this four-star general's equal and was not about to carry his water.

Busby had made his unannounced trip to JETTO to deliver some spectacular news--the administration had discovered Dorothy Rhodes's plot to overthrow the government. He had received a video cube directly from the President only seconds after talking to Dorothy Rhoades. Busby was taken completely by surprise. He had hoped for more time to plan his next move after Rhoades had told him she had put her plan into action.

Thankfully, the general had not been implicated but it was probably only a matter of time. To complicate matters the President had selected him to head the government's effort to crush the plot. His only option was to play both sides of the street and hope for the best.

Busby's world was coming unhinged and he hadn't even thought to call Rhoades after he had seen the video cube from the President. Now he had no choice but to push ahead with the meeting.

General Busby removed the video cube from his pocket, and

placed it in a video player in front of his chair. "What I'm about to share with you is marked 'EYES ONLY.' I received it directly from the President only hours ago." Busby placed his hand over the cube, and it began to glow a bright red. It was scanning the general's palm to authenticate his identity.

After less than a nanosecond, the video cube projected the President's Seal on the briefing screen. "Before I go on, I must put a direct question to you, Mr. Friedman," the general said to the TFI Chief. "You hold the unenviable position of being an American citizen and at the same time reporting to the Chief Justice of the World Court.

"We are all American citizens here who also hold citizenship in the Federation, but unlike the rest of us, your duty is not to this country. If you have any reason to believe we cannot count on you or the Time Force Investigations Unit, I need to know right now."

"General, perhaps you've forgotten, but the Memorandum of Understanding between the government and the World Court gave me direct access to the President. I report to him, but you have my full cooperation in any joint experiments. . . "

"Very good, Mr. Friedman, but I'm afraid we've gone beyond simulations and experiments."

Busby waved his hand over the cube and the President's face appeared on the screen. "Mike, I have some bad news. The FBI has confirmed a plot to overthrow the government. We believe the coup leaders will strike within the next 72 hours. The Federated Legislative Council and the Judiciary are aware of this plot. Authorities at the highest levels of the Federation's government may be involved.

"An escaped convict named Thaddeus Nichols may also be part of the plot. I want you to take the lead on this, Mike. You will have the full cooperation of the entire Federation government. Anything you need, Mike, is yours--no questions asked.

"The World Court Chief Justice has also made the Time Force Investigations Unit available. I expect full cooperation between your guys and the TFI. The World Court has sent their chief prosecutor to provide more information."

Everyone in the room turned their heads as a woman entered the room. She cleared her throat and said, "General Busby, I am Jeanne Hastings, and I represent the Chief Justice of the World Court. Within the next 72 hours the American Federation could very well be destroyed by a group of radicals who wish to re-establish the Confederate States of America.

"If the plot is successful, the United States could become a haven for all those who have no regard for human rights and who will take every opportunity to subjugate those who do. To complicate matters, a convicted time transfer inmate has escaped, and we believe he may be with the plotters. His name is Thaddeus Nichols."

Jason and Dawn looked at each other dumbfounded. Then they made a silent oath to hunt down Nichols, and stop Dorothy Rhoades no matter what the cost.

Still, how had Nichols escaped and where was he? More importantly, were there others helping Rhoades and if so, who were they? Jason Law would learn the answers to those questions and more, but would it be too late?

Chapter Nineteen

Senator Thaddeus Nichols could hardly control himself. He was free and miraculously returned to his own time. He still wasn't sure how it had happened.

Dorothy Rhoades had been hiding Nichols in an abandoned warehouse in Washington, D.C., but it was only a matter of time before he was captured. She took a big chance and went to the warehouse personally to tell Nichols her plan.

"Senator, it's time we make our move. I've arranged to send you back to your own time just before the Battle of Gettysburg. Don't ask how, it doesn't matter."

"I don't care how, Ms Rhoades, but I do care why? Our men fought valiantly at Gettysburg, but unfortunately they were defeated. What can I possibly do?" Senator Nichols asked.

"You can start by finding a backbone!" Dorothy screamed. "You will take this forged letter from Jefferson Davis to General Lee. The letter lays out the Union's order of battle at Gettysburg, supposedly discovered by Confederate intelligence. It will ensure General Lee's victory at Gettysburg, and you will become a hero to your people. I want you to go directly to General Robert E. Lee's camp and convince him you are speaking for President Davis. Can you do that?"

"Of course I can do that, but during the Battle of Gettysburg, I was hundreds of miles away. I was kidnapped by Jason Law and forced to come back to this time to face those ridiculous charges. I certainly can't be in two places at once, can I, Ms Rhoades?"

"There's also the little matter of my death. If you drop me in

General Lee's camp just before the Battle of Gettysburg, I'll have less than 48 hours before I'm picked up by the Time Force Investigations Unit or die from natural causes."

"You're correct, Senator. The laws of physics make it impossible for you to be in two places at once. However, once we place you in General Lee's encampment, a new thread in the fabric of time will be woven, and you will no longer be held captive to the past. You will no longer be destined to die. You'll be free to set your own destiny.

"Of course, it will be up to you to convince General Lee you are acting under Jefferson Davis's orders. If you can do that, the Confederacy will win the Battle of Gettysburg and change history. That's your only chance of avoiding your old fate.

"If you fail, you will die or, worse yet, be taken back to serve your sentence and rot for eternity in that dark, lonely cell. If you succeed, I will bring you back and you will live in luxury. You will become senator for life and you will be acknowledged as the true hero you are. Can I count on you, Senator Nichols?" Dorothy Rhoades asked as she stared into the old man's eyes.

"I put my life in your hands, Dorothy. I will not fail you or my country. I cannot fail. God is with me!"

"Good," Dorothy Rhoades said as she breathed a sigh of relief to herself. Of course, she had no intention of keeping her end of the bargain. Once Nichols had served his purpose, she would have him eliminated, and General Mike Busby had just made that a lot easier.

The military had taken time travel to a new level. Their time jumpers were no longer restricted to observing only while in the target time vector. They could see and be seen. They could actually be part of that time and influence events. That was a huge potential asset but a huge potential problem at the same time. All Dorothy Rhoades could see was the potential for a triumphant Confederate States of America after the Civil War.

Dorothy would send some of her best people with Nichols back to his own time to make sure everything went according to plan. Since they would actually be living and breathing the same air as Nichols, they could monitor his every move. After he had completed his mission, he was a dead man. If she could get her people back, that would be a bonus. If not, well there were always others to fill their shoes.

Rhodes turned Nichols and her three operatives over to a uniformed escort team, who promptly blindfolded all four men. They were transported to an unknown location, and still blindfolded, beamed to a desolate desert base. When their blindfolds were removed the four men were taken to a room guarded by two men and two very vicious-looking dogs.

In the middle of the room was a sealed capsule. There was no entrance and no exit. After going through a brief medical check, the four were led to a small beaming station and were immediately beamed inside the strange capsule. There were none of the paraphernalia usually seen in the ready room at Space Command's cyclotron in Denver.

"Gentlemen, relax and breathe normally," a soft-spoken woman's voice said. The next instant the four time travelers were in the year 1863. There was no wild cyclotron ride whipping them to the speed of light, no mind melding allowing them to reach the Continuum. One moment they were in 2322, and the next they were in Thaddeus Nichols's time. They were immediately beamed outside by the capsule's on-board system.

"I must hurry if I am to save the Confederacy," Nichols said to the other three. They said nothing. Each of them was sworn to make sure the old man succeeded--and then died.

Chapter Twenty

Jeanne Hastings looked at everyone in the room. Her words had just begun to penetrate. "I'm about to show you another video cube that I received from the Chief Justice. It's a Field Bureau of Investigation report on what the coup leaders have named Operation Freedom. As you will see, the name couldn't be further from the truth."

The video cube was a message directly from the bureau chief. His face appeared on the screen and he said, "Mr. Chief Justice, Operation Freedom coup leaders are attempting to change the course of history in their favor and make their planned coup a *fait accompli.* They intend to ensure the Confederacy wins the American Civil War. If that happens, history could be turned on its head and our Federation may never exist. Who knows what catastrophic consequences that could mean.

"We have word the coup leaders are prominent members of the American States Rights Association. Most of the ASR's leaders, including Dorothy Rhoades, have gone underground. We also have information that Mr. Jerry Evans, Senator Nichols's lawyer, is with Ms Rhoades.

"Our own people have tracked down a man we believe to be Senator Thaddeus Nichols and three unknowns to 30 June 1863, hiding somewhere outside Gettysburg, Pennsylvania. As you may know, the Battle of Gettysburg was fought between 1 and 3 July 1863. We have no idea how Nichols and the others were transported to the target time vector. Exactly what Nichols and the others intend to do is an educated guess, but we believe their mission is to turn the tide in the Battle of Gettysburg in favor of the Confederacy.

"We have no good intelligence on how they intend to accomplish their mission. If Rhoades's agents are successful, the Union would stand far less of a chance winning the war, and our world today could be far different. Dorothy Rhoades and her people hope to change history and use it to their advantage.

"It is my considered opinion, and the President agrees, Dorothy Rhoades will settle for nothing less than an independent United States of America patterned after the Confederacy of the nineteenth century. That is an untenable future.

"We need to stop these rebels, no matter the cost. If the Confederates win the Battle of Gettysburg, there is a very high probability that history will not be kind to us."

General Busby was shaken, but his face never revealed his true feelings. He had to let the news sink in before he said anything. Busby counted to five and said, "We'll take a ten minute break and then reconvene."

The general walked towards Major General Leary's office, knowing what he had to do next. "Tim, I'm going to need your office for a few minutes. Have your people make sure I'm not disturbed. I need complete privacy."

"Yes, sir. Don't worry about security. No one can break our jammers." With that, General Leary walked out of his office and shut the door behind him. Leary's security team was the best. There was no chance of anyone intercepting Busby's call.

Busby tapped his communicator and heard the instant connect to Dorothy Rhoades. He was taking a chance no one would walk in on him, but only General Leary would have the guts to do it, and he had just excused himself. Busby was safe.

"Hello, Mike. Everything alright?"

"I'm afraid not," Busby replied.

"You sound a little stressed, Mike. Ever since I told you Nichols's mission, you've seemed distracted, even apprehensive. Are you sure you're all right?"

"Don't worry about me. I know my part. But why not let history play out? Who knows what unintended consequences we may be foisting on the world. We need time to study the ramifications. Besides, everything's come unraveled. I've just been

162

briefed by a World Court prosecutor. Her name is Jeanne Hastings. I've run into her before."

Rhoades remained calm but was very interested in what Hastings had said. "She's the one who prosecuted Senator Nichols. Do they know what we're doing?" Dorothy Rhoades asked.

"Know! Not only do they know, but somehow they've tracked Nichols and your agents to Nichols's own time. They're not sure exactly where your team is, but they'll track them down quickly. You need to call off your dogs! I still may be able to convince the President that this is all a mistake. I can tell him Nichols's escape is just that--an escape by a very clever man trying to get back to his own time, but we've got to move fast. I'll. . ."

"You'll do nothing. Carry out your orders. Do that and when this is over, you will command the world's most powerful armed forces.   Cross me, and you're a dead man," Dorothy Rhoades snarled.

"I want you to go back in that briefing room, tell Harry Friedman you've heard rumors about something called Operation Live Wire, and ask him about it."

"Operation Live Wire? I've never heard of it. What are you talking about, Dorothy?"

"The operation is supposed to be part of something called SMC. That's all I know. Now do your job!"

General Busby sighed and wished he were dead. He understood Dorothy Rhoades was the kind of woman who might make his wish come true.

Chapter Twenty-one

JETTO BRIEFING ROOM,
2322

General Michael Busby motioned for everyone to keep their seats as he returned to the briefing room. "We have a lot of work to do, and we must do it quickly. Mr. Friedman, I've been given a thumb-nail briefing on an Operation Live Wire and something called SMC. Supposedly, your people have been working the project. Tell me about it."

Luckily, Harry Friedman was prepared to give a full explanation. He had already given General Leary a heads-up that TFI had made a breakthrough in time travel and that he would brief it at today's meeting. The two men had developed a genuine liking for each other and this was to be the first time Harry had been willing to share something of importance with the military. Now that the Federation was facing such an imminent crisis Friedman was eager to share it with Busby.

"Certainly. It's called Synthesized Meditation Coupling or SMC. It's a computer enhanced meditation system. When used on a time jump, SMC provides an avenue for our time jumpers to actually interact with the mission time vector's environment. It's still in the experimental stages, but it could give us a way to track Nichols and intercept him.

"One very big problem--it's a one-way trip. We've conducted one live mission we called Operation Live Wire and had no problem sending a TFI agent back in time. He was able to interact with his environment and even struck up a casual conversation with someone he met on the street. We stopped him there. We didn't want to risk any in-depth contact for fear of altering the course of history.

"When we attempted to retrieve our man, he never even made it to the Continuum. He simply vanished when we locked on to him. We've done continual sweeps since then and can find no trace of him."

"That's very disturbing," General Busby sighed. He had been caught off guard by Friedman's update on the TFI's experiments. Of course Busby had his own secrets about time travel but he certainly wasn't about to share those at this meeting.

"Are you saying time jumpers can breathe, talk, sleep--do everything they can in present time?"

"Yes, sir," Harry Friedman replied, "but, as I said, it's a one-way trip. I cannot in good conscience ask another volunteer to throw his life away."

"Harry, I'll go," Jason Law said as he sat motionless in his chair.

"What do you mean, you'll go?" Dawn asked out loud. "You're going nowhere. Think of Jody. Think of me. You're not going!"

"Jason, Dawn is right," Harry Friedman said. "You're not going anywhere. You're the best investigator the Time Force Investigations Unit has ever had, but you're stale. It takes split-second timing to lead a TFI time jump, and you're just plain not up to speed.

"I'm sending you with Detective Sergeant Dick Byrd to do reconnaissance in the Gettysburg, Pennsylvania, area. Detective Sergeant Byrd has already been given his orders. The jump will be not be SMC-driven. You and Byrd's team will observe only. Your mission is to pinpoint Nichols whereabouts and report back to this headquarters."

"Okay, Harry, I'll ask the obvious question," Jason replied. "Why not just grab Nichols and the other three and bring them back? What's so different about this case?"

"General Busby, Mr. Law raises a good point. Once we have Nichols's exact time vector coordinates, we can send Detective Sergeant Byrd's team and bring Nichols and the other three back. Nichols is an escaped Time Transfer convict. The TFI is well-equipped to handle this. You can leave it to us.

"Obviously, you need to track down Dorothy Rhoades and whoever else is involved. You concentrate on that, and my team will bring Nichols back."

"I'm sorry, Mr. Friedman, but that's impossible," the four-star said, trying to sound sincere. "The President was very clear. I will lead our nation in eradicating everyone involved in this attempt to overthrow our democracy. The Chief Justice of the World Court has graciously offered the TFI's help, and I am more than willing to take it, but it will be under my direct orders.

"Detective Sergeant Byrd's team will find Nichols, determine his mission, and report back to this headquarters. We need to know exactly what Dorothy Rhoades intends to do. The best way of finding out is to track Nichols and his goons. Let's see what they're up to and how they intend to do it.

"As of now, I am in command. Major General Leary will establish a tactical headquarters here, and I will communicate any further orders through him. That is all." With that, General Busby bounced out of his chair and almost ran out of the briefing room.

"Harry, that four-star is crazy," Jason said. "The best way to handle this is to grab Nichols now. I'll go along, riding shotgun, while Byrd's team makes the grab, but there's no way we're going to give Nichols the time to do something we may not be unable to undo.

"If Nichols has the chance to pull off this stunt before we stop him, who knows what that could mean? We've never been here before, Harry. No one, not even all those scientists you pay so much, has any idea what might happen. If Nichols is successful, can we undo history? We can't take that chance, Harry. We can't take that chance."

"You heard General Busby, Jason. I'll take up your concerns with him, but for now Detective Sergeant Byrd's team will make the reconnaissance time jump as ordered. The chief justice has taken this out of our hands, Jason.0 I'm sorry. You can go with Byrd's team, or you can go home to Australia. Got it?"

Jason glared at Harry Friedman but only said two words through his gritted teeth, "Yes, sir." Jason Law was ready to burst. "This is a very personal matter for Dawn and me, Harry. Nichols somehow found a way to get into our son's bedroom without being caught. I won't rest until Nichols is back in his cell, or better yet, dead. Now do I make **myself** clear?"

"Very," Harry Friedman said.

Both men stared at each other wondering how Thaddeus Nichols got back to his own time? The answer was at a secret location in the southwest desert.

Chapter Twenty-two

As chief scientist for the Pentagon's National Review Board, Dr. Leo Lehman oversaw all of the cutting edge technology being developed at the super-secret Base One, just outside Las Vegas, Nevada. Centuries ago the base had been called Area 51.

Lehman would never have guessed he would play a pivotal role in unleashing Thaddeus Nichols at the Battle of Gettysburg. Dorothy Rhodes would have been unable to dispatch the Confederate senator and her three thugs if Dr. Lehman had not been so conscientious in carrying out his orders.

Leo Lehman was at Base One to meet an old friend--Dr. Juan Cortez. This was the same Dr. Cortez who had helped pioneer time travel and a path to the future. It was Cortez who had found a way to harness the Philosophy of Transparency that allowed Lieutenant Commander Debe Jackson to travel to the year 3011 where she was confronted by Do Chi.

Cortez was the first to recognize that mankind was not ready for the unintended consequences that travel to the future could mean and how Transparency could be misused in the wrong hands. At Cortez's insistence the government stopped all further Transparency experiments. But that didn't mean time travel was completely off limits to science.

After Leo Lehman passed through Security, he saw Juan Cortez waiting for him. "Juan, good to see you. I'm so happy you agreed to accept General Busby's job offer."

"How could I refuse, Leo. Tell me again exactly what General Busby said to you."

"His exact words were, 'Dr. Lehman, we need to be out front of the bad guys in finding a way to weaponize time travel. The Secretary of Defense and the President aren't convinced yet that time travel should be used for anything except intelligence, but they did give their approval for basic research. Tell Dr. Cortez I have no intention of ever moving beyond the research phase without the secretary's approval.'"

"It will take time to build a team, Leo, and this won't be cheap," Dr. Cortez said.

"You've got *carte blanche*, Juan, but hurry. General Busby isn't a patient man, and this is very important to him. It goes without saying, if it's important to General Busby, it's important to me."

"I'm ready to get to work, Leo, but who's in charge?" Dr. Cortez asked.

"When it comes to the research, you are, Juan. You'll report directly to me, and I'll report to General Busby. As Chairman of the Joint Chiefs of Staff, General Busby is an advisor to the President and Secretary of Defense and he will report your progress to them.

"The last Secretary of Defense gave General Busby operational control of Base One and he still has it. I watch over the science at Base One, but General Michael Busby is the boss, period. One last thing, Juan. Busby doesn't want anyone, especially the people at JETTO, to know anything about this. This is strictly 'need to know'."

"Understood, Leo. I'll make sure not a word goes beyond Base One," Dr. Cortez responded.

Dr. Cortez assembled his team quickly and wasted no time at their first meeting. "Listen up, everyone. We've been tasked to research methods of weaponizing time travel. I know that presents a moral dilemma for many of you. It did for me. But General Busby has assured Dr. Lehman that the Greater American Federation will never be the first to use time travel as a weapon. Our job is research only.

"Our first objective is to eliminate using the cyclotron to reach the speed of light. The cyclotron has served its purpose well, but it's cumbersome and costly, not to mention very risky. We put our time jumpers in jeopardy every time they step into a cocoon. The more streamlined we make time travel, the easier it will be to use in tactical situations. General Busby has designated our research

169

as a priority program. Let's get to work!"

Dr. Cortez drove himself and his people almost to the breaking point trying to find a new way to hurl time travelers to the Continuum. After months of trying, he and his team had little to show for their efforts. Then Juan Cortez had an epiphany! "SORTS. We can use SORTS!"

For several years before coming to Base One, Dr. Cortez had been under a consulting contract with the Pentagon. His major contribution had been SORTS--the Sub-molecular Ordered Refraction System. Its purpose--to move battalion-size units quickly to the battlefront.

SORTS relied on a scientific theorem known as the Cortez Dynamic. Juan had developed it while still in academia. His theorem proved kinetic energy was created as a by-product when a laser beam was reflected off a satellite mirror. The SORTS generator used that kinetic energy to develop the tremendous power needed to beam battalion-sized units where they were needed most.

After briefing his team on his idea, Juan Cortez called Dr. Lehman. "Leo, I think I can use the SORTS generator to beam time jumpers to the Continuum. No more cyclotrons, Leo. Just think of the time and effort we could save by eliminating that contraption. Think of the increased safety for time travelers. Jumping through time still won't be a walk in the park, but once we eliminate the cyclotron, things will be much easier. This won't end up like Transparency, Leo. I can feel it. I know I'm right."

Dr. Lehman was the man who General Busby would hold ultimately responsible for Juan Cortez's success or failure. So he wanted Cortez to understand the pressure he was getting. "All right, Juan, you can explore your idea, but it's both of our heads if you're wrong," Lehman cautioned. "Make sure you're right, Juan, for both of our sakes."

With Leo Lehman's go-ahead, Cortez began his work and, true to form, threw himself into his experiments. Juan was a driven man once again, trying to solve an almost impossible problem. His first objective was to prove a person's DNA flow could survive intact after being funneled through a SORTS station and beamed to the Time Warp Continuum. Ironically, to do that he needed a cyclotron. It was still the only way to ensure a time traveler reached the speed of light, and the speed of light was still the only avenue for reaching the Time Warp Continuum.

Cortez rigged one of the experimental SORTS Stations at Base One to accept sub-molecular DNA flow from the Denver, Colorado, cyclotron. He sent three volunteer time jumpers to Denver where they were placed in a cyclotron cocoon. After reaching the speed of light and attaining a group meditative harmony, they were beamed to the Base One SORTS generator. The generator then "bounced" their DNA flow to the Continuum.

However, instead of regenerating in the Continuum, the three volunteers' DNA flow was hurled into the abyss of the unknown. Base One's instruments gave no readouts of a specific time vector for the ill-fated time jumpers but did keep locked on them. Juan Cortez made a instant decision.

"Let's bring them back," Dr. Cortez said to his chief assistant, Michael Dane.

"Ready, Doctor," Dane answered. The two scientists were working like clockwork, and within seconds the first two volunteers appeared, safe and sound, inside the cyclotron's cocoon. "One more to go," Cortez said. "We'll grab him, and we're home free."

When the third volunteer appeared in the cyclotron's cocoon, he was dead. Juan Cortez slumped over and almost cried but quickly gathered himself. "I have to tell that young man's family," Dr. Cortez told his assistant. "Tell Denver to see to the other two."

Dr. Cortez talked to the ill-fated time jumper's parents for over an hour and promised he would see them as soon as possible. His next call was to Leo Lehman. "Leo, I've got terrible news. We've lost a time jumper."

"What do you mean you've lost a time jumper?" Dr. Lehman retorted.

"I mean he's dead. We were running a live test to see if we could use SORTS to beam three volunteers to the Continuum. One of them didn't make it back."

"Live test? I never gave you authority for a live test, Juan," Lehman replied, trying to hold his anger down. "No more Transparencies, huh."

"Leo, I know you didn't give me authority. Now let me tell

you what happened. I can't undo the young man's death, but I think I know what happened. Let me explain," Juan said.

"Have you notified the family? What about the press? If those jackals get hold of it, we're finished before we start, Juan," Lehman said, now obviously less than happy.

"I've talked to his parents. They're devastated, but they want us to continue. They kept repeating how their son, Daniel, would have wanted it. They won't go to the press, Leo. We can keep this under wraps for the time being."

"All right, tell me what happened."

"Leo, before I decided to do a live test, we had done hundreds of simulations. We dry ran every conceivable scenario, or so I thought. When it came time for the live test, everything went according to plan in Denver. The jumpers reached group harmony and their DNA flow was beamed to a SORTS generator here at Base One. SORTS immediately beamed their DNA flow to the Continuum.

"In all of our simulations, the jumpers' DNA flow regenerated into human form in the Continuum. That didn't happen. Instead all three jumpers' DNA flow bounced off the Continuum like it was a giant mirror, and I think I know why."

"Juan, stop wasting time. **What happened**?" Leo asked, more irritated again.

"We assumed that when the SORTS generator beamed the jumpers' DNA flow to the Continuum, it would be at the speed of light--the same as the cyclotron. Instead, there was no reading of the three jumpers' DNA flow speed at all. I've had the maintenance crews go over everything time after time. One moment the DNA flow registered in the SORTS generator, and the next moment we had no reading of it in the Continuum or any time vector. We double checked and our instruments were still locked on all three of the jumpers. There was simply no reading of where or when they were."

"Juan, this makes no scientific sense. How can this be?" Leo Lehman asked.

"Leo, we know there is a measurable difference in time when DNA flows from the cyclotron's cocoon to the Continuum. It's called 'dead time,'" Juan Cortez continued, trying not to sound condescending.

"There is no dead time when we use SORTS to send DNA flow to the Continuum, none at all. The DNA flow is traveling faster than the speed of light. We can't measure the difference in speed, but I'm convinced I'm correct. I don't know when or if we'll understand how this happened, but it did. The DNA flow bounced off the Continuum and into oblivion. Since we had no target time vector plugged in, we had to retrieve the three volunteers' DNA flow and return it to Denver."

"Perhaps, Juan, perhaps, but how did you lose the one jumper. Did you say his name was Daniel?"

"Yes, sir. Daniel Withers. When we retrieved the three jumpers' DNA flow the cyclotron overloaded. It simply could not assimilate all three of the jumpers from the SORTS generator quickly enough. If we eliminate the cyclotron we eliminate the problem," Juan said. I think I may have an idea how to do just that."

Finally, after what seemed hours, Leo Lehman said, "Juan, this young man's death is your responsibility. I take no pleasure in saying this, but I am referring this matter to the full review board."

Juan didn't really blame Leo. "I understand completely. Daniel's death is on my hands--no one else is to blame, but I know with all my heart that we are on the cusp of a great discovery. For Daniel's sake, we must continue, Leo. We must!"

There was another long silence and then Leo did what few professional bureaucrats are willing to do. He took a chance. "Juan, I'm with you," Dr. Lehman said quietly. "You said you might have a way to eliminate the Cyclotron. Tell me about it."

"I need to think first, Leo, and run some numbers. But I know I'm right. We can open a new horizon in our exploration of time travel. There are risks, big risks, but we must move forward. We have no choice, Leo. We must continue to push the envelope--it's our duty as scientists."

"Agreed, Juan. I pray we're not making a mistake. We can't lose any more lives."

"Of course, Leo, but think what this will mean."

"Think of what this could mean if you succeed and your work ends up in the wrong hands, Juan. Be careful, be very careful."

The two scientists would learn much too soon just how right

Leo Lehman was and what it could mean.

Chapter Twenty-three

It took thirty days of crunching numbers and checking everything again and again before Juan Cortez was ready for another test. He theorized that if he bounced a time jumper's DNA flow from one SORTS generator to another he could keep repeating the process until the DNA reached sufficient speed to reflect off the Continuum to the target time vector. If Cortez was correct there would be no more need for the Cyclotron.

Dr. Cortez had a second SORTS generator set up at Base One and had it cycled with the first generator. After going over the preparations one last time Juan stepped into the first SORTS generator's cocoon and almost immediately heard the hum of the machine's electronics. The next instant he found himself at his target time vector--the Base One front gate exactly 24 hours in the past.

Cortez took a deep breath but still couldn't believe what he was experiencing. Ten fingers, ten toes, two eyes, one nose, one mouth--everything seemed fine. Satisfied, he bent down and grabbed a blade of grass. Seconds later Juan contacted his team and told them he was ready to return. After he successfully reappeared in the SORTS cocoon, he went through a quick checkup and gathered the team to debrief them.

"Welcome back, Doctor," Michael Dane said. "I knew you'd make it, Dr. Cortez, but I must admit we were all a little nervous."

"You, nervous? My son, you have no idea how I was shaking inside before you retrieved me.

"Listen up people. I want to show you something." Juan Cortez dug deep into a pocket and pulled out the blade of now-brown grass he had taken from the front gate. "Thanks to all of you we've taken a big step in our quest to streamline time travel. We can report to the Pentagon that we have moved past using the Cyclotron to find our way to other times. But I have even bigger news. I have just returned from Man's first fully interactive time jump."

Everyone was too dumbfounded to show any reaction. It was at least 60 seconds before Michael cleared his throat and said, "Dr. Cortez, what do you mean fully interactive time jump? How can you be sure?"

Then Michael laughed out loud. "I noticed a big surge in your readings when you arrived at the target time vector, but I thought it was just a hiccup. You actually breathed the air, touched the earth? So that's what that blade of grass is--your proof!"

"Right!" Dr. Cortez responded. "Do a spectrum-age analysis on the blade of grass, and you'll find it was picked 24 hours ago. Do we have the equipment here to do it?"

"No, sir, but the research laboratory at Space Command has everything we need. As soon as we've wrapped up everything here, I'll hand carry the specimen to the laboratory and do the analysis myself," Michael said.

"All right. Make sure you document everything, Michael. I don't want anyone to think we gimmicked this. It's too big."

"Yes, sir, I'll take care of it," Michael said. How can we be sure you haven't disturbed history?" he asked. "No time jumper has ever made physical contact with the past. There's no way to ensure we haven't already disturbed the very time fabric of our existence. How can we be sure?"

"A good question, Michael, but hopefully one that I can answer," Juan Cortez answered. "Once I knew it was theoretically possible to use SORTS for time travel I was almost positive interactive time travel was possible.

"There are rumors the scientists at the Time Force Investigations Unit have been trying to use computer-enhanced meditation to accomplish the same goal. They believe if time jumpers are freed from the intensity of reaching meditative harmony, they may have the strength to make human contact in their target time vector. I think I just proved SORTS is a much more effective system. Either way we can't be sure what impact a major incursion into another time vector will have on history. It's not something we can simulate.

"On a smaller scale, I think I've found the answer. Before I made the jump, I asked the Pentagon's Time Travel Directorate get a *StreamVision* video cube of yesterday's worldwide news carried to the Time Warp Continuum. There is no time in the Continuum, Michael, so the cube could not have been altered by events in the world. We'll compare the cube with a current *StreamVision* video cube and see if there are any changes."

Cortez contacted the time jumper waiting in the Continuum and compared the two video cubes. They were identical. However, there were still questions on how a significant time travel incursion might impact history. "Michael, we know that Dr. Thomas Bing confirmed time is not linear, but Dr. Bing's *Treatise on Linear Applications* states any large disruption along the Infinity Loop may affect all time vectors. It's still a very important open question, but I'm satisfied interactive time travel with limited contact is relatively safe."

For more than an hour, Juan Cortez enjoyed his huge accomplishment. Then Cortez called Dr. Lehman. "Leo, we've done it."

"You mean no more Cyclotron?"

"Yes", Cortez said trying to control himself, "but something much bigger than that has just happened. I just returned from the first interactive time jump, and I did it without disturbing history!"

"Great job!" Dr. Lehman shouted.

"Let me tell you what happened, Leo."

Over the next hour, Juan walked Leo through every detail of man's first interactive time jump. When he finished, he said, "I'm not sure a hard and fast rule never to disturb history is either possible or ethical. We just won't know what, if any impact we might have on history if we interfered in some grand scale.

"I know Dr. Bing was concerned about that very subject. Will we change history if we stop a famine or were we meant to stop the famine, and let our action be part of history? There's still much to be learned and to be debated, but I can tell you interactive time travel is not only possible, it is a part of our new reality."

Leo Lehman wanted to bring Cortez down to *terra firma*. "All right, Juan. Take a deep breath. We have a lot of work to do before we call this a success. I want a plan on my desk within one month outlining a foolproof system of using our newfound knowledge. I mean foolproof, Juan. You'll have to brief General Busby. Something this big will go all the way to the President.

"Once I've approved your plan, we'll schedule you to give General Busby an in-depth rundown on everything. I'll call and give him a quick 'heads up' on what's happened.

"Watch out, Juan. General Busby can be ruthless. Don't play games with him. Others have tried and ended up on the short end of the stick. I'm serious, Juan. When you brief this four-star, be ready for anything. He's not a good man to cross."

"Yes, Leo, I understand, but I'm about to hand him the most powerful military tool in the history of man. Once the rest of the world knows we have it, no one will dare cross us. I leave it to the future to decide how or if we use this discovery, but I'll make my concerns plain to General Busby. Surely a man so powerful wouldn't misuse the discovery I'm ready to hand him."

"I hope you're right, Juan. I hope you're right."

Chapter Twenty-four

Dr. Juan Cortez was pacing back and forth in the waiting room of General Michael Busby's office. Leo Lehman had told Cortez the general wanted to hear all about Cortez's new discovery and how it might be applied to the military. Busby's secretary was becoming annoyed at Juan as he walked back and forth in front of her desk. "May I get you a glass of water, Dr. Cortez? We have the latest news video cube if you'd like to see it."

"No, thank you. I'm fine. How much longer did you say the general would be?"

"As I've already told you, the general knows you are waiting. As soon as he's done speaking to Ms Rhoades, he'll see you."

"Ms Rhoades? Do you mean Ms Dorothy Rhoades?" Juan had been asked to speak at the last annual American States Rights Association conference, and Ms Rhoades had called him personally to invite him. Cortez could think of no legitimate reason for speaking at such a radical organization and declined politely.

"Why would Busby be talking to Dorothy Rhoades?" he asked himself but was jolted out of his musing when the general's secretary told him Busby would see him.

When Juan Cortez walked into General Busby's office, the general was obviously agitated. Busby stared through Juan as if he was deciding the fate of the world. Cortez stood for several moments in front of General Busby's desk and cleared his throat while trying to catch the general's attention. Finally, Juan said, "Good morning, General. I understand you would like an update on our experiments with interactive time travel."

"Oh, yes, yes. That's exactly what I need to hear. Let's get on with it."

Dr. Cortez unsealed a top secret video cube marked, "SORTS4". The acronym was a hybrid of SORTS and the fourth dimension--time. Juan placed the cube in the general's desktop viewer, and General Busby watched the automated background briefing intently. Dr. Cortez did not mention the rumors that the Time Force Investigations Unit was also working on interactive time travel. It didn't bode well for anyone who briefed General Michael Busby and didn't have all the answers. All Juan had were rumors, and he was not about to spread them in front of this four-star.

"As you can see, General Busby, we believe we have a viable interactive time travel system. Obviously, we still have a lot of work to do before we can use SORTS4 in the field, but within 12 to 18 months we could have an operational system. I'm concerned, though, that SORTS4 could destroy the world if we don't establish some hard rules on when or if we should ever use it. I recommend a go slow approach, general. We can't afford to make any mistakes. Who knows what unintended consequences we might set up if we use SORTS4 on a large scale. That completes the briefing, general. Do you have any questions?"

"Only one, Dr. Cortez. How many people know about SORTS4?"

"Counting you, sir, 28. There are 23 staff scientists and technicians at Base One, then there's Dr. Sutton and his boss, Lieutenant General Gains, Dr. Lehman, myself, and now you. Most of our staff have been sequestered at Base One since we began our experiments. My chief assistant, Dr. Michael Dane, is at Space Command personally performing confirmatory analysis on our experiments. No one there knows what he's doing," Dr. Cortez assured the general.

"Good. Get back to Base One and keep SORTS4 locked down tight," General Busby said. "I'll make sure no one disturbs this Dr. Dane. Keep everything locked down until you hear from me personally. Do you understand? Me personally!"

"Of course, General. May I ask why? I understand the need for security, but surely we can let our staff spend a few days at home. I can vouch for all of them. They would rather die than reveal anything about SORTS4."

"Dr. Cortez, I have no time to make myself any clearer. Go straight back to Base One and seal off the SORTS4 complex. Do not contact Dr. Lehman or anyone else. No one gets off base until I say so, and that includes you. You'll be hearing from me within 24 hours."

"I'll do as you say, but remember I have not done an in-depth study on how a major incursion into history might upset the time fabric. It will be months, perhaps years, before we will have a good idea how interactive time travel could impact history. I must stress, sir, these are uncharted waters, and we must proceed with the utmost caution."

"Of course, Doctor. Now please go. I will contact you ASAP. You are dismissed."

Dr. Juan Cortez was confused as he walked out of General Busby's office. He was even more confused when two big marines met him in the waiting room and personally took him to the Pentagon's beaming station. Two more marines were waiting for him at Base One. Cortez only had one choice--obey General Busby's orders and wait.

As soon as Juan Cortez walked out of his office, General Busby called Dorothy Rhoades on his private line. "Dorothy, I've just been briefed on something called SORTS4 and you need to know about it."

For the next 10 minutes Busby gave Dorothy Rhoades a rundown on SORTS4. It was then that Dorothy began hatching her plan to send Nichols back in time to change the outcome of the Civil War. General Mike Busby would do her bidding--he had no choice.

Dr. Cortez's warning about the possible negative impact of interactive time travel seemed trivial to her. "General Busby, I am not concerned about changing history. I want to change history. That's the whole point of sending Senator Nichols back to his own time. But no mistakes, Mike. It will be **both** of our heads if you fail."

Dorothy Rhoades broke the connection and immediately touched the name on her communicator's pad that read, "RAIDER." She took a deep breath and hoped RAIDER would understand why she had to call. "Yes, it's me," she whispered. "We're ready to move, but I thought you should know what we intend to do. Yes, yes, I understand. I'm sure no one else knows about you, but we'll need your support when it comes time... Yes, I'm sorry. I won't call again until it's done."

Dorothy hung up and cursed for allowing herself to lose control. However, she was pragmatic if nothing else, and she realized she had given up any choice in the matter years ago.

In the meantime, true to his word, General Michael Busby had beamed to Base One to give Dr. Cortez verbal ops immediate orders. Cortez would use SORTS4 to send four unidentified men to General Robert E. Lee's headquarters just outside Gettysburg, Pennsylvania. Their entry point--1800 Hours, 30 June 1863. All data records of the time jump would be erased.

All SORTS4 personnel, including Dr. Cortez, would go through an intense debriefing and memory scrub. The general would have Dr. Dane picked up at Space Command and deal with him later. Busby left Lieutenant General Timothy Gains, Dr. Daniel Sutton, and Dr. Leo Lehman completely out of the loop on what was happening. He instructed his aide to contact all three and tell them Base One had gone black on "eyes only" orders from the President. None of the three men were happy about the news, but all three knew better than to press the Chairman of the Joint Chiefs of Staff.

Busby was taking a big chance not having everyone killed, but he might need them before the operation was completed. "There's bound to be some brain damage for some of the SORTS4 personnel after they go through the memory scrub, but it can't be helped," Busby said to himself.

The military technician doing the memory scrub was assigned to General Busby's ultra secret Team Zebra. Busby had set up the team within weeks of becoming the Chairman of the Joint Chiefs of Staff. He personally interviewed and selected each member of the 20-man team. Some he had known since they entered the service; others he had never met before, but all were multi-qualified in a variety of combat and technical specialties and loyal to a fault.

They understood there was only one response when "The Old Man" asked them to do something--"Yes, sir!" The technician doing the memory scrub would do his job and stay quiet. General

Gains, Dr. Sutton, and Dr. Lehman would not ask too many questions. Busby was betting his life on it.

Dorothy Rhoades had promised Nichols he would be part of the new Confederacy, but that was a lie like so many other promises she had made. "Besides," Busby said to himself, "Senator Nichols's future lies in the past. He and the other three will be quickly forgotten."

But Jason Law would not forget so easily as he was about to prove.

Chapter Twenty-five

THE CYCLOTRON,
2322

Jason Law was pacing again. This was going to be his first live jump since he was re-certified for time travel. A young technician walked over to Jason and said, "Sir, it's time." Jason walked over to the cocoon and nodded to Detective Sergeant Byrd and a forensics technician named Kevin Reid. The three time travelers were placed in the cocoon and given the standard briefing by the jump master.

The cocoon began to move slowly around the cyclotron's circular track to nowhere and then began to pick up speed. Once the cocoon hit hyper-speed, the time travelers were hurled into the Time Warp Continuum and then made their jump to Senator Nichols's location. Detective Sergeant Byrd motioned to Jason and said, "Detective Inspector Law, is that our guy?"

Before Jason could answer, the forensics technician interrupted saying, "That's our guy all right. I've already completed my first scan, and that's absolutely our guy."

Jason was glaring at Nichols, wishing there was some way to get his hands on him. "Yeah, that's him," Jason confirmed. "He looks like easy pickings to me, Detective Sergeant Byrd. I say we go ahead and make the grab now. Then we can come back for the other three. If we move fast, we can stop this coup before it starts. I'm calling Harry Friedman."

"No, sir, you're not," Byrd quickly retorted. "I'm sorry, Detective Inspector Law, but we have our orders, and we're going to follow them. You heard Mr. Friedman and that four-star, Busby. We recon the scene and try to confirm Nichols's mission. Then we report our findings and await further orders. If you have a problem with that, I will abort the mission now. There's a back-up team on standby."

Jason was licked. He liked the way this guy Byrd handled himself and Jason Law wasn't about to cut his only tie to Thaddeus Nichols. "All right, all right, but I wish Nichols would make his move."

Just then a Confederate patrol stumbled on Nichols and the other three. During the confusion, Nichols dropped a translucent cylinder to the ground, and it instantly disappeared. Dorothy Rhoades had given the cylinder to him before his momentous trip to the past.

"It's called a camo-drop," Dorothy said. "It's something the military uses on forward deployed missions. I got it from someone very high in the military who shares our views," she said. "Now lay it on the floor."

Nichols did as he was told, and the cylinder vanished.

"It can mimic any surroundings and cannot be detected even by the most sophisticated scanning equipment," Dorothy assured Senator Nichols. "It's been tuned to your aura and can only be opened by you."

Dorothy handed Nichols his forged orders and a sealed envelope marked "EYES ONLY." "Do not open this envelope unless you are facing absolute death before you carry out your orders," Dorothy emphasized. Nichols just shook his head and hoped he would never have to open the envelope.

Detective Sergeant Byrd seemed amused as he watched Nichols and his companions stopped by the Confederate patrol. Sergeant Byrd turned toward Jason and said, "See, sometimes good things do come to those who wait, Detective Inspector Law. Maybe Nichols will do something stupid, and the Confederates will take care of him for us."

"I wouldn't bet on it, Sergeant Byrd," Jason said knowingly. "Before this is over, we'll wish we'd taken care of Nichols when we had the chance."

"Maybe, but we're doing this by the book, Detective Inspector, by the book!" Sergeant Byrd chided Jason. However, Jason Law wasn't a man who followed the rules so easily, and he certainly wasn't going to start now.

Chapter Twenty-six

GENERAL ROBERT E. LEE'S HQ, GETTYSBURG, PA,
30 JUNE 1863

Thaddeus Nichols and his three compatriots appeared just outside Gettysburg, Pennsylvania. They were about 50 yards from General Lee's Headquarters--a beautiful home that had been commandeered by Lee where he directed his Army of Virginia against the Union forces. The Confederate general had been victorious in defending the Confederate capital in Richmond, Virginia, but he understood the Union's mighty armies would return and his out-manned, ill-equipped forces would likely be overrun.

General Lee had two options--maintain defensive positions around Richmond or go on the attack. He decided on the latter. As his army moved north, it began encountering growing Union opposition. Lee established his headquarters outside Gettysburg and began preparing for the inevitable conflict.

Before Senator Nichols and the other three could get their bearings, they were captured by a small patrol sweeping the Southern encampment for infiltrators. "Halt or I'll shoot!" yelled the patrol's leader. The three Confederate soldiers were disheveled--unshaven, with dirty uniforms and bare feet.

"Hey, Corporal, look at those boots. They all got brand new boots. Let's get 'em before anyone else sees them. No one will know and, besides, in ten minutes they'll all be dead. They won't need 'em where they're going."

The corporal snickered, but he had his orders. "You know we cain't do that. Just 'cause we look like heathens don't mean we have to act like 'em. We'll take 'em to the captain. If he says we can have the boots, it's fine with me, but not until."

"Gentlemen, you have made a huge mistake," Nichols said calmly. "I am Senator Thaddeus Nichols of the Confederate States of America. These gentlemen are members of President Jefferson Davis's personal staff. We have great news for General Lee. I demand to be taken to him at once." Nichols and the other three showed their forged papers to the corporal. "Look, each pass has been personally signed by the President," Nichols said to the corporal.

"Sir, I cain't read. We'll take you to Captain Hill, and he'll decide what happens to you."

Senator Nichols was not about to be put off so easily. "You will do no such thing. You will take me directly to General Lee. I have the most important intelligence for him. What I bring will ensure a great victory for General Lee and stop the terrible Union aggression. You and your friends will be able to go home. No more fighting, no more starving. You'll be able to see your loved ones and begin building the Confederacy's future."

"Yes, sir, but not until the captain says so." Moments later the corporal was reporting to his captain. "Sir, I have four captives we found close to General Lee's headquarters. I have no idea how they got through our lines, but they're here, and they claim to be on a mission for President Davis. They even say their orders are signed by President Davis. I didn't know what to do."

Captain Matt Hill was in no mood to go through a long night trying to find out who these four men were and what they were doing in the encampment. Usually, they would undergo rather intense questioning, but if they really were from President Davis, all the rules went out of the book. "Who did you say their leader called himself?"

"Senator Nichols, sir," the corporal replied. "Here's their orders."

"All right, let me see them." Captain Hill had never seen President Jefferson Davis's signature, but the document certainly looked authentic. "Bring in the leader. We'll hear what he has to say."

A moment later the corporal returned with Nichols. "Who may you be, sir?" Captain Hill asked the gentleman in the deep red tailcoat and dark gray pants.

"I, sir, am Senator Thaddeus Nichols on a priority mission for President Jefferson Davis. I demand to be taken to General Lee at once!"

"First, you're not seeing anyone now. It's after midnight, and the general is resting. These are trying times and the general needs his strength. No, sir, you will not see the general tonight.

"Now tell me, why should I believe you? You look like a gentleman and you certainly sound like a man of the South. But looks can be deceiving, and accents can be learned. Tell me what you want to tell the general, and I'll decide if you get to live the rest of the night."

Thaddeus Nichols was calm, very calm. He had very little to lose ad a world to win. "Captain, you will take me immediately to General Lee or you will bear full responsibility for the defeat that is about to befall the Southern cause. You are wasting my time and the lives of thousands of Confederate soldiers. Take me to General Lee **now**!"

"Corporal, take this man out and search him along with the other three. Take every stitch of clothing off them and make sure they're not hiding anything. In the meantime, I'll see what the general's chief of staff wants to do."

Nichols smiled to himself as the corporal took him out to his three companions. He realized he had made a breakthrough. Jefferson Davis's signature on the orders was genuine. Dorothy Rhoades had several Civil War documents with the Confederate President's signature, and it was easy enough for her people to replicate it and use it on the bogus orders. The paper was genuine and the ink a perfect match to the ink used by President Davis's staff.

Senator Nichols could hardly contain himself as the corporal searched him. "In a matter of minutes, an hour at the most, I will see General Lee," Nichols said to himself. "I will convince him that not only are my orders legitimate but that I have detailed knowledge of how the Union forces will be deployed against him and how they intend to meet him on the battlefield. Once the battle is won, the North's will to fight will be shattered. Lincoln will be forced to sue for peace, and I will take my rightful place as the Confederacy's next President. Why should I go back to Dorothy Rhoades and become one of her lackeys? Better to stay here and give the South its future now."

Within 45 minutes Nichols and the other three had been strip-searched, allowed to dress, and escorted to the chief of staff's tent. Captain Hill was inside talking to the chief of staff. "Sir, I'm sorry to bother you, but the most extraordinary thing has happened. We found four men about 50 yards from General Lee's headquarters. Their leader calls himself Senator Thaddeus Nichols. He has orders that he says are from President Davis. They look legitimate, sir. Mr. Nichols says he must see the general now. He says he has information on what the Yankees have in mind to throw at us in the next couple of days. I really think you need to see these men, sir."

Nichols had heard every word Captain Hill said. There was a short pause and then Nichols could hear the chief of staff say, "All right, Hill, but this better be good, or it's back in the ranks for you. You'll be lucky to come out a corporal. Do I make myself clear?"

Senator Nichols smiled. He cleared his throat and began to speak while still outside the tent. "Sir, I am Senator..."

Before Nichols could get the rest of the sentence out of his mouth, a shot rang out and Captain Hill came running out of the tent. Then Nichols heard a second shot. Captain Hill dropped to the ground. Nichols wheeled around to face the menace when he heard three more shots in rapid succession.

All three of Dorothy Rhoades men fell to the ground, and Nichols would be next. He crouched down and ran toward General Lee's headquarters but was met by even more shots from Confederate soldiers guarding the headquarters.

Nichols saw a stand of trees behind the Confederate picket lines and began running toward them. If he was lucky, he might make it to the trees in the confusion. As he was running, he saw three figures running from the trees toward the Union lines, but he wasn't the only one to see them. A Confederate sharpshooter had the lead man in his sights and brought the Union infiltrator down with one shot. The other two kept running for their lives and disappeared in the darkness of the night.

Thaddeus Nichols could never try to see Lee now. The Confederate general's staff wouldn't believe his story even with his forged orders. He would be seen as a provocateur leading a Union skirmishing party which was hoping to rattle the Confederate troops before the battle. He made it to the tree line where he and his three companions had first appeared. Nichols only had seconds to decide what to do next. First things first. He ran to where he had secreted the camo-drop, and it instantly appeared. Nichols marveled for a second at the gadget but quickly opened the cylinder and grabbed the envelope.

Then he saw the fallen Union soldier. He was alive but barely. Nichols stripped off the soldier's jacket and grabbed it along with the Yankee's cap and rifle. He took a quick look around and began running toward the Union lines.

When he was out of earshot from the Confederates, he threw off his tailcoat and put on the soldier's jacket. Luckily, the soldier had been shot in the groin, and his jacket had not been damaged. Nichols tied his handkerchief on the soldier's rifle barrel and began running again toward the Union lines.

"I'm still alive, and I still have a chance. I am God's instrument of punishment in this time or any other," he whispered to himself. Nichols reached into his shirt and found the envelope marked "EYES ONLY." Inside were a note from Dorothy and a forged letter from Jefferson Davis to Abraham Lincoln. Then Thaddeus Nichols understood what he must do. "I will strike fear in our Northern brothers and sisters. No one will feel safe!"

Meanwhile, back at the Confederate encampment, General Lee had been awakened by the uproar and was not in a good mood. His chief of staff ran into the general's sleeping quarters as Lee was screaming at the top of his lungs, "Can someone, anyone, tell me what's happening! Tell me, what's all the ruckus?"

"Sorry for the disturbance, sir," Lee's chief of staff said breathlessly. "Some crackpot claiming to be on a mission for President Davis was trying to get in to see you. He said he had details on how the Union intended to attack us. He claimed to be a Confederate senator named Thaddeus Nichols.

"Before I could get any more information, all hell broke loose. A Union infiltrator got Captain Hill and the three men who were with Nichols. We killed the infiltrator, but Nichols escaped. We're looking for him now."

"If it really is Thaddeus Nichols, I'd just as soon see him

dead," General Lee retorted. "He's a strange man, treats his slaves badly. President Davis told me personally he believed Nichols is insane. Senator Nichols bears watching. President Davis would never entrust him to send me a personal message.

"If you find him, hold on to the man. I don't have time to deal with him now. Besides, what could one man do?"

That was exactly what Jason Law was asking himself as he and the TFI recon team watched the deranged madman make his way toward the Union lines, plotting his next move. All Jason Law could do was look on helplessly.

Chapter Twenty-seven

TFI HEADQUARTERS,
2322

"I will not shut up!" Jason screamed at Harry Friedman. "We had him! It was just a matter of making the grab and bringing him back. What's happened to you, Harry? I have no idea where Nichols is heading. We tried to get a look at whatever was in that cylinder but no luck. Even when he pulled out that envelope, Nichols's aura was too strong for us to get close enough to him.

"We need to do something now, Harry. I've never seen you take a back seat to anyone, but you treat this General Busby as if he's got something on you. Is that it, Harry? Has he got something on you?"

"Detective Inspector Law, you will leave my office at once, or I will have you thrown out. No one has me in his pocket, least of all that four-star blowhard. Now leave my office!" Harry Friedman screamed.

Things had gotten way out of control, and both men knew it. Jason was the first to speak. "Harry, I'm sorry, but Dawn and I are going crazy. That madman, Nichols, made it clear he was coming back for our son. I won't let that happen, Harry. Now Nichols is back in his own time and your guys tell me we can't track him! How can that be, Harry? You've got the most sophisticated tracking system in the world. There has to be some way we can find him."

"I'm afraid not, Jason. The Court upheld Nichols's cease and desist order, and he was never fitted with a cerebral implant. The tracking chip the authorities implanted when he was moved to Prisoner VIP Quarters must have been disabled somehow.

"We could have triangulated his position if he hadn't lost

himself among the Union forces at Gettysburg. The upcoming battle has put a tremendous stress on the corporate psyche of both the Union and Confederate forces. It will take at least 48 hours before the flux subsides, and Nichols has less than that much time to live.

"In the meantime, Nichols can't be traced. The good news is he has very little chance of making it through the Union lines. Even if he does, I doubt seriously he can turn the world upside down in that little time.

"Give my people time, Jason. They'll find him and then you can grab him. No more hands off. You'll lead the grab team, and we can make sure Nichols never gets a chance to stir up trouble again."

"Okay, Harry," Jason said, "but I'm sticking around here until we find out what Nichols is trying to do. Maybe Dawn and I can figure some way to speed things up. Agreed?"

"Agreed," Harry said. "Just keep Detective Sergeant Byrd in the loop. I've been ordered to the White House. The President has called a special meeting of his Emergency Action Council. General Busby and I will be briefing them. In the meantime, if you need something, you can contact me on my implant."

"I don't know, Harry. You could be locked away in the Situation Room for days. Even an ops immediate message can't get through that place. I may not be able to wait that long. Why don't you just give me a video-cube telling everyone what you've decided. That way there'll be no mistakes.

"Oh, and I'll need to be brought up to speed on that new SMC time-jump system. Just say I'm to be given the cook's tour on the SMC project and given a few practice runs in the simulator. That's all I need."

"I can do that, Jason, but don't get any funny ideas. I've already told you SMC time travel is a suicide mission. I will not authorize any such mission without the expressed approval of the President," Harry said.

Harry touched the "video record" icon on his desktop holographic screen and began speaking. "To All Personnel: Detective Inspector Jason Law will be provided a complete briefing on Synthesized Meditation Coupling. Simulated time jumps authorized." Harry entered his classified PIN and sent the text to Jason's cerebral implant. The TFI Director stood up, and the two men shook hands.

Jason walked out of Harry's office and motioned to Dawn who was talking nervously on her communicator. "What is it? Who's on the line?" Jason asked.

"It's Doc. He says Jody's still having those terrible dreams. Jody keeps asking when we'll be home."

"Let me talk to Doc. Hello, Doc? Yeah, things couldn't be much worse here. I can't talk about it over the communicator. How's Jody? Okay. Dawn's coming home right now. I'll have her at the beaming station in ten minutes. Tell Jody Mum will be home before he wakes up from his nap. Can you pick her up at the station? Great! See you soon, Doc. Yeah, me too. Keep your head down."

Dawn had heard everything and was torn between leaving her husband in such an emergency and wrapping her arms around their little boy. "Jason, are you sure? You won't do anything silly, will you? Can I really go home, right now?"

"Right now. Grab your things from the lounge, and I'll meet you in the beaming station." Ten minutes later Dawn hugged Jason goodbye and was beamed less than 10 kilometers from their home outside Sydney, Australia. Jason took a deep breath and walked quickly to TFI crew quarters. He was looking for Detective Sergeant Byrd.

Chapter Twenty-eight

Jason Law walked into the TFI Crew Quarters and spotted two agents who had just returned from an assignment. "Either of you seen Detective Sergeant Byrd?"

"Yes, sir. He's in the shower. Can't you hear him? He's got the worst voice on the force." The two TFI agents laughed and pointed toward the decontamination shower entrance.

Jason heard Detective Sergeant Byrd humming a well-known tune, trying and failing miserably to stay on key. "Byrd, is that you?" Jason yelled.

"Who's asking?" came the reply.

"It's Jason Law. I need to talk to you. It's important. Hurry up!"

In less than 30 seconds, Detective Sergeant Byrd came out of the shower with a towel wrapped around his body and a distinct frown on his face. "Detective Inspector Law, what's so urgent?"

"We've lost Nichols. He's on the run, and Harry Friedman says there's no way we can track him. Harry's authorized me to drop in behind Union lines and track him down," Jason lied.

"Are you saying Mr. Friedman has authorized you to use the Synthesized Meditation Coupling System? That's a one-way trip, and you know it. Friedman would never authorize it. Besides, if you do find Nichols, what are you going to do with him? The TFI technical staff has already confirmed there's no longer any record from 1865 of Nichols dying. Our internal records still show you grabbing him, but in the year 1865 Nichols is alive and well. If you go after him, who knows how that could upset history. It's too risky."

"Look, Byrd, I have my orders, and I'm going to carry them out. Here, take a look." Jason fed Harry Friedman's message to Detective Sergeant Byrd's cerebra implant. It was the same message that Friedman had entered into Jason's implant with one important change. The word "simulated" had been erased.

Harry Friedman had made the oldest mistake in the book when he entered his classified PIN. He gave Jason a chance to watch him. Then and there Jason Law had his hand in the cookie jar.

"I don't believe it," Detective Sergeant Byrd said. "This is some kind of mistake. Mr. Friedman would never allow such a thing without talking to me first. I'm calling him to verify this."

"Go ahead. He should be in the White House Situation Room by now. He was headed to the beaming station the last time I saw him."

Detective Sergeant Byrd tried to connect to Friedman's cerebral implant but couldn't get through. Instead, he received a computer-generated White House Message on his communicator that Friedman was attending a national security meeting and was unavailable. "I'll try him again in an hour."

"You do anything you want, but right now I get my SMC briefing, and you put together a team. We'll all make the jump to the Continuum, but I'll be the only one making the jump to the target time vector."

Detective Sergeant Byrd was a very suspicious man, and he knew something wasn't right, but he also knew he had just seen the TFI Director authorize Detective Inspector Law to make a SMC-driven time jump. "If you want to kill yourself, that's up to you. Everything else is so screwed up around here, why not send you? All you could do is turn history upside down and change the whole course of the world. Sounds great!" the Detective Sergeant said sarcastically, "Just great."

Chapter Twenty-nine

TIME WARP CONTINUUM

"You've still got time to change your mind, Detective Inspector Law. We'll find another way to stop Nichols. You're throwing your life away with no good reason," Detective Sergeant Byrd said to Jason Law who had successfully passed into the Continuum.

Jason Law already knew he was throwing his life away. Unfortunately, he couldn't think of another way to stop Nichols. Dawn and their son Jody had made his decision almost easy.

"No time to talk, Byrd. Make sure the TFI geeks are dropping me in the right place. I'd look pretty silly in this Union uniform behind Confederate Lines." The "geeks," as Jason referred to the TFI scientific staff, had indeed done their jobs. They had done their research very carefully to ensure Jason was being sent to the right time and location.

Jason had done his own research to ensure he had the appropriate uniform--Pennsylvania Infantry. He wore the rank of major, and he hoped anyone stopping him would buy his story that he was a foreign volunteer. There were a number of them fighting on both sides. Jason had the appropriate identification papers and a set of orders saying he was to be given full cooperation in carrying out his mission--hunting down a notorious Confederate spy.

"Let's get on with it, Detective Sergeant Byrd. Tell TFI Headquarters to pull the trigger."

Byrd did as he was told, and a moment later Jason Law found himself about two miles from Gettysburg, Pennsylvania, behind Union lines. "So far so good," Jason whispered to himself as he scanned his surroundings.

He was standing in a small field about 100 meters off a dirt road. The road was congested with wagon after wagon of supplies being moved toward the front. Jason counted 10 wagons move by in less than 10 minutes. In between the wagons were Union cavalry soldiers making sure the traffic kept moving and no looting took place.

"Come on, come on," Jason said under his breath. He had no idea where Nichols was, but he felt certain the Confederate senator would get as far away from the front lines as possible. "My only hope is to find Nichols the old-fashioned way. I'll hunt him down like I would any other rat." Jason had been very lucky when the Chief of Detectives in Sydney had asked him to come back to the police department. His time there had given him the chance to sharpen his detective skills, and he would need all of them if he was to track Nichols down. But where to start?

"Hey, Henry? You see something moving over there?" one of the mounted escort soldiers said to his partner. "There's something moving over there. You know what the captain said. Nobody goes unchallenged. Let's go see who that is." The two soldiers trotted their horses toward the small field where Jason was moving back into the dark. "Who goes there?" cried the first soldier.

"Halt or we'll fire!" shouted the other soldier.

"Hold on, mates. No reason to get upset. I'm coming; I'm coming," Jason said as he stepped forward.

"Hands up, mister," said the first soldier. "Who are you and what are you doing in that field?"

"I'm Major Thomas Edwards, First Pennsylvanian," Jason said as calmly as he could.

"You sure sound funny for a Union officer. Keep your hands up. Where you from?" the second soldier said.

Jason did as he was told and kept his hands in the air as he stepped closer. "You're right, corporal. I do sound peculiar for a Union major. I'm a foreign volunteer."

"Foreigner, huh? Where're you from?" asked the second soldier.

"It's called Australia. Belongs to the Brits," Jason said nonchalantly. "Here are my orders," he said as he slowly reached into his tunic and pulled out his set of forged orders.

Detective Inspector Law became Major Thomas Edwards at that moment. "Come on, man. I don't have the time to be polite. I'm on a very sensitive mission, and I need to be on my way."

"Will you come with us, sir?" the first soldier said in a deferential tone.

Within minutes Jason Law and his two escorts had made it to the front of some supply wagons where they found Captain Paul Meade. He was in his mid-20's and had received his commission on the battlefront. He was old beyond his years and treated every stranger with caution.

"Captain Meade, this here fella, I mean officer, claims he's on an important mission, but we found him in that field back there keepin' kinda outta of sight. Seemed a bit strange. He talks awful funny, too, sir." With that, the corporal handed Jason's orders to Captain Meade.

Paul Meade looked at Jason Law and then at his orders. "Sorry, sir, but we can't be too careful. Says here you're looking for a spy. What's he look like?"

"He's wearing a Union tunic and civilian pantaloons. He's past middle age and speaks with a distinctive Southern drawl. His name is Thaddeus Nichols but may be using an alias. Have you seen him?"

"Maybe, maybe not, but my men were correct. You do speak with some kind of strange accent. Just where are you from, Major?"

Jason took a deep breath and said, "Australia, Captain. It's a British colony, located. . ."

"I know where Australia is, Major. What are you doing in the middle of our war?"

"I'm in your country fighting as a volunteer," Jason responded. "It's there in my orders. I know you have your duty, but you're holding up a very important mission. I've got to stop that spy before he has a chance to do any mischief. If you don't have the authority to make a decision, take me to someone who does."

Major Edwards was a lucky man. Meade had seen the spy within the last 30 minutes. "Sir, I saw your man less than a half hour ago. I thought he looked awfully strange, but you know the way it is. Many of our guys haven't had a chance to rest in months. Their uniforms are rags, and they make do. Your man wasn't the first soldier I'd seen without a complete uniform. This is the front, sir. We grab what we need and worry about the niceties later. Why do you want this guy, Major?"

"All I can tell you is he's wanted at the highest levels. Which way was he heading? Was he on foot?"

"Yes, sir. He was running toward the rail yard. Looked like a deserter to me. My men searched for him but couldn't find anything. We reported him to the station master and that was that. I can get you a ride to the station if you want."

"Yes, that would be fine," Jason said to Captain Meade, but inside Jason feared there was a good chance it would not be fine. Jason had already given up his future with his wife and son. His life meant nothing to him. "I'll see us both in hell first," Jason said to the man that wasn't there. Meanwhile, on a freight train headed for Washington, D.C., Thaddeus Nichols was running out of time.

Chapter Thirty

General Mike Busby was not used to being called on the carpet, not even by the President of the Greater American Federation. He certainly was not comfortable answering the pointed questions the President was asking. "Sir, I have no idea where this man you call Thaddeus Nichols is. I've never heard of him," Busby lied.

"General, you have exactly 10 seconds to come clean, or I'll see you in one of the secret military detention centers you've been hiding from me. Ten, nine, eight, seven...," the President began counting. The secretary of defense stood silently next to the President.

General Michael Busby knew when to hold and fight and when to surrender. This was definitely the latter. "All right, all right. I know who Thaddeus Nichols is, but I have absolutely no idea where he is. I swear to you, sir, I don't know where he is."

Busby was telling the President the truth. Before Dr. Juan Cortez had sent Nichols and the other three back in time to Gettysburg, Pennsylvania, Cortez had told General Busby there was no way to track them. The aura energy levels produced by the thousands of Union and Confederate soldiers under the stress of the upcoming battle were just too intense to get an accurate reading of where Nichols was.

Busby hadn't bothered to tell Dorothy Rhoades. A big part of him didn't want her plan to succeed, but another part realized her plan was his only chance for survival. "Do a brain scan. Do whatever you want. I don't know where he is, Mr. President."

"Good idea, General. I'll use your own methods to find out what you know. How long do you think it will take those guys of yours in black to get it out of you? Yes, I know all about your so-called "intelligence teams." Did you really think you could keep everything from me? How long have you been working for Dorothy Rhoades? Where is she? Who else is in this with you? Where is Nichols?"

The President had only learned about Mike Busby's treason within the last 24 hours. The secretary of defense and Busby's vice-chairman, a Marine four-star named Arthur Fielding, had been suspicious for some time and had finally found out about the secret work Dr. Cortez and his team had been doing at Base One.

General Fielding had grilled Dr. Leo Lehman, chief scientist for the Pentagon's National Review Board, who told Fielding the whole story. Busby had mistakenly thought Dr. Lehman was in his back pocket and posed no threat. The bottom line--General Busby failed to have Lehman go through the same memory scrub Dr. Cortez and his team were forced to endure. Thankfully, Cortez had not suffered any permanent brain damage as so many of his team had.

"I know all about Dr. Cortez and Base One, and if you know anything else I'll find out," the President said menacingly.

"How did Leo Lehman find out about what I did? Cortez couldn't have told him, and the Team Zebra memory technician would rather die than say anything," General Busby said. The four-star was genuinely confused.

"Come now, General. We both know there was someone else. Did you really think Michael Dane would keep quiet? He's a good man, Busby, no thanks to you!"

"Michael? No, no, he wouldn't. Everything I've done, I've done for him. You're lying!"

With that, the President cleared his throat and spoke softly into his office communicator, "Martha, please show them in."

A moment later General Busby's only son, Michael Dane, walked into the Oval Office with Dr. Leo Lehman and Dr. Juan Cortez. The young Michael had drifted away from his father and had taken his mother's name years ago.

He glared at his father as he approached him. Busby had

spared his son the dangerous memory scrub that the staff at Base One had endured, believing his son could never forsake him even after their long separation. "How could you believe I would stand by and let you get away with **treason?**" Michael said to his father.

General Michael Busby stared at his son and reached out to him, but his son turned his back on the disgraced military leader. "Take this traitor away!" the President said to two FBI agents who had just entered the Oval Office. "Turn him over to General Fielding." The President turned to Busby's son and said, "Michael, I know this has been extremely difficult for you. You have given us a chance to stop Dorothy Rhoades and that madman, Nichols. However, there's much more work to be done if we are to save our country."

With that, the President asked his executive secretary to come into the Oval Office. "Yes, Mr. President?" she asked as she entered the office.

"Set up a meeting for me. I want this face-to-face in the Oval Office, not one of those holographic virtual meetings. I need General Fielding and the head of the Time Force Investigations Unit. What's his name?"

"Mr. Harry Friedman, sir."

"Yes, yes. Get them here within the hour. Tell them to drop everything. General Fielding can deal with General Busby later. General Fielding and Mr. Friedman here in one hour, got it?"

"Yes, sir, one hour," Martha said as she left the room.

"You should have seen this coming," the President said quietly to the secretary of defense. "I'll deal with you later. You are excused, Mr. Secretary."

"Yes, sir," the secretary replied and walked out of the Oval Office. The secretary's days as SECDEF were numbered and he was already calling his wife to give her the news.

The President turned to Dr. Lehman, Dr. Cortez, and Busby's son, Michael. Gentlemen, I'll need all of you to be here in an hour, too. I'm afraid I'm out of ideas. I'll fight this with my dying breath, but if Dorothy Rhoades pulls this off, we're all finished. Any ideas?"

"Yes, Mr. President," Dr. Lehman said. I have a friend who I think may be able to help us. His name is Dr. Pirramuar James--a professor of archeology at the University of Sydney in Australia."

"Get him here as soon as possible if you think he can help, Dr.

Lehman.

"I do Mr. President. Dr. James is probably the world's most foremost anthropological authority on the American Civil War. I believe one of his ancestors was a slave somewhere in the deep South. I'm not sure where. His historical perspective could be invaluable in trying to anticipate the coup leaders' next move."

"Fine. Anyone else have any other suggestions?" the President asked.

Dr. Cortez cleared his throat and said, "Yes, Mr. President. Pray."

Chapter Thirty-one

Jason Law jumped off the Union wagon and quickly found the station master and asked him if he had seen Nichols.

"No sir, I saw no one matching that description," the station master said. "But this is a big rail yard, and there's no tellin' who might have run through here. Union soldier's jacket and pantaloon pants, huh? No, sir, I haven't seen him, but I can check with the yard crew, Major Edwards."

"No, that won't be necessary," Jason said. He still felt very uncomfortable in the Union uniform, but he was slowly becoming accustomed to being called Major Edwards. "When did the last train leave the station?"

"An hour ago, sir. It was a freight train dead-headin' back to D.C."

"Dead-heading? I'm not sure I understand," Jason said to the station master.

"It was travelin' back to the D.C. freight yard to pick up more supplies for the troops. Should be there in a couple of hours."

"When does the next train leave for the Capital?" Jason asked.

"There ain't no more trains runnin' in or out of D.C. tonight, Major."

"I need to get to D.C. right now. Any suggestions?"

"If you're in that big of a hurry, I might be able to help. If it's for the war, that is."

"I've already shown you my orders. If I don't get to D.C. soon, the war will be over, and the Confederates will be on the winning

206

side. Get me to D.C.!"

"Yes, sir. I've got a yard locomotive and an engineer to get you there, but I'm afraid you'll have to stoke the engine. We use the locomotive to move cars around the yard. It's full of coal and topped off with water. Not the prettiest girl in our stable, but it will get you to D.C."

"Take me to it. Tell the engineer to break a speed record. There's a madman loose in the Capital, and there's no telling what he intends to do."

Chapter Thirty-two

Thaddeus Nichols had barely made it out of the D.C. rail yard without being seen. He had stripped off the Union soldier's jacket and left it in the empty freight car he had hopped at Gettysburg, but he kept the two-barrel derringer he found on the soldier. Dressed in his undershirt and pantaloons, Nichols looked anything but inconspicuous.

He moved along a dark street as quickly as he could when he heard the sound of a wagon. Thaddeus was in luck--he hitched a ride with a waggoner who had just dropped off a load of plain pine coffins headed for Gettysburg. "Looks like you're a working man. Where you headed?" the waggoner asked in a casual voice.

"Towards the White House," Nichols replied.

"Dressed like that? I don't think so, mister."

"You're right," Nichols said. "I'm just heading that way. I'll let you know when we get close," he lied.

The waggoner let the subject drop and said, "I have the terrible duty delivering all those caskets, but it's a pity not all of our good men will have the honor of being buried in a decent coffin," the waggoner said. "The men who end up in those pine boxes are the lucky ones. If the number of dead gets too high, they'll just bury them in mass graves. Pity."

"Yes, a pity," Thaddeus agreed. The senator was trying to say as little as possible to not give away his Southern drawl, but his attempt to limit the conversation was a complete failure.

"Say, mister, where did you say you were from? You sound like a Rebel for sure. Maybe we should head for the police station and let them listen to you. You ain't some kind of spy, are you?"

"Me? Gracious, no. Just an old man down on his luck." I come from down close to the Mason-Dixon Line, that's all." Nichols was gambling the waggoner was too tired to care and would give up this line of questioning, too, but he kept pressing Thaddeus.

"I'll tell you what, mister. We're only a block from a police station house. We'll just stop there and let them sort this out. Then we'll be on our way." The waggoner gave his horse team a gentle nudge with the reins, and they picked up the pace. It would be the last move the waggoner ever made.

Nichols could see the station house lights and knew he had to act. "No, I'm afraid I don't have time to waste with the police," the senator said to the waggoner. Thaddeus grabbed the waggoner savagely and threw him into the wagon. The waggoner struck his head on the way down and was obviously seriously injured. "You stupid man," Nichols whispered as he grabbed the horses' reins and calmly pulled into an alley only a half block from the police station house. "You wouldn't leave well enough alone. Well, it's God's will."

Thaddeus stuck his right hand deep into one of his pantaloon's pockets. He searched until he found the Aborigine holy man's bone cross that Nichols's father had confiscated when Thaddeus was just a boy. Nichols stepped into the back of the wagon and placed his hands on the still breathing waggoner. Nichols began to squeeze the man's throat, gently at first and then tighter and tighter. The waggoner tried to struggle but there was no fight in him.

In seconds it was over, and Thaddeus Nichols felt the same rush and total release he found each time he took a person's life. He quickly went through the man's pockets and found a 10 dollar gold piece. Nichols pocketed the money and stripped the man's shirt from him. "Not the best, but it will do until I can find better," he muttered.

Thaddeus Nichols hopped from the wagon and began running down the alley until he was several blocks from the police station house. The police would find the driver's body soon, so he would have to move quickly. Nichols had been to Washington, D.C., a number of times before the war began. He was well known in the Capital, and would be spotted quickly if he wasn't careful.

He needed a set of gentleman's clothes if his plan was to

succeed. "Where can I find suitable attire at this time of night?" he said to himself. "There's no place open and besides I'd be recognized at any of the stores that catered to gentlemen. Where can I go?"

During his long hours of prison time locked in that hideous cell, Nichols had read all he could about the American Civil War and its aftermath. He had been particularly struck with Abraham Lincoln's assassination at Ford's Theater. Thaddeus made an instant decision--he would find what he needed at Ford's Theater. "How fitting," he chuckled to himself. Nichols knew the layout of the Capital from before the war and found his way to the theater easily. He saw the stage door and quietly opened it. He could hear the performance but couldn't make out what the actors were saying. As Thaddeus shut the stage door quietly, the stage doorkeeper saw him.

"Who are you?" the old man asked Thaddeus. "I don't remember seeing you before. Have you got a pass?"

"Why yes, right here," Nichols said as he reached into his pants. "Oh no, I can't find it. I must have dropped it as I was hurrying to the theater. I'm Seymour Ferguson. Perhaps you've heard of me?"

"Can't say that I have. What are you doing here and what gives with those clothes and that drawl?"

"I'm in character. I've written a play about that rebel Jefferson Davis and his crowd. I want to show those rebs for what they really are. I'm supposed to speak to your artistic director after tonight's performance. I can't find my pass."

"No pass, no entry. Sorry, but those are the rules. You should know that if you are who you say you are."

The old man began to walk back to his chair. Nichols took a quick look around, saw no one, and grabbed the old man from behind. Thaddeus put his hand over the old man's mouth and dragged him toward a dark corner.

Then Thaddeus grabbed the cross from his pocket, placed it in his hand, and began squeezing the stage doorkeeper's throat. "Quiet, quiet, it will be over too soon. You have been blessed. You are being called home by the Almighty, and I am his Angel of Death." Thaddeus felt the old man go limp and waited for the euphoria to overtake him. "No one is beyond my reach. No one can stand against me. Not even President Abraham Lincoln."

Chapter Thirty-three

Jason Law jumped from the locomotive as it began to stop at the rail station. "Thanks for the ride!" he said to the engineer but didn't wait for a response. Jason ran to the station's doors just as a middle-aged, obviously tired man was locking them. "Pardon me, I need to see the station master immediately! This is an emergency. I must see the station master immediately!" Jason managed to get out between deep breaths of air.

"You found him. What can I do for you, Major?"

"I'm Major Thomas Edwards, and I am hunting for a Southern sympathizer. He's dressed in a Union soldier's jacket and a gentleman's pantaloons. He may be going by the name Thaddeus Nichols. This madman is trying to overthrow the United States government. Have you seen him or had any reports from your men about anyone fitting that description? This is of the utmost importance. The country's future may depend on it."

"You've got my attention, Major, but I haven't seen anyone like that in the station and my men sure haven't told me they've seen anyone like that in the rail yard. In fact, it's been a pretty quiet night. We haven't had a problem."

Jason was running out of ideas. How could he ever track down Nichols? "Surely there must be someone you can check with, someplace you could look?" Jason pleaded.

"Sorry, Major. Believe me, I'm a patriot, and I'll do anything I can for the Union, but we haven't seen anyone out of the ordinary tonight. Sorry." The station master turned back to the doors and took a large key from his vest. As he was locking the doors, bells began to ring from the police station house just a few blocks away.

"What's that?" Jason Law asked.

"Sounds like one of the police wagons. Something big must have happened. The station's just up the road."

"Thanks!" Jason yelled and began running in the direction the station master pointed. It was a slim chance, but any chance was better than none. Jason had almost made it to the station house when he noticed a police wagon and a number of people in an alley. "What's going on?" Jason shouted.

One of the onlookers turned and said, "Some guy's been strangled. Don't know who he is. Looks like a working man, though."

"I need to speak to whoever's in charge?" Jason said loudly, and a police sergeant turned to answer.

"That would be me, Major. I'm Sergeant Holt. Why do you ask?" Sergeant Theodore Holt didn't want some Union major thinking he could start ordering him around.

"I'm Major Thomas Edwards, and I'm on a highly classified mission. I'm looking for a man. I'd like to take a look at whoever that is to see if it's him."

Sergeant Holt had no problem letting this major take a look, especially if it would get him on his way. "That will be fine, Major, but what's your unit? I never heard an accent like that."

"Australian volunteer. Now let me see that man." Jason walked past several police officers and saw a man's body lying in the alley. "Damn," Jason said out loud. This was certainly not Thaddeus Nichols. Jason began to turn around and then, for some reason, turned back to the body and bent down. "Don't be touching anything until Captain Roberts gets here, Major."

"Absolutely," Jason said as he bent over the body. Then he saw it--a deep purple bruise in the shape of a cross on the man's neck. "How long ago did you discover the body, Sergeant?"

"Just a few minutes ago. He ain't been dead long. Probably no more than a couple of hours. Did you see that bruise? Kind of strange."

"Any witnesses?" Jason asked Sergeant Holt.

"Not so far, Major. Okay, you've had your look. Is that your man?"

"No, I'm afraid not, but he's the one who murdered this

man."

"Are you sure?" the sergeant asked. Holt was now much more interested in the major and was about to question him more when everyone turned towards the sound of more police alarm bells.

"More trouble?" Jason asked Holt, and the sergeant shook his head. Before Sergeant Holt could stop him, Jason jumped on one of the police wagons and grabbed the reins from the driver. He had never seen a horse wagon before, let alone driven one, but he cracked the reins and the horses began to move quickly toward the sound of the other police wagons.

Seconds later Jason careened around a corner with the horses more in control than he was. He saw Ford's Theatre with a large crowd huddled around the stage door. Jason somehow stopped the horse team, jumped from the wagon, and ran towards it. "Move out of the way. This is official government business. Move out of the way!" Jason yelled.

As he got closer to the stage door, he saw more uniformed men standing in front of it. "Who's in charge? Who's in charge?" Jason yelled as he made his way to the front of the crowd. "I'm Major Thomas Edwards, and I need to speak to whoever's in charge!"

From inside the theater Jason heard a loud voice call out, "I'm Captain John Roberts, and I'm in charge, Major. What's so important?" the police captain said as he walked into the alley.

"Sergeant Holt sent me," Jason lied. "He's at a murder scene of his own waiting for you. He has a victim who was strangled. The man has a deep bruise mark on his neck in the shape of a cross. How about your victim? I'm looking for the man who probably killed both of them."

"Who said anything about someone being dead. We have a victim, but he's certainly not dead. Has the same strange bruise mark, though, and he's dazed, but he should make it."

Jason started moving toward the stage door and said, "I may still have a chance. I need to talk to your victim now, Captain. This is a matter of national security! Now take me to him."

"Number one, you don't tell me to do anything. Number two, this guy can't talk. We've got a doc looking at him, and he says this guy won't be able to talk for several days."

"Is he awake? I can communicate with him. Just let me see him. Here are my orders."

"All right, Major, but I really don't think you'll get much out of the old man. He's the stage doorkeeper and he's pretty shaken, but, all right, give it a try."

Jason made his way past the stage door to where Thaddeus Nichols thought he had killed the doorkeeper. The old man was propped up against a wall choking and trying to get his breath. The doctor was attending him and looked sternly at Jason as he approached. "I'm Major Edwards. Captain Roberts has cleared me to see this man. It's a national security matter," Jason said to the doctor.

The doctor didn't say a word but moved out of the way. "Looks like you've had quite a rough evening, sir," Jason said to the old man as he patted him on the shoulder. "I need to take a look where you were strangled, all right?" The doorkeeper nodded slowly, and Jason saw the same deep bruise in the shape of a cross.

"Did the man who did this say anything?" Jason asked the old man. The doorkeeper nodded, and Jason motioned to Captain Roberts for a paper and pen. The old man shook his head, "no."

"He can't read or write, Major. Looks like you are out of luck," the police captain said. Just then the doorkeeper motioned to Jason to come closer. Jason bent down and the old man tried to whisper, but couldn't utter a sound. Jason looked deeply in the his eyes and patted his shoulder. The doorkeeper grabbed his throat to force out a sound and with one final effort managed one word, "Abe."

Jason turned around and yelled, "I need to get to the White House now! Someone, anyone, I need to get to the White House now! He's going to kill President Lincoln!"

Chapter Thirty-four

The police wagon was rushing through the streets of Washington, D.C., on a direct route to the White House. "It's taking too long. Why can't we go faster?" Jason screamed at the driver.

"Major, if I push these horses any harder, they'll drop dead. Just shut-up and let me do my job. That man, Nichols, won't get past the guards, let alone see President Lincoln. The President is completely safe, Major. Believe me, I've been to the White House before. There's absolutely no way Nichols will get to President Lincoln. I guarantee it."

Chapter Thirty-five

THE WHITE HOUSE,
1863

Thaddeus Nichols had hailed a carriage for hire as soon as he left Ford's Theater. He was dressed in the gentleman's clothes he had stolen from the costume department at Ford's Theater. "Take me to the White House," he said to the carriage driver.

"Yes, sir," the driver responded as Nichols jumped into the carriage. As the driver was pulling the carriage into the street, he and the senator were both startled by the bells of several police wagons heading for the theater. A police wagon was rushing toward them with a Union major driving. "Don't see that every day, Mister. Wonder what that Major fella is doing with the police? Don't you?"

Thaddeus Nichols shot a quick look at the police wagon and saw Jason Law on it. Nichols almost panicked but quickly regained his composure. "It's no concern of mine. I told you, I need to get to the White House." The senator pulled the 10 dollar gold piece he had stolen from the waggoner's body and said, "Make it fast, and this is yours!"

"**Yes, sir!**" The driver pushed his horses to a gallop, and Thaddeus pulled his collar around his face.

"Hurry, man, hurry!" Thaddeus cried out. Then Thaddeus began mumbling quietly to himself, "God has shown me the way. I will strike down Lincoln with my own hands and force the Union to sue for peace. I will have my rightful place in history. To hell with the future! To hell with Dorothy Rhoades! My hands are the hands of God! I will strike down Abraham Lincoln and see the Confederacy victorious, so help me God!" But it wasn't God who had twisted Nichols' thoughts. It wasn't God who had decided to take a direct

216

hand in changing history. It wasn't God who had manipulated Thaddeus Nichols's every thought since that fateful day when a small boy choked the life from an Aborigine holy man's wife. It was an evil power stronger than any man.

That spirit, that evil was also working in the future. His willing subject was a man Dorothy Rhodes called RAIDER.

Chapter Thirty-six

WASHINGTON, D.C.,
2322

Dorothy Rhoades was frightened. No, she was terrified! Everything that could go wrong had gone wrong. General Michael Busby was in custody and most likely telling everything he knew. The American States Rights Association had been shut down, many of its staff arrested, and its membership rolls under scrutiny, not only by the FBI but by state and local authorities throughout the nation.

Dorothy had gone to ground in a small apartment not far from the Capitol building. She only had one chance--talk to RAIDER. "He'll either find a way out of this for me, or he'll go down with me," she said out loud. There was no covert way of reaching RAIDER. All communications in the city were being monitored under a declared state of emergency. Those people with cerebral implants were under the additional threat of having every thought screened by the government. Fortunately, Dorothy had never allowed herself to be fitted with one.

The deposed head of the ASR waited until dusk and then left her apartment disguised as a sanitation robo-supervisor. In the twenty-fourth century, robots took care of most the mundane tasks, including office cleaning and trash hauling. However, even robots needed someone to check in on them and robo-supervisors filled that role.

Dorothy headed directly toward the Capitol building. She made it to the employee entrance without being stopped and pulled out the fake identification card RAIDER had given her, a card only for the most dire emergencies.

Rhoades had given herself a complete facial and body transformation with a portable plastic surgery scanner, but it was impossible to beat the aura security checks at the Capitol. She only had one choice--bluff."Good evening, officer," Dorothy said in the monotone voice used by many of the over-worked, underpaid hourly employees who worked at all the government facilities throughout the nation's capital.

"Evening," the officer replied in the same monotone voice. His name was Brad Ewing, and he was a middle-aged military retiree "double-dipping" from the government trough. The guard was no more interested in this woman than any of the other people who had passed his post during the last eight hours. Brad had four more hours to go on this shift--part of the increased security required under martial law.

He was about to wave the woman through when a buzzer went off. "Why me?" Brad griped to no one in particular as he held his hand up and said, "Sorry, lady, but the computer says we need to do a full screening. Won't take too long. Just come this way, and I'll hand you over to my supervisor."

Dorothy Rhoades didn't wait to be told what to do. She grabbed a handheld communicator from the guard's desk and struck him over the head. Blood began streaming down his face as he cried out, "Stop her. She tried to kill me. Stop her!"

Two Capitol Hill staffers waiting behind Dorothy tried to grab her, but she spun around and began running.

The two staffers started chasing Dorothy with one of the two Capital police officers who had been standing behind Officer Ewing. "Halt. Halt or I'll shoot," the first officer cried out. He was out of shape, and had no chance of catching Dorothy. A die-hard jogger, Dorothy was easily out-pacing him and the two staffers.

"Halt or I'll shoot!" the officer yelled again as he stopped and pulled his hand weapon. He aimed toward Dorothy and let the weapon's automatic tracking system take over. In less than a second, the weapon had locked onto Dorothy, and the officer fired. Dorothy slumped to the ground.

"I told her to stop. You two are my witnesses. I told her to stop." The officer had never fired his weapon in the line of duty but was well trained on what he had to do next. He pulled out his communicator and hit "Alert."

"Sarge, get over here quick. I just killed some woman. She's dressed like one of those capitol robo-supervisors. I have no idea why she ran, but I've got two witnesses that saw everything. I gave her the two warnings, and she just kept running. Yeah, I know what this means, but I swear I did everything by the book."

Sergeant Ray Bower had been on the Capital police force for too long and understood he had a long night ahead of him. After getting the emergency message, Bower called his captain and said, "Yes, sir, that's all I know. I'll go down and make sure the area's secured. No, sir, I won't let anyone touch a thing until the crime scene guys get there. Yes, sir."

The sergeant hurried from his office to Dorothy Rhoades's body and, after surveying the area, told Officer Ewing to report to the captain for debriefing. Then Sergeant Bower turned to his other two officers and had them brief him on everything. He asked one of the officers to escort the two staffers to the captain's office and told the last officer to rope off the scene.

Sergeant Bower went over to the body. He was going to take a big chance. If the captain found out what he was doing, it could mean his stripes, but if the Crime Scene Unit discovered something that pointed to a "bad shoot," it would definitely mean his stripes. He put on sterile gloves and covered Dorothy's body with a standard issue body cover from his emergency kit. He looked over his shoulder and made sure the security cameras were still pointed toward Officer Ewing.

The sergeant patted down Dorothy's body and found only one item--a business card from the chairman of the Senate's Internal Security Committee, Senator Clay Sheen. Bower was over his head and he knew it. "There go my stripes," he said to himself as he pulled out his communicator.

"Captain Raymond, this is Bower. I found something you need to see."

"What is it?" the captain asked nonchalantly.

"It's a business card from Senator Sheen, sir. We found it in one of the woman's pockets."

"Interesting, but before we do anything else see if you can confirm her identity."

"Yes, sir. I just thought we should check with the Senator's office to make sure he's okay."

"Good idea. Hold on."

Sergeant Bowers could have lied to his captain and told him the card was in plain sight, but there was no way that explanation would fly. Eventually, the security camera digital files would show the truth. Besides, Bower had known Captain Jay Raymond since they attended the academy together, and the sergeant knew better than to cross the other man. A few seconds passed before Captain Raymond got back on the line.

"Bower?"

"Yes, sir."

"The Senator is out of the office and no one there has any idea where he is. They're trying to find him as we speak. I'll follow up."

"Yes, sir, I'll get on with my report and let you handle the protocol. Thank you, sir."

He didn't like it but Captain Raymond understood this time he had to be by-the-book. He would inform the division commander of what had happened and await further orders. However, the man called RAIDER was absolutely not by-the-book, and he was ready to prove it.

Chapter Thirty-seven

WASHINGTON, D.C.,
1863

Thaddeus Nichols had to make a decision quickly. It would be impossible to make it inside the White House before Jason Law caught up with him. "Pull over here. I've changed my mind," Thaddeus said to the carriage driver.

"But I still get the ten dollars, right?"

"Don't worry, you'll still get paid," Nichols said and tossed the 10 dollar gold piece to the driver."

The carriage driver was confused--why would the gentleman pay him 10 dollars for not getting to the White House? It didn't make sense, but he certainly wasn't going to argue.

"Yes, sir," the carriage driver said. "People with money," he thought to himself. "I can't figure them out." But it didn't pay to be too inquisitive if a person wanted to make good tips, and the carriage driver certainly did. The driver heard police wagon bells again and waited to let the wagon pass. He turned to say something to the gentleman but his passenger had disappeared.

"That's strange. I'll have to make sure to tell the wife about everything tonight. Too many people, too many bells, too many police. When the war's over, I'm taking the family back home. Yes, sir, back home to Front Royal."

Thaddeus Nichols had made it through the perimeter of the White House grounds and had hidden in a large thicket only about fifty feet from the mansion's main gate. Within seconds he heard the police wagon swing into the entrance and a guard shouting, "Halt. Yes, sir. Are you sure the President's in danger, sir? Let's show your orders to the corporal of the guard. Follow me, sir."

Seconds later Nichols could hear a sentry cry out, "Search the grounds. There's an assassin on the grounds!"

Nichols looked up to the second floor of the White House and saw President Lincoln looking, almost staring back at him. Then someone pulled the President away from the window. "I have failed," the Confederate senator mused.

Suddenly Thaddeus saw Abraham Lincoln and a black servant running out of one of the service entrances. Both men appeared to be scanning the grounds when the servant spoke to President Lincoln. "Sir, you cannot stay out here; it's too dangerous. Something's not right, Mr. President. I can feel it. There's evil in the air."

"Now, James. You sound just like Mrs. Lincoln. I told you I saw a man's face out here, and I know him. I just can't place him. Go find the captain of the guard and bring him to me. I'm not going back until I speak personally to the captain. I don't want someone shot, maybe killed, unnecessarily. I **know** I've seen that man before. Now bring me the Captain of the Guard. I won't move from here."

"Yes, Mr. President," the man Lincoln called James said. The Aborigine was making a mistake, but so many years of slavery had taken their toll. The emancipated slave did as he was told.

Thaddeus Nichols watched the servant leave and thought to himself, "This is the work of God. I will kill Lincoln with my own hands and strike down a nation. Only then can the Confederacy survive."

Nichols could hear loud voices at the main gate, and he realized it must be Jason Law. "I must strike quickly," he said to himself as he circled the President to come at him from the rear.

Abraham Lincoln was peering into the dark, trying to find the face he had seen briefly from his window. "Come out! Come out, whoever you are. I promise you won't be harmed if you will come out and show your face. I am the President of the United States, and I give you my word you will not be harmed!"

"What's the use?" Lincoln said to himself and turned toward the service entrance to go back inside the White House. As Abraham Lincoln turned, he came face to face with Senator Thaddeus Nichols of the Confederate States of America.

"You! Thaddeus Nichols. What are you doing here? Do you

have a message from Jefferson Davis?"

"No, Mr. President, I have a message from God! You must die to save the South. Long live the Confederacy!" Nichols shouted as he grabbed Abraham Lincoln's throat with both hands and began to squeeze. "Die. Die!" the crazed psychopath screamed.

Lincoln could feel himself losing consciousness, but he was helpless to stop the blackness overtaking him. He slumped over with Nichols's hands still wrapped around his throat. In that moment, Thaddeus Nichols felt a complete release of any decency he still possessed. He let the President fall to the ground and then jumped on top of Lincoln and began choking him again.

Suddenly, Thaddeus was grabbed from the rear and thrown off the President. Jason Law was on top of him, hitting him in the face. "You'll wish you were dead before I'm through with you, Nichols!" Jason screamed as he struck again and again.

The black servant came running up to Jason with the captain of the guard and several soldiers. The servant went straight to President Lincoln, and the captain yelled to one of the soldiers to find the President's doctor. The servant known as James began chanting over the President's body in a foreign tongue as he rolled the President over and struck him twice on the back. The President took several deep breaths but did not regain consciousness.

In the meantime, the captain of the guard told a soldier to get the Union major off the assassin. "Don't you kill that madman, Major. We need to know who sent him and if there are any more of them around," the captain said to Jason Law.

"All right, all right, but watch him closely," Jason said. The man from the future stood up and rushed over to the President. "Is the President all right?" Jason asked the servant. For the first time, he looked into the black man's face.

"Yes, Jason, he will survive," the freed slave replied.

"How do you know my name?" Jason asked, now confused more than ever.

"We are brothers, Tagai," the first Pirramuar said. "There is still danger, Tagai. I can feel it. Be on guard."

"I'm sure there is, but we're safe for now," Jason said and patted the old Aborigine on the shoulder. Jason turned toward Thaddeus Nichols. The Confederate senator was sitting on the ground guarded by one soldier. Jason stared at Nichols and saw the eyes of insanity. Nichols's face was beet red and the veins were sticking out from his forehead.

Thaddeus Nichols asked the guard for a cup of water, but the soldier ignored him. Nichols began swaying back and forth on the ground humming a hymn, and the soldier warned him to be quiet. Nichols replied, "Of course, Sergeant. I won't make any more trouble," he said as he pulled a derringer from his jacket sleeve and pointed it at Abraham Lincoln.

The President was still unconscious, lying on the ground. Nichols raised the handgun quickly and pointed it at the President's head. "You'll not escape God's hand this time, Mr. President," Thaddeus Nichols said as he pulled the trigger.

It was not Abraham Lincoln's time to die. Another assassin's bullet was destined to strike him down. The Union major jumped in front of the President's body as Thaddeus Nichols pulled the trigger on the derringer he had concealed so expertly. Jason Law was dead.

Chapter Thirty-eight

Jason Law lay dead on the ground between President Abraham Lincoln and Senator Thaddeus Nichols. The Confederate senator pointed the derringer at the President again, but before he could pull the trigger, the black servant grabbed the handgun and wrenched it from Nichols's hand.

President Lincoln was rushed into the White House by the captain of the guard, into the waiting hands of his doctor and the soldier who found him. The one remaining guard had been knocked unconscious as Jason Law threw his body between Nichols and the President.

"I have been waiting for you," Pirramuar said to Nichols as he jumped on top of him, "but I thought I was meant to take your bullet, you Son of the Devil!" Then Pirramuar lunged at Nichols and the two men struggled for the gun. Nichols fought like the madman he was, but the freed slave was strong--very strong.

Within seconds the servant had wrestled Nichols to the ground. "I have waited for this moment a long time, Thaddeus Nichols. Don't you know me? I am the one your father stole from the Outback and brought back to this land in chains. I am the one your father called 'James.'

"Do you still not recognize me? Or am I like all of the others your father held in bondage--a man with no face, a woman with no voice? Someone you could choke the life from with no fear of retribution?

"You were wrong! I am the one who will take retribution! I will take your life and feed it to the Underworld. I will see you dead!

I will give my wife peace!"

The black man pointed the derringer at Nichols's head and slowly began to pull the trigger when he saw the imprint of a cross bulging from Nichols's pant pocket. Pirramuar ripped the pocket open and grabbed the cross. He took the cross that had been his so many years ago and placed it on Thaddeus Nichols's throat. Then Pirramuar, Aborigine holy man, began to squeeze the life from the coward's body. Slowly, very slowly, Pirramuar applied more and more pressure as Nichols' face turned red, then purple and finally as black as the Aborigine's own face.

In what was an eternity for both Nichols and Pirramuar, the end finally came and Thaddeus was motionless. The Aborigine holy man began praying for the man he had just killed, and understood they would both be judged in the next world for what they had done.

Pirramuar heard someone coming, and he quickly moved away from Nichols's body. It was the President of the United States and the captain of the guard.

"Are you all right, Mr. President?" Pirramuar asked.

"I'm fine. You and the major saved my life. How's the major?" Lincoln asked.

"I'm afraid he's dead, Mr. President," the captain said. "Senator Nichols, too. Looks like he's been strangled. There's some kind of mark on his neck."

"Neither of you will say a word about this. Do you understand?" the President said sternly to the soldier and the servant he called James.

"Yes, sir," they replied in unison.

"The world will never hear of this," Lincoln said. "These times are too troubled for the world to know what happened this night. Now cover the body of that assassin and swear you will never say anything about what you may or may not have seen tonight."

"Yes, sir," was their reply again.

"Good," the President said in a quiet voice.

"I'm sorry the major lost his life. He was a very brave man. If it hadn't been for him, I would be dead. Is he new? Why haven't I met him?" President Lincoln asked no one in particular. "Do either of you know him?"

"Yes, Mr. President, I do," Pirramuar said. "I have been

waiting for him."

"Waiting for him? What do you mean, James?" President Lincoln asked in a warm voice.

"Don't listen to him, Mr. President," the captain said. "He's been saying something about going home for over a month. He says he's from someplace called Australia. Can you beat that?"

"Never mind," the President said. "James, you say you know this man? Do you know how we can notify his family? Can you help?"

"Perhaps, Mr. President. Perhaps," the black man said as he bent over the body of Jason Law.

Chapter Thirty-nine

COLONIAL HEIGHTS SUB-DIVISION,
2322

Dawn Law was sobbing uncontrollably. Harry Friedman was trying to comfort her as best he could, but Dawn would have none of it. "Why, Harry, why? It's your fault Jason's dead! You knew he might try something crazy like this! Send someone back to get him. That new system at Base One can bring him back safely. There has to be a way to revive him. We can save Jason! We can save him!"

Harry replied, "You know we can't do that, Dawn. He's gone. Once he died no one could do anything to bring him back. His body wouldn't survive transport. I know you want him here. You know I'd do anything I could. He's gone; Dawn, he's gone."

"Why, Harry, why?"

Harry looked into Dawn's face, but he had no answer. He looked over to Doc Francis, Jason's adopted father, and said, "Doc, you know I'll live with this burden the rest of my life. Dawn's right. I should have known better. I should have made sure there was no way Jason could pull such a stunt. I don't know what to say to either of you. I'm sorry. I don't know what else to say."

Dawn looked into Harry Friedman's eyes, and she realized he was almost as heartbroken as Doc and she were. She took Harry's hand and said, "Harry, I know you loved Jason. I know you're sorry, but right now I need to grieve. Doc will look after me. But you need to go back to the States and find the man who's responsible for Jason's death."

"Dawn, I've already told you. Nichols is dead. He was killed by one of President Lincoln's personal servants."

Dawn shouted, "I'm not talking about that madman, Nichols.

I know he pulled the trigger, but someone much more powerful than Nichols is behind this. Someone more powerful than Nichols, Dorothy Rhoades, or anyone else in the American States Rights Association."

"Dawn, we know who was behind everything. The police found his business card on Dorothy Rhoades's body. It's Senator Clay Sheen from Missouri. The FBI is tracking him down as we speak. It's just a matter of time."

Dawn looked up and gave Harry a small smile and patted his hand. "Thank you, Harry. Now go. Doc and I have arrangements to make and somehow find a way to tell Jody his father won't be coming home. Then I have to find Pirramuar and tell him what happened."

Pirramuar James, however, had already been told what had happened. He had been visited in his sleep by another Pirramuar who had told him everything. The two holy men would meet in the Dreaming and pray for Tagai the Warrior. They would pray for him and lead him to the next step in his journey. Jason Law was dead in this world, but Tagai the Warrior and Jason Law were both very much part of the next.

Chapter Forty

Senator Clay Sheen had made a very hard decision. Somehow the FBI had traced his secret funding of the American States Rights Association. He had been siphoning off special earmarked appropriations meant for his state for years and getting the money in Dorothy Rhoades's hands. She had used it to build up a network of over 5,000 Confederate loyalists who were supposedly ready to lay down their lives for the new nation.

However, all that loyalty went up in smoke when the 5,000 were rounded up by the Pentagon's special forces and thrown into an internment camp set up at Base One.

Clay Sheen realized he would be apprehended within days if not hours, so he decided to leave the world as the true coward he was. He overdosed himself with anti-depressants and finished off his cocktail with pure grain alcohol. In the end, he was alone with a bottle of pills in one hand and a pint of booze in the other.

Chapter Forty-one

THE DREAMING

Jason Law was confused. He was hovering over a scene of the Whitehouse grounds in the year 1863. He had watched the same scene play out at least three other times and each time it ended the same. "This can't be real. I'm hallucinating. I must have been shot when I jumped in front of Lincoln. I'm delirious. That's the only answer. I must be delirious."

"No, my son, you're not delirious. You just haven't come to grips with what happened. The Jason you were is no longer," Pirramuar, the man he had once called James, said.

Jason turned his face from the scene below and looked into the eyes of his protector, his shield, and said, "You mean I'm dead, Pirramuar?"

"Dead, yes, dead to the world you left behind, but this is just as real and is the next step in your search."

"Search?" Jason said. "What search? I don't understand."

"You are not ready to understand. Take this step and more will be revealed. That is all I know, Tagai."

Jason was still confused. Why had Pirramuar called him by his Aborigine name? Then he looked down and saw that he had become Tagai the Warrior, and he allowed himself to accept his fate. Suddenly Tagai saw another Aborigine standing next to Pirramuar. "You're the servant who helped President Lincoln regain consciousness after Nichols tried to kill him," Tagai said.

"That man is part of another world, Tagai," the black man President Lincoln had called James said. "But we are all on a quest. We all seek the answer to the question that cannot be answered until we have walked further on the path of knowledge. Man has

232

fought wars, tortured the bodies of innocents, left the unfortunates to die in the streets. We have all been part of that carnage.

"But Man has also done good," the first Pirramuar said. "How the two balance is a riddle that can only be answered on your journey. There is no going back; there is only now."

Tagai looked at the two Aborigine holy men. Even after death Tagai and Jason could not reconcile themselves. Tagai was ready to take the next step toward his fate. Jason, however, still cursed God for taking his father too soon and allowing his mother to suffer so badly at the hands of a madman.

"I must see Dawn one more time before I face God to condemn Him. I call on hell's guardian to strike a bargain--my soul, my eternity for a moment with Dawn, and to touch her face."

"Done!" a voice cried out from the darkness. "Do not listen to these so-called medicine men. I can show you the way back."

Jason turned his head and saw Thaddeus Nichols. The senator was smiling almost a boyish smile, and his eyes were open wide. Jason was being pulled back by his almost uncontrollable yearning to be with Dawn. Then Jason saw the deep bruise mark on Nichols's throat and forced himself not to listen to the old man.

"No! I was wrong. I would rather burn in hell than accept your offer."

"That can be arranged, Jason, but why do we argue over such trifles?"

Jason looked again at the spirit that had been Thaddeus Nichols. The spirit was now Do Chi, the Himalayan monk who had corrupted himself and then tried to do the same with the world.

"I can be anyone you wish me to be, Jason. Or do you prefer 'Tagai'?" the voice of the one some call the Lord of Darkness said. "These two Aborigines have only told you part of the story. There are many paths you may choose. Some lead to glory; some lead to ruin. It is your decision. You may continue to the unknown or you may stop now and take the comfort of knowing your search has ended.

"I can give you anything you want as long as you come with me now. A step further on this path is a step farther from Dawn and the others you love. The choice is yours--falling into the arms of the one you love most or walking into the unknown."

"Do not listen to the voice of temptation, Tagai. Choose the path that will bring you peace, and in the end you will be with Dawn. She must take her own path, but if your love is true, nothing can keep you apart," the Aborigine said.

Satan was quick to respond. "Why not take the easy way, the way that takes you home, Jason? Your son Jody cries out for you in the night. His mother cannot comfort him. He needs your strong arms to protect him.

"Remember, Thaddeus Nichols promised Jody he'd be back. If you come back with me now I can see to it that your son is never bothered again. You will be able to see your son, hold him, and watch him fall to sleep in peace. You will be able to kiss your lovely wife and tell her again how much you love her."

"And then what?" Jason asked.

"Why, you will come with me."

Jason paused before he spoke. The temptation to see Dawn was growing stronger, and he realized it would soon consume him. "No! I choose the course that leads to the Light. I choose Understanding. I choose God," Jason said in a loud voice.

"You choose God, do you?" the devil said mockingly. "God has no use for your kind. Did you really believe you had any choice? The moment you left the other world you gave up your right to choose.

"I had hoped you would come with me willingly, Jason. Then your torment would have been the greater. There was never any hope for you, never any Dawn, never any tomorrow. There is only the torture that is now and forever.

"You are dead to Dawn and your only son," Satan spat out. "You are dead to God. You are mine. The clock can never be unwound, you pitiful fool. I have been patient long enough," the ruler of hell said almost softly. "We are leaving. Come."

Jason was beaten. The man who had fought all of his life, and even after death could fight no more.

But the Aborigine warrior within him could. Jason began shouting. "In the Dreaming you are not king. Here you can be beaten, Satan."

"Hold on, Jason," the holy man of Jason's youth shouted. He took the fishing net from his waist that Tagai had used to snare the Do Chi of the future. Pirramuar swirled the golden net above his head and cast it over Jason. At that instant Jason Law and Tagai the warrior were united for eternity. The next moment Jason was standing with both of the holy men called Pirramuar. Before any of the three could speak a bright light surrounded Jason whose heart held the spirit of Tagai. Jason smiled briefly, and then vanished in the light on the next step of his journey.

The boy who had struggled so hard with the inequities of life, and the man who had damned God so many times had surrendered to God's judgment. And with God's judgment came hope.

BOOK THREE

~ BOUNCEBACK ~

Chapter One

It had been six months since Jason Law's death. The Federation had moved quickly to deal with the last holdouts of a revolution that had never really begun. There were still vocal critics of the Federation within the United States--a few were extremists, but most were patriotic citizens with legitimate issues. The President of the United States was personally chairing a conference on those issues with loyal Americans from all walks of life.

Before the conference began, the President had gone on a live broadcast and said, "My fellow Americans, we are on the way to a re-birth of our nation. For too long we have allowed our freedoms to be subjugated within the Federation. I make a solemn promise that we will re-establish those freedoms within our sovereign borders and once again allow those freedoms to burn brightly. We will remain a willing partner within the Federation, but we will no longer allow our freedoms to be taken away one step at a time. "Once we have formalized our recommendations, and they have been approved by Congress, we will convene a Constitutional Conference and begin the ratification process. Each of you will cast your vote on how our nation will move forward.

"We have lost our way. Too many times the human rights we all took for granted have been stolen from us. No more! God bless the United States of America." Those last words had not been spoken by an American President in over a hundred years, but throughout the country there was a collective "Amen."

During the FBI's clean-up operations, Dorothy Rhoades's

personal assistant, Paul Radford, was found hiding at Rhoades's home. The FBI Agents also found Jerry Evans there, still in a deep cryonic sleep. Radford was arrested with no incidents, and Jerry Evans was taken to the nearest hospital where he was revived.

At the President's direction, the attorney general informed the United States Supreme Court the administration would no longer support the World Court's use of multiple life sentences for serial killers from the past. After a quick hearing the Supreme Court issued an unanimous opinion that multiple life sentences constituted "cruel and unusual punishment." The opinion was immediately forwarded to the World Court which agreed to set a hearing on the subject in their next session. There was little question the World Court justices were more than aware of the U.S. President's stance on the subject and would adopt the Supreme Court's opinion quickly.

The world would sleep a little better, at least for a while. But a recently widowed woman named Dawn and her son Jody were still finding it very hard to look to the future. Two men would soon bring a message to them from Jason Law.

Chapter Two

Dawn and Jody were in the back yard of their home outside Sydney, Australia, with Doc and Pirramuar James. They had just finished a late dinner and everyone was laughing--everyone except Dawn. She told herself she had to get on with her life. It would be what Jason wanted, but she couldn't leave his memory behind so easily.

The Time Forces Investigations Unit had put out a statement lamenting the death of Detective Inspector Jason Law but gave no details. Only a few of Dawn's closest friends had been told the truth.

The history books remained the same. There was no word of the attempted assassination of President Lincoln or the heroic part Jason had played in saving the Federation. There was, however, a short story buried in an 1863 Washington, D.C., newspaper recounting how a freed Aborigine slave working in the White House had been repatriated to Australia with his two daughters.

Dawn could feel Jason's touch as she awoke each morning. She could hear him laugh as they both ran down the beach. She could see his pride as Jody grew, but Jason was dead, and a part of Dawn felt as if she were dead, too.

"Still having trouble, Dawn?" Doc asked her quietly.

"Yes, I'm afraid so, Doc. Time heals they tell me. I just don't know when," she said with a sigh.

"Why don't you let me set up with another appointment with Greg Hoffman. He's one of the best psychiatrists in Sydney, and you said he helped the last time."

"No, Doc, I don't think he can help me anymore," Dawn said.

"Pills can only do so much, and I need my wits about me since Pirramuar helped me land that job at the university."

Pirramuar walked over to the other two and put an arm around Dawn. "Come here, you two. I have something I want to give Jody." The three adults walked over to Jody who was lying on the grass looking up at the evening sky.

"Look, Mum, it's the Southern Cross," Jody said staring into the stars. "Pirramuar says you can only see it from the Southern Hemisphere. He says Dad's up there someplace."

Dawn smiled, and Pirramuar bent down over Jody and handed him something. "What's this, Pirramuar?" Jody asked as he looked down. In his hand was an old cross made of bone.

"It is a cross that an ancestor of mine carved hundreds of years ago. I told you about him. His name was Pirramuar, too. He carved the cross to remind himself about the two sisters climbing to the sky to be with their father. You remember the story, don't you?"

"Yes, I remember. But why did you give the cross to me?"

"In a few years I will offer you the same opportunity I offered your father--to become one of my people. It is a very rare honor few are ever given. Until then I wanted you to have this to remember your father. I wanted you to know he is still on his journey."

"What journey, Pirramuar?"

"That's a discussion for another time, Jody. For now, keep the cross close to you."

"Yes, yes, I will!" squealed the small boy.

Pirramuar turned to Dawn and said, "You weren't ready for this until now. Jason asked me to give it to you if anything should ever happen to him."

Dawn looked at the bright blue feather and saw it was a perfect match to the one she kept on the mantle. "Where did Jason ever find it? Oh, Pirramuar, I miss him so. I pray God will let us be together someday."

"A part of you is already with him, Dawn. Jason is on a journey that you will take some day. Until then he wants you to accept his fate. He has."

"Thank you, James. This is very special to me." Dawn turned to show her son, but he was gone. "Jody, come here. I want to show you something."

Doc patted Dawn on the shoulder and said, "I think he went to his room. Do you want me to get him?"

"No, Doc, it's alright. He just needs some space. I'll show him later."

Chapter Three

JODY'S BEDROOM

Dawn was right. Her young son needed to be alone to try to sort out the chaos that had become his life.

As he entered his bedroom a soft voice whispered, "Shut the door, Joseph. I told you I'd be back."

TO KNOW GOD YOU MUST KNOW YOURSELF.
TO KNOW YOURSELF YOU MUST SUBMIT TO GOD.
TO SUBMIT TO GOD YOU MUST KNOW GOD.

ABOUT THE AUTHOR

J. R. Simmons is a retired Air Force officer whose duty assignments included one short and two long tours of duty at the Pentagon. He graduated from the University of Nebraska in 1966, and entered the Air Force that same year. Colonel Simmons's understanding of the inter-workings of the Pentagon and the relationship between the government's civilian and military leadership were invaluable in writing his first book. The author lives in Southwest Virginia where he continues to write.

www.ingramcontent.com/pod-product-compliance
Lightning Source LLC
Chambersburg PA
CBHW030142200626
46812CB00015B/647